# ONE
# HUNDRED
# BULLETS

by

E.J. Findorff

*To Marie Louise Chenet,*
*my 10X-great grandmother,*
*born in New Orleans in 1756.*

Prologue


Twenty years earlier.


In a fog of sleep, Nick thought his mom had sat at the foot of his bed, but only her ghost could create that possibility. *Maybe, it was real*. However, the light from the hallway glowed behind a silhouetted figure much larger than his mother.

"Nick, wake up." His father pulled at his feet, as if not knowing how to be gentle.

The eleven-year-old propped himself on his elbows. His Spiderman alarm clock read 2:13 a.m. "Dad? Is it time for school?"

"No." His father snapped his fingers, waiting for Nick to gain clarity. "You know I loved your mother."

Nick processed that sentence despite the thickness of his confusion. He didn't want to give the wrong response. "I know."

His weighty palm landed on Nick's thigh like a brick. "Get up, we have to go somewhere."

Nick didn't ask questions as his father retreated to the door. The ceiling light exploded from above. He dropped out of bed wearing only underwear. Lego's under his feet forced him to hop forward. Unbalanced and squinting, he dragged his feet to the dresser for an outfit. Without warning, it slammed shut of its own accord.

His father towered above him while holding a gym bag. "Just put on some sweatpants, a coat, and some shoes. And throw an extra change of clothes and shoes in the bag."

"What for?" his wispy voice asked.

"Don't question me, Nick. Do it, or you'll get the belt." His father plodded out the room again. Nick could hear him pacing.

The rattling of keys in the front room caused Nick's stomach to turn. He pulled up his Spiderman sweatpants. They had been his favorite *reoccurring* gift from his mom. Every Christmas, she would replace the old sweatpants with a pair to fit his growing frame, always the same web-slinger pattern. She would never do that again. After tying the drawstring with shaky fingers, he slipped into a pair of Converse. His coat was last, pushing his arms through the tight sleeves. He needed a bigger size.

Once properly zipped, he packed a pair of new Saints sweatpants, a tee-shirt, and his basketball shoes in his gym bag. Was this a trip? He met his father by the front door. With the green padded leather jacket, his dad looked like a Marine super-soldier.

"Let's go. We don't have all night."

The chilly air ignited Nick's senses. The moonlight painted a bluish hue as he walked to the passenger side of the red Mustang, placing the bag gently into the back seat. The car had been idling the whole time, radio volume set just low enough to hear.

"Sit in the front from now on." His father squeezed into the driver's seat.

Nick had never experienced the passenger seat before, even when his mom wasn't riding with them. The vents blew hot air, but he continually rubbed his hands over his sweatpants, smoothing out the goose bumps. They wouldn't go away. His father eased along the deserted street, still without an explanation.

At the first major intersection, Nick spotted a police car parked on side the road. The officer seemed to be watching them – he *was* watching them. At the next light a half-mile down sat another squad car. That was Mr. Gary, for sure. Why were they out here this late? The heat brushed his face as he yawned.

Nick's eyelids closed despite his best efforts, but not for long. He jolted awake as the tires bounced on a raised driveway. They had pulled into a small parking lot of an abandoned strip mall. The Mustang crept into the complex with the headlights off. His father parked in a spot as if going shopping. The engine continued to run while stationary, under the cloak of an immense oak tree.

While the heater ran, his dad put a large hand on his shoulder. He spoke in a low tone, "Remember how I told you I'd get the guy who killed your mom?"

"Yes," Nick whispered, easing from his grip in order to put his face near the car's vent. It was February in New Orleans, Mardi Gras season, and the cold could get bone-deep.

"I keep my promises," he finished.

The engine ceased, indicating the night was far from over. Why his father woke him at two in the morning was a mystery he didn't want revealed. Nick looked out the windshield at the run-down strip mall, not recognizing where they had stopped. It looked like a scene from an apocalyptic zombie comic book.

The driver-side door swung open, but his father didn't step out. The cold intermingled with the car's warmth, and the darkness disappeared when the overhead light flicked on. Nick observed his dad's sharp-angled profile while still bound by the seat belt. A gust slapped his cheek.

His father inhaled, expanding broad and dense, like one of those *old-timey* football players that wore the leather helmets. He had a wide face, with large, angry eyes. His buzz cut was already turning gray at the age of forty. "Let's go, Nick."

"Dad, why are we here?"

"This is not the time for questions." He secured a flashlight and exited the car. The door shut with an easy click.

Nick watched the man walk around the front of the darkened hood. His father opened the passenger side like a chauffeur. Nick unhooked his seat belt. Forcing his legs out, he looked at the parent who had been absent most of his life, whether it was from working or frequent separations from his mom to *get his head straight*.

"Where are we going?" Nick looked for an open store. The huge windows had newspapers taped to the insides.

"There's something I need you to see." His father pointed at the nearest door, guiding Nick with a hand on his back.

The broken neon sign clearly said *tacos* in the name. Graffiti tagged the walls, and garbage had collected in the corners. A couple of windows were shattered, boarded up with plywood. Rows of weeds ran in the cracked concrete like the tributaries he had read about in Geography class.

"Is this place open?"

"The whole strip mall is abandoned. It's hard to keep a business going out here in the East."

Nick stopped at the door, as if making a stand would matter.

His father reached for the rusted, grimy handle. "Don't worry, it's safe."

"I'm cold. I don't want to go in."

His dad faced him. "I wouldn't want to go in either, but we need to. There's something we need to do for your mom."

"But, mom's dead." His eyes watered.

"I know." His voice changed as he pointed. *"Now,* Nick."

Nick remained hesitant, despite fearing punishment. He flinched as his father's massive paw palmed his cold cheek. It was quite the opposite sensation from being smacked with it. With that, his small frame was nudged inside. Nick stumbled into the darkness, stopping when his feet stuck to the floor. He inhaled something like sour milk from behind the school's cafeteria.

The flashlight exposed cheap aluminum framing and missing drywall. The empty room contained a long counter running along a wall and discarded trash lying about. A small creature scurried into the back room. The far corner revealed a person lying on their side while bound to a chair with rope and duct tape. There was a sack over the man's head.

Nick froze, as fear stole his breath.

His father put the flashlight on the counter, but kept it pointed at the prisoner. He stepped up to the mysterious man and without much effort, pulled him upright using the back of the chair. The person instantly came to life, fighting the restraints like a nudged cockroach on its back.

"Don't be scared, Nick. He's not going to hurt you."

Nick swallowed hard. "W - who's that?"

"That's Harold Sanders - *Slimeball Harry*. This is the man that killed your mom." His father slapped Harold's head. "Slimeball Harry here thought he got away with it… until now, that is."

"That's the man that killed mom?" Nick cried.

His father pulled off the bag. Nick had seen Harold Sanders leaving the courthouse after the judge let him go, found not guilty due to *circumstantial evidence*. He remembered how confused he felt - how angry. On the television, Harold Sanders had been caught laughing in relief. Now, his beat-up face wasn't smiling at all under the duct tape.

His father returned to Nick's side. "Do you know what a vigilante is?"

"Someone that takes justice into their own hands."

"That's right." His father knelt. "It's when a man like you or me gets justice by taking the law into his own hands. When the legal system fails us, when laws fail us, sometimes we need to take care of things Biblical-like. We're vigilantes tonight."

"But, you're a policeman."

"Not tonight, I'm not." His dad roughed up Nick's hair, then stood straight.

"Are we going to beat him up?"

"Not exactly. There is an old saying, *an eye for an eye*. I believe in that." His father had found a new level of serious.

Nick hesitated. "He's going to die because mom died?"

His dad's expression fell flat. He magically produced a gun that Nick had held several times. He placed it in Nick's hand. "Time to use what you learned at the firing range."

"You want me to shoot him?" Nick held the gun flat in both his palms.

"Yes, I do." His father directed Nick to stand in front of the bleeding man. "Just point it at his head and shoot. Or point it at his heart. You choose."

"I don't want to." His arms grew tired under the weight.

His dad's calm demeanor vanished. He stomped and roared, "He killed your mother! He's the reason you and I live *alone*. He's the reason you stay with your *pawpaw* when I'm at work. Aren't you angry? I know I am."

He nodded, having no other option. "Yeah."

"Then, do it. If you loved your mom at all, you'll *pull – that – trigger*."

Nick took in a staggered breath. He raised the gun, still using both hands. The man's eyes grew wide, and he trembled. Slimeball Harry tried to say something, but the tape wouldn't budge. The man's head bobbed forward, as if trying to tip himself over. Harold Sanders took away his mom and didn't go to jail. His father wanted him to be a vigilante, to make things equal.

*An eye for an eye.*

The barrel of the gun hovered a foot away from the man's face. Nick closed his eyes. His father yelled something that fell silent in his ears. What would happen if he didn't shoot the man? He had never seen his father so… obsessed. Nick put pressure on the trigger if only to make the night go away.

*Click.*

No explosion came. The man squealed under the tape. Snot flew from his nose. A very alive man cried in relief. Nick put the gun gently onto the ground, numb and confused.

"That was good." His father picked up the empty weapon.

"Nothing happened." He wiped away falling tears.

"It was a test of manhood, Nick. I didn't want you to kill him. I'm proud of you."

"Dad…"

"Don't call me Dad anymore. You're a man, now. Call me Lou."

It took a moment for that curve ball to register. "Like you call your dad Shelly?"

"Exactly. Call me Lou. Call pawpaw Shelly. Say it."

"Lou." His voice quivered. The name sounded alien coming from his mouth.

His father… Lou… smiled. "Not many men would have been able to that. You did right by your mom." He bent over to speak face to face. "But, that doesn't mean Slimeball Harry isn't going to pay."

"How?" He really didn't want to know.

"I need you to promise me something. Will you promise me?"

"Okay, Dad… Lou."

"You saw the blue and whites on our way here, right? The squad cars?"

Nick nodded hard.

"Those are the guys from the poker game. They're keeping an eye out for us. They're going to say we were with them at our house playing poker all night into the morning. They're going to say you were there, too. Everyone will believe us because we're all policemen."

"Why are we lying?"

"Because we might get asked questions by a lawyer or some other policemen about what we were doing tonight. You have to promise me that you'll tell them I was playing poker and you were playing video games and went to bed at nine. We were never here. Can you do that? Keep our secret?"

"Yeah."

Lou nodded with satisfaction. "I'm so proud of you. Go back to the car, but don't get in, okay? Do *not* get in. I know it's cold, but wait for me. I'll be right there." He pointed the flashlight at the door.

Nick's tired, thin legs carried him toward the exit. He closed the shop's door behind him, but instead of going to the car, Nick hugged the brick wall until reaching a window that had newspaper missing at the corner.

He could barely make out his father's large figure with his arm stretched toward the man in the chair. The flashlight wasn't pointed at Harold Sanders anymore. The inside looked like a grainy black and white television show.

A firecracker seemed to go off in his father's hand, and Slimeball Harry stopped moving. Nick pushed off the wall and sprinted to the car. A moment later, his dad casually stepped from the store as if he had just bought a gallon of milk. Nick stood with his arms folded high and tight across his chest.

Lou reached inside the back seat for the bag. "Take off your clothes."

"Why?"

"Because we need to get rid of them. Everything."

"My sweatpants?" *My mom's special sweatpants*?

Lou grabbed him by the coat. "Yes, your sweatpants. Everything." He shoved a plastic bag into his chest. "Put everything into this bag. Quickly."

They both expelled their clothes under the shade of the oak at the edge of the parking lot, out of sight from the road. Nick ignored the day-old welt from Lou's belt on his back and the healing bruise on his thigh. They replaced each article with a new one from the gym bag.

"You didn't bring another coat or socks?" Lou scolded.

Nick shook his head, trembling, not daring to complain.

"Oh, well. Live and learn."

Lou left the bag of clothes under the oak. As the Mustang drove toward the exit, a cop car pulled into the lot. They passed within a foot of each other with a slight wave. Lou turned onto the street and they headed home. Nick welcomed the returning heat. He rubbed at his Saints sweatpants in order to subdue the goose bumps. It took all his effort to not think about his father killing that man. Instead, he let himself mourn the last gift his mom ever gave him.

Chapter 1

Present day…

The dispatcher's voice crackled over the radio. "Forty-two in progress. Alley between thirty-two and thirty-four Elysian Fields. Be advised, suspect is armed with a knife."

"That's right down the block." Nick brought the two-way to his mouth. "Car 1099 responding."

"Affirmative 1099," the dispatcher returned. "Be advised, secondary units also responding."

Officer Belinda Goodman jerked the squad into gear, making a U-turn with the flashers, but no siren as that would announce their arrival. They intended to catch the guy at the scene, rather than take a chance of him getting away by running through the neighborhood. It would be too easy to get lost in the mix of tourists just six blocks away. They sped past once proud, beautifully neglected houses positioned behind a line of oak and magnolia trees. At the given address, they located the activity in a gangway. The secondary units had yet to arrive.

"There they are," Belinda said with urgency, but continued forward until they were out of view from the alley's perspective.

"Be quiet. We don't know if he'll hurt the girl if he sees us coming." Nick quietly opened his door.

"Could be on something, too. Might panic," Belinda agreed.

Nick put his finger over his lips as they exited, leaving the doors open. The two Georgian houses had faded, colorful paint peeling off their columns and shudders. The four-foot wide gangway supported a wide open, decrepit wrought iron gate. No residents nor tourists were visible.

A young, black male in a push-up position hovered over the female. His pants were down to his knees. The knife appeared to be in his grasp, although partially hidden in the shadows. The victim's arms and legs moved slow and aimlessly. Nick took position behind Belinda as they approached the entrance. Nick drew his Glock with caution, but Belinda crouched like a sprinter in the blocks, with one hand on the ground.

Without communicating her actions, Belinda shot forward and tackled the male. Her muscular weight knocked the attacker off the woman. She landed on him like a wrestler, causing his knife to skid across the concrete. With her knee on the back of the suspect's neck, she retrieved her gun and pressed the barrel against the back of his head. Nick jumped over the moaning woman, placing his weight on the small of the man's back. He had a hard time pulling both his struggling arms together.

Belinda released pressure from the rapist's neck, and he almost pulled from Nick's grasp. The man's voice was strained. "Let me the fuck go, you stupid white bitch."

He bucked hard, almost contacting the gun. His head bobbed and turned like a contortionist, brushing Belinda's gun. She flinched, and her weapon fired into his cheek. The man's weight fell flat. Nick and Belinda froze. They looked at each other, sandwiched in the deep shade of the towering homes. A smattering of blood speckled Belinda's uniform

"Belinda, what the fuck?"

"I didn't... I mean... he resisted."

Nick stood, running his fingers through his hair. He glared at her, then surveyed the front and back vantage points for potential witnesses. The sidewalk was clear, however, both houses had windows. He whispered, "That's going to be the story? Resisted?"

"What else is there?" She rose, stumbling backward.

"I have to call this in. We can't wait, or they'll tear us apart in the investigation." Nick ran out to the street, putting his radio to his ear. "Dispatch, this is Car 1099. We need an ambo at our location. We have an unconscious female. Shots fired. The suspect is down. No other casualties."

"What is the condition of the suspect and victim?" Came back over the speaker.

Nick glanced at body. "Suspect critical... fatal. Victim conscious, but delirious."

"Affirmative, 1099."

Nick heard sirens in the distance. He secured the radio back onto his belt. "We tell the details as they actually happened. No reason to make anything up, Belinda."

"I know. He resisted. He made a sudden, aggressive move." She paced.

Nick knelt at the dazed woman's side. She seemed uninjured, besides the lump on her cheek. "Unbelievable."

Belinda leaned against the lime green house with blood splatter dotting her face. "You can take care of this, right? Your people?"

Nick felt at the cuffs on his belt. "My people? Who do you think I am? You're a white woman that shot a black man in today's America." He looked at the victim to make sure the lady was still out of it. However, his eyes caught movement in the window above. Behind the curtain, a black woman locked eyes with him... *and nodded.*

Belinda continued, "He's a rapist with a weapon." She finally expressed real panic. "Jesus Christ."

Nick kept his voice down. "Someone was watching us in that window."

"Shit. Just great. Witnesses are unreliable." Belinda glanced at the window, where the lady had been.

The cut and bruised woman on the ground moaned, trying to roll onto her side. She wore jogging gear that was torn and displaced on her body.

"Pull your shit together," Nick commanded as the ambulance pulled onto the curb, as well as the secondary unit.

"You got my back, don't you?" Her face was finally calm, almost pleading.

He answered quickly, "He resisted. Yes, he resisted. We could end up having a problem with that witness, but we have to risk it."

"And you'll make sure it goes away, right?"

Nick squeezed his eyes shut, looking away from his partner. Had she shot the rapist on purpose? The way she took him down was fearless, if not reckless. She always denied being on steroids, and he had believed her, but was *roid-rage* even a thing anymore? Lou was going to have a fit that Belinda was involved in something like this.

The medics squeezed into the gangway to take care of the victim, realizing the suspect was a lost cause to be left for the coroner. Neighbors gathered with their cell phones extended. Belinda tried to keep it together near the curb. She wiped her slightly bent nose that had once been broken. It added character to her tough, yet feminine face.

Nick's stomach pinched, knowing this could turn into a heap of shit.

But, maybe this *needed* to turn into a heap of shit.

Chapter 2

Nick had found shade under a neighbor's Magnolia tree, attempting to keep balance on the roots while kicking the hand-grenade looking seed pods littering the ground. He watched the well-dressed investigator, Sergeant Bagley, approach yet again. She had been summoned from her lofty office at Headquarters to investigate the *officer involved shooting*. As with any OFI, a homicide supervisor, sergeant, or any rank above had to take lead. She had told him twice to call her Mary Ann. One house over, Belinda stood with two uniformed policemen under her own tree, waiting.

"Let's go through it one more time, Nick," Sergeant Bagley said on approach after just having spoken to the homeowner. Bagley wore a blue skirt and smart white blouse, and kept her wavy, dark hair cropped to the shoulders. She exuded the confidence a black woman needed to climb through the ranks of the NOPD. She had an expression like she could never be surprised, or not know the answer.

"C'mon Mary Ann, we've been here for two hours. I've told you my account three times." He turned in a slow circle. The entire block had been barricaded, leaving the press to guess at the goings on. Nick wiped at his face, glancing at the Crime Scene Unit as they went about their business.

"Humor me."

He faced her again. "You just want to trip me up."

"Maybe I just love the sound of your voice." Her tone was sarcastic, yet she comically raised an eyebrow. She had a certain disarming charm.

Nick repeated the story for a fourth time, ending with their mantra, *he resisted.* The CSU team zipped the black body bag just as he finished. He asked, "Will we have to speak with Internal Affairs?"

"Sure. Probably. We'll see." She had no problem rattling off the uncertainties. "You're required to take three days. Turn in your gun before the end of watch and you still need to write a very detailed daily thingy."

"Daily thingy?" He watched her shrug with indifference at her choice of words. Nick threw his hands up. "Fine. I've been through the routine."

With a reassuring nod, Mary Ann Bagley told Nick to sit tight, and returned to Belinda at the other tree to get her version again. He found it odd that she had no recorder or notebook. All she did was listen. Nick conjured a strange image of Mary Ann acting like a boxing referee, bringing Belinda and him together from their respective trees to fight to the death.

Belinda seemed to answer the investigator's questions while they stood in the hot shade. Nick couldn't hear, but his partner's flailing arms attempted to help her argument. Her eye contact with Sergeant Bagley was minimal. Hopefully the investigator wasn't an expert in body language.

Surely, Lou had heard about this by now.

Chapter 3

Miles outside the French Quarter, the summit of the Haynes levee was his safe space – his *peace*. Nick leaned on the chain link fence, which reached skyward, embedded in a waist-high concrete base. In the distance, through the diamond pattern of fencing, Lake Pontchartrain's horizon seamlessly met the night sky. He and his mom had once enjoyed long walks atop this levee before they built the safety barrier. Sometimes, he could feel her hand in his. The clouds leisurely covered the moon in a slow game of hide-and-seek. Breaking of water on the large stones could be heard below.

The six-mile long hill, carpeted with a patchy mix of wild grass and weeds, hugged the north side of the wide boulevard. It protected the New Orleans East neighborhoods from Lake Pontchartrain during storm surges. Parallel to the shoreline, between the levee and the rocks, were railroad tracks where he had flattened many a coin as a kid. He and his father had sprinkled his mom's ashes in the water not fifty yards away.

Upward of sixty camps built on pylons had inhabited the edge of the lake, but Hurricane George destroyed all but six of them a little over two decades earlier. Nick's parents had been part owners of one of those charming, rustic camps, and they had spent many fun-filled weekends on the water entertaining other cops. His parents would never fight at that camp. She would have wanted her remains spread near the remaining stubborn, split, and splintered pylons rising from the water.

The breeze lifted his hair. Something jumped in the water. Nick had orchestrated three eradications, *three murders*, which would be scoffed at by the original ten members of the *Tribunal*. He knew the elder's murder count to be in the hundreds, committed over the past twenty years. Thankfully, no one kept a scorecard, or maybe they did? Nick always suspected Lou maintained a journal of details, but if the feds hadn't found anything yet, maybe there wasn't one.

His mom still offered advice through the years, albeit through his subconscious. However, he never spoke to his mom aloud, like in the movies. His truth remained silent in his head, knowing she could hear that just as well.

*Don't worry, Mom. I know I'm not the man you would have seen me grow into. I can imagine you'd slap Lou for how he raised me, but I'm an adult now. I know what's right and wrong. I have the ability to make those choices. Lou made sure to destroy the decent part of my soul, the part you gave me. But, I'm going to make you proud.*

Nick turned away from the lake to face the New Orleans East neighborhood that extended along Hayne Boulevard, otherwise called *Haynes* by the locals. Stretching in both directions was a mix of houses, restaurants, and other assorted businesses. None of them were modern looking. They were disjointed at best, haphazard, built with cheap brick or wood frames. In the days of the camps, those businesses along Haynes had thrived. Now, it seemed as if the magic vanished.

Directly below, across from where Nick stood was *Shelly's*, his grandfather's self-named bar. It was a small, two-story box-framed structure with weathered, white aluminum siding. Under the large front window, a row of unattractive bushes survived the occasional urination or vomiting patron. In front of the bushes was a wooden guardrail that couldn't stop a bike much less a car, but it kept clueless drivers from crushing the foliage.

His grandfather lived on the second floor. Stricken with agoraphobia, Shelly hadn't left the bar for the past five years - that anyone knew about, anyway. Luckily, there was one old-school doctor still willing to come by the bar for check-ups.

Lou's classic red Mustang pulled into the small ten-car lot made from the compaction of clam and oyster shells. He parked next to Nick's squad car in front of the window, just short of the wooden guardrail. Their cars were the only two this late evening. The *open* sign reflected neon green off Lou's shiny hood. Nick watched from atop the levee as his father walked around his trunk. His belly extended a little farther every year, and his hair was graying, yet still thick and wavy. Lou would be retiring from the Third District in a few years and it was killing the old man. His father entered Shelly's ancient screen door with his piece attached to his belt. He'd know Nick was up on the levee as soon as he saw the empty bar stool.

Nick had changed from his uniform into loose jeans and a tee-shirt at the Eighth District in the French Quarter, getting well wishes from his peers, knowing he would be gone for three days. He carefully stepped down the uneven slope, dropping onto Haynes when the passing cars weren't dangerously close. He trotted over the four lanes, directly onto Shelly's property where remnants of shells crunched underfoot.

The scene inside was a carbon-copy of his previous visit. The unassuming bar had the qualities of an old-world mafia hangout, akin to a mom-and-pop deli in New York, where life and death decisions were made at a small table next to Italian meats. Locals never realized one of the most influential, if not powerful men in New Orleans was having a beer on any given day. Occasionally, policemen in plain clothes would come in and their stares would be obvious. Sometimes, they were invited to leave.

With the door on the far right, customers hooked an immediate left upon entering, lest they bump into the end of the take-out counter. The antique, gold-trimmed bar formed the letter L, splitting the middle of the room. The interior was dark, like the lake, with several chrome tables against a wall supporting Saints paraphernalia and retro Dixie and Jax beer signs. Near the front window were three beat up video poker machines with outdated digital graphics.

A Queen song floated from the corner speakers. Nick found his duct-taped stool and scooted it close to Lou, who had a full Coors Light on a cork coaster. Lou wore baggy shorts and a tank top, showing his faded array of tattoos, some military. Sparse, gray hairs escaped from his collar.

Shelly appeared from the back room and automatically placed another beer on top a Dixie coaster. The eighty-year old man still reveled in full mobility, with muscles that refused to abate. He offered a sprite greeting. "Looking good, grandson."

"You, too, Shelly," Nick reciprocated in kind.

"You up on the levee again?" Lou inquired. His eyes were trained on the television hanging behind the bar.

"Yep."

"I miss her, too." Lou rotated his finger in the air at Shelly. "Turn the music up a bit and give us a little privacy." He turned on his T-9 bug detector, which looked like a small walkie-talkie. He put it between them, satisfied Nick wasn't wired.

Nick searched the empty bar as classic rock pumped out the speakers. "So, I'm clear?"

Lou finally turned his apathetic face. His voice was low. "Just swept the place. We're clean, but a bionic ear could easily pick us up from out there."

*So paranoid.* "I didn't see any suspicious vehicles."

"Then, we *must* be safe." Lou smirked.

"Alright, don't be a jag."

"Then, don't be stupid." Lou eyed him for a contradictory remark like when Nick was ten, then continued, "What happened?"

"Hold on." The chilled beer went down in several swallows. "Ah, shit that's good."

Shelly marked up the tab, which was a joke since Lou covered most of the bills. But it made Shelly happy to keep his accounting. He listed inventory, monthly fluctuations in heat and air, and he even counted how many patrons were served every day. Nick figured it kept him from going stir crazy, cooped up in the bar. If there happened to be a *Tribunal* ledger, he wouldn't doubt Shelly kept it up to date. The old man walked to the antique jukebox and adjusted the volume on the wall speakers, turning up Frank Sinatra's *My Way*.

"What happened?" Lou asked, under his breath.

Nick sighed. "Didn't your source tell you?"

Lou straightened up, inspecting a Coors Light label that he could probably recite word for word. "You better lose this bitchy attitude."

His teeth clenched. "She shot the rapist."

"Was it justified?"

Nick took another swallow from the bottle. "Subjective." He waited. "She didn't need to shoot him, but what if she didn't? He was squirming, fighting me. What if he wiggled loose and there was a worse turnout?"

"Any video?" Lou's expression remained quizzical.

Nick spoke low while looking away. "Not that I know of. She expects it to be swept under the Tribunal rug."

"I'm told Mary Ann Bagley has the case."

"That's right."

"I know her. You'll be fine." He pretended to watch the game show on the television.

"Belinda?" Nick asked.

"We'll see." He paused, "What did you tell Bagley?"

"That we responded to an aggravated rape in progress. While Belinda and I had the suspect subdued, he struggled to break free."

"Subdued. Not cuffed?"

"I was in the process," Nick lied. "Belinda shot him before I could."

"Big guy?"

"Big enough." Nick leaned in closer. "It wasn't the worst misuse of force I've seen."

"No tasers were out?"

"No. Didn't want to risk hitting the victim."

"Didn't care about a bullet, though?" Lou didn't give him time to answer. "We'll make sure you two don't have to talk to Internal Affairs. Thankfully, there's no budget for body cameras. Time served with your leave, I'd guess."

"There's more."

"What?"

"The 9-1-1 caller saw the whole thing from out her window."

Lou held his surprise. "My *sources* told me there were no witnesses."

"Chalk it up to public support. She gave me a nod from her window like it was fine, and told Bagley that she didn't see anything. Only heard the gun fire."

Lou blew air from his lips. "Lucky. If she changes her story, she'd be considered unreliable. Belinda will probably get out from under this if the story sticks. Shit, it'd probably be better if she went down. I'm tired of her trying to weasel her way in."

"I know."

"You better go over that story in your head every chance you get, just in case. Bagley might come back for a follow-up. Don't offer any imaginary details. You can never deviate."

"I'm rock solid." Nick finished his beer. "So, now I'm on leave for three days."

"Try to enjoy it." Lou swirled his bottle. "Second order of business. Gavin Jones."

Nick thought of his mom again. "Our murdering local resident, Gavin Jones? Have the boys voted? After three years, isn't Cooper up in the rotation?" Nick waved at Shelly for another beer.

"Cooper *is* up, but there's been a change of plans. I want you to do it.

Chapter 4

"If Cooper is up in the rotation, why do you want me to do it?" Nick glanced at the ESPN silently playing out on the television.

Lou huffed. "Do you have to question everything?"

"It's a big deal, Lou. It's taking a life."

"You haven't done one in years. I want to make sure you still got it in you."

"You would think I'd be the one you trust."

"One day you'll be ordering members to do eradications. I need to make sure you're well adept at performing them."

Nick tried to sound convincing. "Fine. He's guilty. He deserves it."

"Well, I admire the enthusiasm." Lou reached for the remote. "Do your research."

"Always." Nick's stomach turned. "Let's go over it again. What do we know so far?"

Lou's head dipped, and his eyes closed. "He's only been in New Orleans five years."

"Not a native," Nick stated.

Lou's thick frame leaned closer. His voice was deep, but breathy. "He's been arrested for piddly stuff here, and West Virginia…" Lou faced Nick like they were on an intimate date. "...then he goes and commits murder in our town."

"He killed his girlfriend. Hid the body. With a history of domestic abuse. He'll get another girlfriend and kill her, too."

"Probably. You need to tell me the day it's going to happen. Cooper says he hits the Winn Dixie by Belinda's house every Monday around noon. Use it."

"What if an opportunity presents itself?" Nick wiped his palms on his thighs, a nervous habit he had acquired on that fateful night of Slimeball Harry's murder. He stood to stretch, but only to get away from his father's stale breath.

Lou spun on his barstool to face him. "Haven't I taught you anything? You plan everything. Everything!"

His jaw clenched. "My first three went off perfectly."

Lou laughed over the music, but his eyes never relaxed. "The feds have been quiet, which scares me more than anything else." Lou smacked the bar top with unneeded drama. "Assume you're being watched out there. Assume people are recording your conversations."

Nick said, "I've seen the pictures documenting his abuse. He beat the shit out of her, consistently."

"You were always overly sensitive to the domestic abuse victims. Just 'cause you saw me hit your mother one time."

"Yeah, the *one* time." Nick stared at Lou until their eyes met, but he didn't falter.

"Keep it civil, boys," Shelly interjected on approach. "There's no shot at a trial with this asshole?"

Lou looked at his father. "The DA didn't want to touch it. It's up to the Tribunal." He slowly turned toward the muted television on the wall.

Nick despised the word *Tribunal*, which had started on social media after the FBI released their findings to the press a decade earlier. The word embodied arrogance and superiority, much like Lou. "Do we even need to keep the Tribunal going?"

"Are you kidding me?" Lou twisted in order to gently place his palms on each side of Nick's head, ready to debate. "That day we got revenge for your mother started something that has changed the city, changed the way the world looks at us."

"I know," Nick said a bit too loud. He backed out of Lou's hold.

His father continued, "What we've been doing for the past twenty years is working. Do I need to remind you that New Orleans has the lowest murder rate in the country per capita? We have the highest high school graduation rate ever. The lowest unemployment rate - ever. The highest volume of tourists - ever."

"No, you don't have to remind me, but you always do."

"I'm proud of that." The police captain put his meaty fingers on the back of Nick's neck. "I know I wasn't always there for you during your formative years, but you've done alright for yourself. One day the Tribunal will be yours."

Nick cringed inside. "Sometimes I feel your legacy is the only reason you kept me around."

Lou offered a rare smile. "If you didn't have it in you, I would have guided you to a more… safe career."

"You didn't guide shit. I chose to be a policeman."

"Sure, you did."

"I did." Nick's jaw set. "It's all Marcus and I talked about."

Lou ignored Nick's protesting. "The city is over the hump. Our job is easy, now. What did we have – only four eradications in the past six years? Back in our fifth year, we had seventy-three." Lou inhaled, concluding his point.

Nick had killed a child molester, a murdering gangbanger, and a heartless drug dealer. Despite his reluctance, he convinced himself these men deserved their fate. Each time, he imagined the gun would just click like when he had been eleven, but it never did. He admitted to his best friend Marcus that it had gotten easier to detach from his emotions.

This *honor of eradication*, as Lou had put it, was bestowed on members of the Tribunal based on each cop's location, availability, and rotation. However, it was also about loyalty. He had memorized alibis for the old Tribunal members, as well as the new. They faked a dinner on a certain night or saw a particular movie together. Eventually, a cold, hardened criminal would mysteriously be murdered and thankfully, Nick had never been called to testify.

"I gotta go. Cali's probably waiting up for me."

Lou snagged his shirt. "One more thing. About your woman."

"Still can't call her Cali?"

"Something's always bugged me about *Cali* not having any family."

"That's not so unusual."

"I did some more checking."

"After six years? Really? What is wrong with you?"

Lou ignored the question. "It always bugged me that I couldn't find a complete history."

"In rural Alabama? No shit. Six years, Lou." Nick rubbed his temples with his eyes closed.

"There's a Cali Maddox that was registered to St. Andrew's Academy in Alabama."

His eyelids popped open. "This isn't new info."

"Funny thing. The registrar states she was there, and yet, there are no class pictures of her in each of the four yearbooks. Not a candid shot. Not a one."

"How did you find her yearbooks?"

"Easy enough to track down."

Nick was tired of calming Lou's suspicion about his fiancé. "She told me about that."

Lou's eyes widened. "Oh, do tell."

He tried to drain an already empty beer bottle. "I mentioned this before. Her mother didn't want her picture in there. They were in hiding from her mom's abusive boyfriend. She was too scared the bastard would find them."

Lou took that in, noticing two older, bearded guys entering the bar, laughing. "I do remember you saying that. Makes sense." He swallowed some beer. "That would explain why I'm not finding much. Nothing else you want to admit to?"

"Accuse me first, and we'll see." Nick waited, but no accusation came. "We done?" He stared at an empty beer, wanting to avoid more questions.

Lou stood. "I'm going home." He put one hand on Nick's shoulder. "But, we're far from done."

Nick watched the door close behind Lou. He looked at Shelly. "Was it something I said?"

Shelly pulled up his own flimsy stool he kept behind the bar. "He has a lot on his mind."

"Don't we all."

Shelly's eyes twinkled, seemingly gaining life without his son around. "You going to go through with it?"

Nick shrugged. "Has to be done."

Shelly made sure the two new patrons were out of earshot. "Be very careful with this Jones fellow."

Nick glanced over at the interlopers, too. "You know something I don't?"

The old man frowned. "Come by sometime while you're on leave... while Lou's at work. We'll talk."

Chapter 5


The streets of New Orleans East belonged to Nick. He *owned* them, *reclaimed* them, and made them available to good citizens once again. It was a typical, boring neighborhood with modest ranch houses and the occasional two-story. It was nothing like the historic Marigny or Treme neighborhoods people were used to seeing on the television. Even nearing midnight, driving home from his meeting with Lou in an area once known for its violent crime, he didn't witness that sinister activity from long ago.

The potential for danger had waned. Clusters of youths weren't hanging out on corners, or congregating in front of convenience stores, daring anyone to go inside. Gangs hadn't disappeared entirely, but the drive-by shootings and drug wars were virtually non-existent. A group of teens in hoodies at two in the morning didn't mean automatic trouble.

What he *did* notice was a young, black couple holding hands as they strolled along the sidewalk. Farther down the block, an elderly white man in pajamas walked his Labrador Retriever. Independent businesses extended their hours until late in the evening. There were less sirens wailing in the distance - no helicopters chasing down suspects. Those reminders made his relationship with Lou tolerable.

One mile later, Nick arrived home. Cali's Jeep Fit was parked on the street, near the mailbox perched on an iron pole. She resisted parking under the carport for fear of being cornered by an unsavory character. She kept a registered firearm in her purse and knew how to use it, which made Nick feel better.

Nick parked the blue and white behind his Sonata already tucked under the lit carport of the small, red-bricked ranch house. His address was just two blocks from the levee, but a mile down from Shelly's. Some days he walked to the levee, stopping to chat with neighbors who spent time outside. He knew their cars, their kids, and their pets... the way a neighborhood should be.

He stepped out from the squad car and walked to the lawn. The grass had gotten to be three weeks long, but he hardly felt guilty for not cutting it. Sometimes, he paid a neighborhood kid, but he hadn't been around lately. He checked the street by habit, then retreated inside.

All the lights were out, except for a single bulb over the kitchen sink. Cali's organizational skills were displayed from the spices to the utensils lined up against the aqua green backsplash. Nick meandered to the refrigerator where he gulped from a jug of sweet tea until satiated.

The kitchen decor was Cali's vision, but she didn't have a lot to work with. The cabinets were outdated and yellowing, along with all the appliances. If something worked without having to curse at it, then it stayed. The kitchen space was small for an island, but Cali improvised with a tall, distressed, antique table with a shelf underneath for pots and ceramics.

This Gavin Jones eradication came from left field. Nick could argue, but it was futile. The Tribunal was virtually a police mafia and once in, you didn't leave unless you retired, which three members had to this point. He put his hands on the chipped kitchen counter and took several deep breaths, shedding Lou from his shoulders.

Procrastinating in the kitchen, Nick pulled out his department registered Glock and placed it on the table. He kicked off his shoes and unbuckled his ankle holster containing a personal snubnose revolver, leaning it on top the other gun. He sat at the dining room table in the dark, staring at the intermingled weapons, like a centerpiece at an NRA wedding. He flicked the handle of the snubnose with his finger, trying to get it to spin like a bottle. He only stung his fingernail.

After a few minutes of pondering, he put the guns in a hidden safe in the pantry. Hiding a gun was unnecessary and dangerous when it only took three seconds to punch in a key code, not including the two seconds to cross the room to get it. Luckily, they never had a home invasion.

He stripped to his boxers in the en suite with the door opened a crack. Cali never stirred while he brushed his teeth and washed his face. She had finally cleaned the sink after days of his procrastination. That made him smile. He had used every excuse not to, often claiming exhaustion, and like they both knew she would, Cali caved.

Nick crept into the bedroom and stood in front of the dresser. He took out a folded pair of adult sized sweatpants. They fell open in his hand and he could just make out the Marvel superhero pattern. The Christmas after his mom's murder, with his own allowance, he had bought the only pair of Spiderman sweatpants left in the Target. It was an imaginary Christmas present from his mom to himself. However, they were adult-sized and not the right art. Nick made them work with office clips until they fit properly. Lou hadn't even noticed.

He clutched the sweatpants under his chin and told his mom goodnight, then put them back, folded nicely. He glanced to Cali lying on her side. With half of her face in the pillow, the blanket covered her nose, leaving one eye exposed… and it was open.

"Sorry," he said in a whisper, closing the drawer.

Her eye squinted in what he hoped was a smile. "Are you okay?"

"Fine. Let's talk about it tomorrow."

Cali moaned when Nick slid under the blanket, melding his body to her backside. The warmth instantly enveloped him. A sweet strawberry fragrance wafted out the top of the covers. She pulled his hand across her firm stomach, shifting into a perfect spooning position. He smoothly maneuvered that same hand under her tee-shirt, resting his forearm between her breasts.

"Sorry, so late." He managed to use his other hand to move a length of blonde hair in order to kiss her warm, slender neck. "Thanks for cleaning the sink."

"Are you turned on by that?"

"It's the rubber gloves."

"I'll go put them on," She cooed, sniffing into the air. "Beer? What were you doing all night?"

"Uh, cheating on you?"

She flipped to face him. "You can't cheat with anything less than a nine or I'll be insulted."

"He was a nine... inches." Nick smiled as she laughed. He traced the length of her arm.

"Where can I find this guy?" Their giggles subsided. "I know you were at Shelly's with Lou."

"As usual."

Her finger drew slow, wiggly lines on his chest. "Don't be one of those brooding cops that can't talk about his day." It was a statement requiring a response.

"We were talking about how Belinda's mistake affects my making detective." Nick offered several gentle kisses.

"Was it a mistake?"

"Depends on who you ask. I don't think she meant it."

"Does it affect your making detective?"

"Shouldn't. I can't wait to wear normal clothes everyday instead of that uniform."

"Just don't ever show up in my E.R." Cali kissed him softly.

"Can't promise you that *Nurse* Maddox, but I'll do my damnedest."

Nick and Cali had been dating for six years, engaged for one. Neither were in a hurry. In the first few months, when the relationship had gotten serious enough for Nick to bring her around his cop buddies, cautious Lou needed a background check. Nick insisted she was legitimate, but Lou vetted her anyway. According to his father's intel, Cali Maddox was an authentic nurse, having graduated from The University of Alabama School of Medicine. She had been born and raised outside of Montgomery, Alabama. Her mom was deceased, father unknown. Lou had stopped his investigation at that point, or so he thought.

"You're tense." Cali squeezed the base of his neck.

He closed his eyes, rolling his head with the motion. "God, that's good."

She backed away and pointed for him to lie on his stomach. Her legs straddled his torso and she dug her fingers into his back, using her palms to push muscle back and forth. After five minutes, the massage finished with a barrage of kisses across his shoulder blades.

Nick could only hum into the pillow.

"That was the appetizer," She said, softly.

Cali lifted her leg, balancing on her other knee to allow him room to roll over. When he settled on his back, she squeezed her bent legs against his hips, using her nails to till the length of dark hair down the center of his stomach.

The passion never dissipated after all these years, emotionally or physically, concentrated in her green eyes. Two percent of the world had that color, calculating in terms of gender it meant Cali was basically one in a million. She had never gone through the motions of sex, or forced cuddling, or shied away from public displays of affection. He had yet to detect disinterest while she listened to his obscure opinions about menial things.

The real question was; *why was he waiting for it?*

She arched her back and pulled off her nightshirt. Her lengthy hair whipped upwards, falling gently back to her shoulders. He watched her face in the glow from the moonlight. The way she looked at him sometimes, it made him scared to lose her. It made him scared for the things he would do for her, if she would only ask.

Chapter 6

The digital alarm clock would be turned off for three days. Nick woke at first light every morning, anyway. Heat from the sun filtering into the bedroom had yet to give the window unit a challenge. He groaned. His exposed skin prickled. He had been meaning to install thick curtains to block the light, one of many little jobs to complete.

Nick's head searched for warmth on the pillow. His arms were wrapped around his exposed torso. The blanket had collected at his knees, which had never happened his entire life. Without opening his eyes, he reached for the covers, however something blocked his hand. His eyes focused to find Cali facing him, lying on her side dressed in hospital scrubs. Her extended arm bent so as to prop up her head, leaving her blonde ponytail to sway.

"What are you doing?" he asked with a dry mouth. "I'm cold."

She glanced at his boxers. "What were you just dreaming about that has you so excited?"

He didn't have to look. "The Saints winning the Superbowl."

"That explains it." She fiddled with his hair. "Men get an erection almost every hour during sleep."

"What is going on with you?" He played with her ponytail. "You're acting silly."

"Just in a good mood. I got something for you."

"Again? Well, let me go pee first and we'll see what happens."

Cali conjured the sound of a buzzer on a game show. "EEHHH. Wrong answer." She popped off the bed like a gymnast with a dismount. "Unlike you, I have to go to work. Meet me in the kitchen. I'll make you coffee as a consolation prize." She blew him a kiss as she left the room.

"Thanks," he groaned.

Nick returned to the dresser after a bathroom excursion, taking out the sweatpants he had held the night before. Putting them on, his toes attempted to avoid the holes, but he stumbled, and his foot ripped the aging material. When he caught his balance, he faltered at the sight. Gingerly, he finished putting them on, wondering if he could sew up the gap that exposed his thigh.

A coffee with milk and sugar waited as he entered the kitchen, almost limping as if injured. Cali gazed down at his exposed thigh. "Oh, my."

"Yeah."

She leaned against the counter with a smile. Her scrubs hid her figure, but she was sexy despite them. Her body eclipsed an unfamiliar bag on the counter with a strange pocket watch logo. His hands warmed on the cup. "What's that behind you?"

Instead of answering that question, she kissed him quickly on the lips, patting down his hair. "Shave, will you? You're scratchy. By the way, I think you need to lose those sweatpants. You look like the Hulk busting out of Spiderman's costume."

"Yeah, just did this with my razor blade toenail. But, I can't throw them out. I told you..."

"I know," she interrupted, repeating the story she'd heard a dozen times, "You bought them when you were thirteen. It was the closest pair you could find to match the ones your mom gave you."

He sulked. "I haven't found anything close. They don't make them anymore."

"Do you still have that picture of you wearing them on Christmas Day?" She gravitated toward the counter, securing the mysterious package.

"You know I do."

"Get it. I want to see it."

"Now?" He sipped his coffee, squinting at her over the cup.

"You ever want to have sex again?" she threatened.

Nick put down the coffee. "You're choosing to play that card now? With this?"

"Damn straight."

"I thought it would be with getting a dog or a seeing the ballet or something. But, I know you're up to something." He hiked an eyebrow and left the room, returning to face her with a small binder opened to the middle. "Here. I hope sex is back on the table. Or on the sofa. Or on the floor."

"You hold the binder." She opened the bag, giving another order. "Hold it up, so I can see."

"Don't tell me you found..."

"Just do it."

Exasperated, he obeyed. "What I do for lovin'..."

Cali brought her hand out of the bag, raising a pair of sweatpants that matched the pattern in the picture exactly. "Are these what you were looking for?"

Nick threw the book onto the table without aiming. He took the sweatpants and inspected every inch. "Where did you get this?"

"As Time Goes On, retro shop on Magazine Street. All kinds of shit from the 1800's on up."

"Unbelievable." He inspected the material in better light.

"I wanted to wait until Christmas, but with your current state of affairs…" She waved her hand at the shredded cotton weave. "You need these, sweetie."

"It's my size. And the exact pattern." He wrapped his arms around her as his eyes filled. She caressed his back until he released her. "Thank you."

Her fingers wiped his cheeks with reluctant tears in her own eyes. "You're welcome. You okay?"

"More than okay. Love you."

"Ditto. But, I have to get to work."

He scooted out of the old sweatpants and put the new ones on. "Perfect."

"We can do a before and after picture." She smiled. "What do you want to do for dinner?"

He mimicked porn music with a wink. "I'll think of something."

She tapped his chest with a hard finger. "Yeah, yeah. Make a plan. Something with candles and forks and conversation. See you tonight. Love you."

"I believe you."

The door closed. The colors on Spiderman's suit were still vibrant, as if the sweatpants had never been worn. He almost rubbed his hands across his thighs. *No, that insecure habit needed to stop.* Nick held the sweatpants in a new regard, as a way to not only remember the good times with his mother, but to also be reminded of how much he loved Cali.

He returned to his coffee again. With a new surge of energy, he picked up his cell phone and dialed. "Hey, Belinda, how are you?"

"I don't know. I keep replaying it in my head."

"You want to talk about it? I'm no head-shrink, but I've shot two suspects before. One died. I do understand."

"Yeah, I know. No. I feel fine. You want to meet me at your gym?"

"You want to work out? Really?" He sipped his coffee.

"I have to do something. I'm going crazy here. I don't have a boyfriend to take my mind off it. I need the distraction."

"Sure. Why not?" He headed for the bedroom to change clothes while listening to her.

"You think it's safe to show our faces? We were mentioned on the news."

"Yeah, but there's nothing damning yet. They're not screaming for our heads. Haven't seen any protests either. The report favors us. He was raping the woman and he had a knife."

"And he resisted."

Nick let out a silent breath. "I'll go, but on one condition. We don't talk about the shooting or your obsession with the Tribunal. I just got Cali to stop asking if I know anything; I don't need it outside the house, too."

Chapter 7

Nick trained at The Crowder Gym, named for the street where it was located. It would never be called the *crowded* gym. He appreciated the daily release of his pent-up aggression from playing peacekeeper. An officer's restraint could be either frustrating or draining when dealing with public grievances and disturbances. If he couldn't body-slam a douche-bag during a traffic stop, then he had to free that pressure valve somewhere else. Unfortunately, Belinda had released her valve in the worst way.

He entered the gym expecting to be hounded by press, but it was clear. Belinda was stretching on a mat near the treadmills when he arrived. "You're right," she beamed, none the worse for wear, "No one recognizes me."

"Cool. Chest and tri's today?" Nick asked, joining her in the warm-up. He put his towel and water bottle near hers.

Belinda kept her dishwater blonde hair styled short like a Vogue model. At five-foot ten, she had been an athlete at Dominican High School, playing varsity soccer and volleyball. After graduation, she became an MMA fighter, signing a three-year professional contract. In her fifth match, having two wins and two losses, a severe concussion ended her short-lived career. Law enforcement wasn't her first choice, but it was a natural fit.

Nick was particular about his gym memberships. He preferred independent owners, but the profit margin was so small, sometimes they fell quickly into decline. The Crowder gym kept its equipment new and clean. A staff member rotated on the floor, assisting anyone that looked lost or had poor form. Belinda set her bag by an open bench. Nick dropped underneath the empty bar and slowly pumped out ten reps to get the blood flowing. Too much weight too soon could cause injury.

"What's going on with Gavin Jones?" Belinda asked, taking Nick's place on the bench.

*Damn it.* "What do you mean?"

"The boys have a pool going on him. Fool deserves it if he's too stupid to get out of town." Belinda pumped out the easy reps.

He let the statement linger as he slid a twenty-five pound plate onto the bar with a clamp. Belinda did the same on the other side. The weight would grow with each set. He measured her. "I told you, don't start with that shit."

She swung her arms in a circle and looked around, but anyone nearby had earplugs. "You think what happened will help my chances getting in?"

"You probably need to be *asked*, from what I understand."

"You're a broken record."

"And I always will be. I don't know why you try."

"Okay. As an *informed outsider*..." She rolled her eyes. "When did it all start? I mean, I have an idea from the news articles, but you... you know more than me."

"Ah, a new tactic." Nick smiled. "You just want to get me talking." Nick needlessly wiped off the bench.

"Just conversation." She took her turn under the barbell after exchanging out the plates. "There's no harm in giving me history, right?"

"History. Okay. *From what I'm told*, the feds first got involved about fifteen years ago."

"Suspicious deaths of criminals," she said while pushing.

He kept both his index fingers under the bar. "Yeah, I mean, gang members are killed by rival gangs. Hookers are killed by pimps or johns. Spouses are killed by other spouses or lovers. And child molesters and rapists are almost never found murdered, and yet, they were all turning up dead. So many at one point, the coroner couldn't keep up. I think it's one of the reasons they finally sprang for a new facility."

Belinda eagerly switched the lighter plates for heavier ones. "And the feds?"

"Their *Violent Crimes* squad moved into the lakefront field office to set up shop. The NOPD closed ranks and was less than hospitable." He offered a wry smile.

They switched places and Belinda enthusiastically spotted Nick. "When did the feds suspect it to be cops?"

"About ten years ago." Nick spoke clearly, barely straining with the early reps. "Interviewing the family and friends of these murder victims got nothing but speculation and finger pointing. The feds switched from a group of underground vigilantes to a multiple insiders theory."

Belinda nodded. "So, for the past decade, the Bureau figured that it was a cop or group of cops responsible, given how pristine the crime scenes were."

"Yep."

She caught the bar on his last rep. "And no one ever slipped up. Amazing."

Nick stood. "I would assume they don't slip up because they don't talk."

"Just like you." Belinda placed fingers over her smile. "Sorry. Go on. Please."

Nick shook his head. "The feds got support of the *cop* theory from some of the families of the murdered criminals."

Belinda had a total of eighty-five pounds on the rack, including the bar. She sat. "And the legend of the Tribunal was born."

Nick stopped for water. "Then, came the day the FBI *showed their ass*, according to Lou. After the widely publicized murder of a serial rapist, the FBI held a press conference, hoping to cast the entire NOPD in bad light."

"I remember that. The city was relieved when the guy was found dead, but not the feds."

"You know the FBI started out as a super Christian organization. They attempted to appeal to the moral, conscientious majority. Nola being mostly Catholic, the FBI even pleaded to the religious to do the right thing. But, the public wasn't having any of it. The Bureau found the police more protected than ever."

She took the time to concentrate on her set. She finished, wiping her brow with a towel. "So, the Feds had to change their approach, right?"

Nick indicated he wanted two forty-five pound plates on each end. "They stopped asking questions. They send out a fed once and a while to fish, but they've been stalled ever since."

"Crazy that all of America knows about it, but *we're* so close to it."

"Crazy."

He didn't expand further as the workout progressed. He could have added that as another few years passed, the Bureau enacted several undercover operations that yielded nothing but embarrassment. Outsiders with an agenda could be smelled coming like a sack of oysters. The circle was too tight. As ludicrous as it sounded, the city grew to love the NOPD.

Nick had heard all the hushed whispers of how the high-and-mighty FBI couldn't infiltrate the lowly NOPD. It seemed like a ridiculous notion, but every player in this game of chess did their job and nothing more, leaving the FBI chasing shadows.

Chapter 8

The showers at the gym were Petri dishes Nick avoided. Plus, a few immodest regulars enjoyed being naked way too much. The day he saw a member blow-drying his shaggy butt-hair was the last day he went in the locker room. After a long, steaming shower in his own bathroom, he ate a turkey sandwich while spread out on the sofa listening to his playlist. He kept the television on mute in case a story broke about Belinda's shooting. The anticipation surfaced again about Gavin Jones.

Could he commit one more murder in the name of justice? There wasn't any Gavin Jones intel left to memorize. The man changed his appearance as often as Lady GaGa. One police photo showed a long-haired black man with a dead stare. Then, while in custody for questioning, the man wore his mangy hair parted down the middle. His skin glistened as if oiled up for the beach. The most recent photo displayed a buzz cut and a budding beard.

A few of the eradicated were suffocated and some were drowned. Each Tribunal member had their own preference with how they killed their mark. Violent targets were usually shot in the heart, sometimes the head. Rapists or child molesters might catch one in the groin first. Lou preached against torture – against emotion. Get in and get out. A passionate kill invited mistakes.

Gavin Jones once worked as a FedEx driver until he didn't show up one day because he was in Orleans Parish Prison. Currently, the convict was unemployed, so he couldn't be taken out at his job. In the early days, Lou had loved the drive-by while accompanied by another Tribunal member - a barrage of shots from a stolen car by two men with hoodies. Witnesses were eager to say bangers. Besides, there were neighbors and traffic cameras to worry about. Everything got recorded nowadays.

Lou and Mr. Gary once joked about the *Fight Club* movie. The first rule of the Tribunal is to never speak of the Tribunal. Despite knowing each member and socializing from time to time, the members were never to become friends. Relationships muddied the process. Protecting your best friend wouldn't look good on the witness stand. Nick and Marcus had been an exception, however, as they have known each other since childhood, and Lou gave his stamp of approval with Mr. Gary's apprenticeship of Marcus.

The Jones situation brought back his initial eradication, as expected. Nick had taken great measures to cope with the events of killing a child rapist name Elliot Green. Those mental exercises hadn't worked. It was better to just let the memories come, then pass, like so many thunderstorms.

With the emotional detachment he'd developed over the years, he let the Green memories surface. It always started with Marcus giving his face a motivational slap. Marcus had used his squad car to drop him off at Green's van on a cool, overcast day. The molester violated parole having been parked near the recess yard of an elementary school. The children were screaming and laughing, and Nick's blood boiled at the implications of this guy doing it again.

The vehicle had been a white utility van with no side or back windows, just tinted ones in the front. The panels were dented, rusted near the wheel-wells, and dirty enough to write a message with your finger, something like *kids stay away* would have been appropriate. Marcus positioned the squad next to the van.

The tall, imposing Marcus had distracted Green on the driver's side with a typical warning. During that exchange, Nick opened the van's passenger door and climbed into the seat complete with a black ski mask, causing the vehicle to wobble. If the door had been locked, Marcus would have instructed Green out of the van, which would have unlocked all the doors at once. Without hesitation, Nick slapped his cuffs on Green's wrist, securing the other end to the steering wheel.

A string of expletives had left Green's mouth. He wore a loose janitor-style gray jumpsuit. The standard concealing glasses and ball cap completed the ensemble, as if molesters had a dress code.

"Not another word." Nick had aimed his gun. "Roll up your window."

To outside observers, a policeman had casually walked away from a citizen sitting in a parked van. Marcus disappeared in his squad, leaving Elliot Green pulling at his tethered arm. The mug shots didn't do his complexion justice. Green looked as if he went at his pimples with nail clippers. His nostrils were long and narrow. His lips pink.

Nick straightened his ski mask. The disguise itched his face initially, but the sensation faded just minutes later. At that moment, Nick couldn't feel anything but his fingertips on the gun. He had glanced at the supplies in the back of the van with a frown. Duct tape, rope, dolls, and stuffed animals.

*A kit.*

On television and in books, the characters were allowed a monologue to explain things, but in real life, if one person wanted the other dead, the trigger would be pulled, and the problem solved. Nick hesitated with the gravity of the situation, leaving Green to plead for his life. As the man ran out of steam, he caught on to the situation. "I know what this is." Elliot had lost his breath. He bowed his head and stifled a sob. "You're Tribunal."

Nick reached over, pulling the guy's cap and glasses off. Green had a face that must've been beat up on the playground. Before Green's initial arrest, he had been fired under suspicious circumstances from Reed Elementary. He was hired by Little Tots Day Care only to be accused of molesting a five-year-old boy. Green served three years with a three-year probation with a plea. The judge was soft because of the kid's shaky testimony. Nick had no doubts.

"You have a mask. You can still leave." Green's cheeks had burned red.

"Nope." Nick jabbed Elliot's nose, sending the back of his head against the window. "A young male came forward to tell the judge you molested him, so you plead down. Too bad he was an unreliable drug addict with no proof. I spoke with his family. You had contact with the boy."

Green had bawled like a coward. "I'm within a hundred yards of a school. I'm breaking probation. Just arrest me." He tried to stop crying, but his face was still wet.

"I'm torn, Elliot. You're going to be my first eradication. That's what we call it in the Tribunal. *E - rad - de - cation*. Never done it before. I actually didn't know I could up to this very minute." That had been the truth.

The creep grasped at that glimmer of hope. "You don't want to do it. You kill me and you're no better than I am - a criminal. You're hesitating for a reason."

"I'm waiting for that recess bell to ring. It'll cover the shot."

"The bell?" Saliva had sputtered through the child molester's lips. Tears flowed. "I need help," he squeaked. "I was abused as a kid... molested by my uncle. Where was *my* help?"

"If you were molested, then I'm sorry. That's a shame. But, at a certain point in adulthood, you have to choose between right and wrong. Because you *know* what's right... and what's wrong."

"And you think this is right – what you're doing?"

The recess bell had rung from the back of the school. Green's head snapped toward the sound. He tried to form a word but only stuttered. Nick fired three shots into Elliot's stomach as the teachers collected the children. Just like that, Elliot Green was slumped on the steering wheel, eyes half-open. All of Nick's blood seemed to drain into his legs, leaving his torso and brain and empty husk. He got the chills, and pinpoints of light shot across his vision.

He had killed a man.

He had killed a *child molester*.

Every one of those children had made it home that day.

There hadn't been a party, nor a celebration. No Tribunal member had ever mentioned Elliot Green again. After the eradication, Nick arrived at Shelly's where Marcus had situated himself on a stool by himself. Their non-verbal communication conveyed solidarity. They each faced their beer, sitting shoulder to shoulder, not speaking, but content in the understanding of what had transpired. After a minute, they clinked their longnecks.

Lou and Mr. Gary, several stools over, hadn't disengaged from their animated conversation. Nick knew to expect apathy from its members. Lou had brought Nick into the fold, and Mr. Gary had mentored Marcus. Those seasoned cops had killed in the double digits, laughing as if those memories were locked away in the blackened cellar of their mind. There was something unsettling about that.

Nick let the Green memories evaporate into the present. With hair still damp from the shower, Nick started planning as the day was sliding by. Cali had mentioned dinner with forks and conversation, but he thought to do one better. He needed to run down the street to the Winn Dixie for the proper groceries to make his rare masterpiece – seafood gumbo. Cooking was an excellent way to keep his mind off all things Tribunal.

Did he have another choice of vocation as the son of the Tribunal leader? Like Elliot Green, he had to know what was right and what was wrong. Yet, Nick made the choice to end the child molester's life, so he must have thought it was right. But, someone conditioned to Tribunal life would think that, wouldn't they? It wasn't a black and white answer.

## Chapter 9

Known as the Holy Trinity in Cajun cooking, the chopped onions, bell peppers, and celery were tossed into the roux. Nick followed his mother's gumbo recipe exactly. The half-crab for seasoning, shrimp, Andouille sausage, and other spices were lined up in wait. U2 at Red Rocks blared from a Bose Bluetooth speaker. A glass of sweet tea was slowly savored.

The lawn had been reluctantly mowed under the late afternoon sun as the gumbo cooked. The aging Sonata got washed and Gavin Jones' documents were shredded. Nick set the dining room table with tall green candles, plates, and silverware. A vase of assorted flowers was positioned nearby. Sitting at the corner of the table was a fancy, chrome bucket filled with ice and a six-pack of Abita Amber.

Nick waited until Cali was due home to cook the white rice. She would need a bit of time to settle in, anyway. He showered a second time, shaved off the *scratchy*, and cleaned the kitchen the best he could, stirring his tasty creation while waiting.

Cali entered the front door right on time with a loud remark that traveled through the house. "Something smells awesome. What are you cooking?"

"My special gumbo. Get ready for the best meal of your life."

Cali entered the kitchen inhaling deeply. Her blue scrubs hung loose on her frame. "Wow. You've made this – what, four times? You should go on administrative leave more often." She gave him a kiss, squeezing his butt. "I thought you might've worn your sweatpants all day."

"I wanted to."

"Let me go clean up. Be ready in a bit."

Fifteen minutes passed when Nick heard Cali pad into the dining room. He peeked from the kitchen to see her in thick socks, dressed in a tight Saint's shirt and shorts. It dawned on him that the *black and gold* were playing tonight. She sat at the decorated table wiping her palms together in anticipation.

When Nick brought the pot into the dining room, she was rocking enthusiastically in the chair, like a kid getting a birthday cake. "I was expecting to dress up and go out, but honestly, this is so much better after a rough shift. And I'm starving."

"I know you don't like to go out to dinner when you're tired, so I brought the restaurant to you. Although, we won't need forks like you said." He held up a gumbo spoon.

"You, me, gumbo, Abita, Saints." Her green eyes twinkled. "Nice."

Nick poured a scrumptious moat of gumbo around an island of rice. Bubbles rose to a foamy head on beer served in tall, refrigerated glasses. He sat only when Cali had everything she needed. They ate and talked about their day, which he genuinely enjoyed. Cali gave him a sense of normalcy in a life that touched on all levels of disturbing.

"You ever talk with any of your friends back in Alabama?" He dipped a block of store-bought cornbread into the gumbo as if the question was no big deal.

She lost her smile. "Never had any good friends there. They would have visited if I did. Why?"

*Because Lou was digging again.* "I worked out with Belinda today. She asked who might be sitting on your side at the wedding. Besides your friends from the hospital as bridesmaids, I really didn't know how to answer." He tested the beer.

"Obviously, I won't have any family there."

He touched her hand. "I know."

"We should start rounding up a guest list. It's funny, people cannot believe that I don't have any social media accounts. I don't get the allure of people knowing all your shit."

Nick consumed a large spoon of gumbo. "I hear Facebook is on the decline. I just see it as a constantly updating contact list."

"There'll be some people from the hospital I'll invite. Besides…" She dove into the gumbo. "…Your friends are my friends, right?"

"Right." Nick let that subject end.

The meal had been consumed with gusto. With both bowls cleaned, Nick cleared the table and told Cali to take position on the sofa. The Saints were playing on Sunday Night Football, which had come with plenty of invites earlier in the week to watch at other venues. Nick had declined. He carried two Abita Ambers into the living room where Cali had embedded into the cushions.

He handed her a cold bottle and scooted his ass next to hers, like a magnet. There wasn't a gap between them as they reclined together. They snuggled, kissed, and drank while watching pregame.

"I'm surprised you're not watching with the boys at Shelly's." Cali stared at the huge screen mounted on the wall.

"Thought I'd throw you a bone and keep you company."

"That's sweet." She slapped his leg.

"I *should* spend more time with those bastards." A few seconds passed before they both laughed at his offhanded joke. The police spending off hours together was practically a requirement. He finally answered her question seriously. "I wanted to do something special for you… and relax a bit."

"You cut the lawn. Washed your car. Surprised you're not in a coma."

"Edged, too."

"I don't understand how you're in such great shape and yet you're too lazy to do anything around here."

"I cooked, too," he exclaimed.

"I know, and my poor baby must be exhausted." She pinched his cheek.

"I need a staff. If I had to choose, I might rather have assistants than be rich."

"But, if you're rich, you'd have assistants."

Nick sighed. "But, it's not the same. If you're poor and have assistants, you appreciate them so much more."

"You're so pretty," she said, playfully.

"It's logical to me."

During halftime, and after the food had time to digest, Nick put the remaining dishes in the dishwasher and took out the trash. He opened the last two beers from the melting ice bucket and delivered them to the sofa where Cali waited.

A news teaser came on about Belinda's shooting, and activists calling for an outside investigation, given there were no witnesses or video. One sound bite mentioned the Tribunal by name. After some silence, Cali spoke, "I'm curious."

"Sometimes, I just blurt out stuff about myself, too."

She laughed. "Shut up. No, I'm wondering if the Tribunal's going after Gavin Jones."

He stared forward. "Why are you wondering that?"

"It's been a while since the Tribunal has been in the news."

"I told you I don't know anything."

"I think cops talk." She lifted her head to see him. "I wouldn't doubt you know someone who knows someone. Hell, if you're involved, I'd applaud."

"Didn't you take an oath to do no harm?"

"It's the Nightingale Pledge. If a Tribunal target comes into my emergency room, I'll try to save him. But, nurses and doctors who've been there for the past twenty years tell me how it used to be. A steady line of bangers and innocent bystanders with gunshot wounds coming through. Kids. Tourists with frantic relatives filling the waiting rooms." She shuddered. "Whatever's going on, it's saving lives and saving taxpayers money."

A Saint's play gained seventeen yards on a run up the middle. Nick and Cali performed an automatic high-five above their heads without looking. They agreed that Saints games would be the only time for that cheesy move.

"Would you tell me if you knew?" Cali asked between plays.

"Probably. I mean, if it didn't put you in danger. There's enough speculation out there. Cops spread gossip more than the press. We have no idea who they are. Like friggin' Illuminati or something."

Cali leaned forward, stretching to put her beer on the coffee table. She leaned closer if that were possible, flattening herself against him. Her hand palmed his chest. She looked at him with wet, hypnotizing green eyes. She bit her bottom lip, something he'd seen her do during sad movies.

Nick also put his beer down and held her tight. "What's wrong?"

"Nothing. Nothing's wrong." She kissed him, pushing her lips into his, but keeping her tongue in check. It wasn't meant to start anything. Nick understood, taking his cue from her.

Cali lightly touched his cheek, and a wave of memories came to him. He had been slapped there twice by a woman named Tanya. The sensation unearthed a buried secret from long ago. He pretended to watch the game, but drifted to a time just days after the murder of Slimeball Harry – to the predestined meeting with little twelve-year-old Tanya Sanders, Slimeball Harry's daughter.

Chapter 10


Nick had been eleven-years old when he stumbled upon Tanya Sanders.

The police had found Harold Sanders decomposing in the abandoned strip mall three days after his murder, according to the NOPD press conference. Some kids riding their bikes noticed a bad smell and investigated. No one had attempted to question Nick. But, what would an eleven-year-old know about it?

Still, that hadn't stopped Nick from checking around every corner. Cop shows on television made him nervous, picturing himself as the criminal being hauled away in cuffs. Marcus and other friends were eager to speculate about Harold's murder, wanting Nick to give them insider knowledge. He feigned ignorance, saying his father wasn't part of the investigation.

Lou hadn't seemed any different after blowing a man's brains out, even kind of happy for the first time since Nick's mom was killed. There still hadn't been any hugs or other displays of affection, verbal or otherwise, but the punishments with the belt had stopped. His father had even slapped his butt once like a football player. Nick tried to process that event for hours, wanting to determine if it meant *good play*, but it was much better than a new bruise.

A few days after Lou's buddies had cleared the strip mall, Nick found the online obituary and funeral services for *Slimeball Harry*, as Lou had called him. The obituary didn't inform the public of the crime he had allegedly committed. The man that killed Alison Campbell Rush was survived by a wife named Tiffany. And he had a daughter named Tanya, age twelve. Harold's only child was a year older than him. How did *she* feel about her father? Did she still love him? Hate him?

Harold Sanders had worked as a plumber for most of his life, and if that damn pipe hadn't started leaking under the sink, his mom would still be alive. The man had come into their home, invited even. He checked out the place, saw something he wanted, and came back to take it. He took everything Nick held dear.

Sanders had been cremated due to the autopsy and his body's deterioration. His memorial for close friends and relatives was happening just three miles from his house. Apparently, they believed he was innocent, as had the clueless court system. Lou had railed about the city becoming desensitized to the violence. Murders happened so often in New Orleans that it was no longer a tragedy, it was merely a shame.

Nick cleared the obit search history before turning off the computer. A framed picture of him and his mother walking on the Haynes levee faced out from the dresser. He studied it as if he was going to war and might not return. Lou certainly had faults, but he also had a few redeeming qualities, too. His father let Nick keep a password to the computer and his phone. Lou said someone had to trust you first in order to earn it. His father was too much of a prick to believe something like that, so he stayed cautious. Nick charged to his closet and folded up a set of dress clothes and put them in his backpack.

In those rare times he had lied to Lou, he learned it boosted his self-esteem and he found ways to inject little white lies when he could. This, however, was a big one. Nick stuck his head into the garage where Lou's sandaled feet protruded from under the red Mustang. Its two front tires were raised on individual ramps. *What if it fell and crushed him*? The engine hoist hovered above, unused at the moment. Classic rock played from inside the car and two empty beer bottles had been rolled near the garbage can.

He knocked on the doorframe. "I'm going over to Marcus'. That okay?"

A tool whacked something from underneath. "You don't want to see what I'm doing under here?"

"Sorry, Dad. The new comics are out."

"Comics," he scoffed. "You finished your chores? You got the new jacket you had to have?"

"Yes, sir." he pulled at the brand new Northface as if Lou could see. Being early March, it was still chilly out.

"You said you like Camaros, right?" Lou asked without sliding out.

"Sure." He waited for a follow up statement. "Love them."

"My pal is going to sell me his '75 Camaro. It's a fixer upper. I figure you and I can restore it together. A little project we can do on the weekends at Hoover's junkyard."

"A car for me? I'm only eleven."

Lou finally slid out far enough to peek his face. "It doesn't run. Needs a lot of work. By the time you're old enough to drive, it should be cherry. And you'll appreciate it so much more than just buying a junker off a lot."

"That sounds great."

"Great." He slid back under the car. "Tell Big Hoover hi for me. Tell him about the Camaro, too. He'll be glad to have you back at the junkyard. Be back by supper."

Nick hopped on his blue Huffy with no intention of seeing Marcus, but he would have to tell his best friend to cover for him. He peddled from the garage with his backpack on his shoulder. The farther he journeyed, the lighter he felt. The absence of Lou allowed him to fly. The biting wind stung his face, but he endured. He managed to stay on side streets for most of the way, jumping curbs and cracked sidewalks, crossing one major intersection with the help of a red light.

Stopping a block from the Holy Cathedral Church, he chained his bike to a rack at the Circle K and headed for the soiled bathroom. He changed his clothes without touching anything gross and warmed his beet red cheeks with a working hand drier. A little water from the dripping faucet helped his hair lay flat.

He stepped out of the bathroom and inhaled the fresh, cold air. Leaving his bike at the store, he hoofed it a block until seeing a sprinkle of people talking outside the steps of the church. For the first time, he wondered why he came. Was he going to *boo* the attendees? What if someone noticed him and started asking those questions Lou warned him about? But, these people would have no idea his father had killed this man.

The nicely dressed mourners made their way inside at different speeds. One rugged guy hurried on a cigarette while another woman power-walked in heals, holding onto a man in a loose suit. Teens wore jeans and collared shirts. Some had tennis shoes. Nick's knees trembled while approaching the base of the steps, giving witness to the gigantic, carved wooden doors.

"Who are you?" A soft voice said from behind.

Nick stiffened and turned. A pretty girl about his age had snuck up on him. She had straight dark hair with bangs in a perfect line over her eyebrows. He wasn't used to seeing girls her age with makeup, but she sported a little on her lips and eyes. His jaw locked. He considered himself lucky not to be drooling.

"Well? Can you talk? Are you a mute?"

"I'm Nick," he almost choked. *Shit*. He gave his name. But, how could she know who he was?

"I'm Tanya." Her sad face hadn't smiled. She only held out her hand.

Nick took her fingers, feeling the charge travel through his body. This was *Slimeball Harry*'s daughter. He wanted to run, but his legs were frozen, either by fear, or her face.

"Sad," he finally said.

"Who are you here with?"

"My dad. He's inside. He's a plumber. He's an old friend of Mr. Sanders." Nick didn't understand how he could lie so easily.

"Why are you standing out here in the cold?"

He looked at the intimidating doors. "I don't like churches. My dad said I can wait out here."

She nodded, focused on her feet. "I don't like churches, either. Especially now." They waited through a moment of silence. "They don't know who killed my dad. So many people think he murdered that woman, but he didn't."

"All that matters is what the judge thought." A true enough statement.

"What matters is what one evil freak thought." Her arms wrapped around herself as a tear dropped. Her voice came out loud and shrill. "Whoever killed my dad is going to hell, and I hope he dies from a hundred bullets."

"They have no idea who killed him?" He wanted to hold her, and wipe away her tears.

"I hear my relatives whispering. They think it was that woman's husband… the cop, and it was a cover up. Maybe I'll prove he did it."

"That would be something." *Why was it so hard to comfort her?*

"If we all know he was innocent, why doesn't that policeman, Louis Rush? He got it so wrong." She used a tissue to blow her nose.

"You sure your dad was innocent?" *Did that come out of his mouth?*

Shock registered on her face. Rage filled her perfect eyes. With clenched teeth, she slapped him across his cheek. "Because he is! Because he was."

He stood in shock, not feeling anything but the sting on his face. She pushed past him and bounded up the steps. It took effort, but she pulled open the immense door and disappeared inside. He could have crumbled into a ball right there on that spot. At the time, Nick had thought he'd never see her again. He thought she'd never get a chance to slap him again. Man, was he wrong.

*She wanted Lou to die from a hundred bullets.*

Chapter 11


The second day of banishment was upon him. Nick took the time to do his *research*. He watched from a distance as Gavin Jones drove his sun-ravaged, 2001 beige Volvo into the Winn Dixie parking lot. The man's current appearance consisted of a high fade with inch long blond tips at the top. The grocery store monopolized the corner of an immense U-shaped strip mall with security cameras facing the entrances of the individual establishments. Once Jones entered, Nick followed, only moments behind.

Nick wore a pair of shades and a Saints cap into the cold store. He selected a red basket with handles instead of the buggy, checked his watch, and stayed a safe distance. Nick read food labels to procrastinate. Jones walked certain aisles with a rattling buggy, picking ready-to-eat items, and not wasting time browsing. Milk, Hamburger Helper, soup, cereal, and Coke among other things. This was typical male shopping; purchase what you need in a short amount of time.

There were several pretty women Gavin passed by and made comments to, but Nick was too far away to hear. By the women's reactions, it wasn't a welcomed exchange. The way Jones leered back at them, at their chest and posterior, made Nick feel pity for that type of man. He certainly had a vile vibe about him.

Gavin ended his shopping on the back aisle. He chatted with the butcher, friendly enough with a male, and then made his way to the checkout. He pushed in front of a shocked elderly lady to get in line. *What a gentleman.* The hair on Nick's neck stood on end as something wasn't right. However, he didn't see anyone paying him undue attention. He shook it off.

Nick stalled by inspecting bags of red kidney beans on an end-cap display near the cash registers. Would it be like this if he made detective? Could he observe human behavior and properly judge if someone was a scumbag without concrete evidence? Jones was pretty obvious.

Someone spoke to him. "Wow, I see you more off the job than on."

He recognized his partner's voice. He *was* being watched. Belinda was dressed in an Under Armour muscle shirt and shorts. Her rounded shoulders and sharp lines were enough to turn off insecure men, but to Nick, it was something to admire. "Belinda."

"Beans?"

The bag of kidney beans spread out in his hand. "How's it going?"

"Makin' groceries. I usually do it late at night when it's dead, but I'm out of Moon Pies." She looked at the array of health foods in her buggy. The Moon Pies was a joke.

"Nice selection."

"This isn't your Winn Dixie." She waved around her, muscles responding with each movement.

"Mine was out of my favorite beans." He glanced at Jones standing in a checkout line.

"A Winn Dixie is out of Camellia Beans? Is that right?" Her hip shot out with incredulity.

"Just running errands and found myself driving by. I'm also shopping for Shelly. He's out of Moon Pies." He reminded himself he needed to have that talk with Shelly about Gavin Jones.

"Weird, that agoraphobia thing. What do you think that stems from?"

"Habits and insecurity? I don't know. Won't talk about it." He found it hard to focus on her.

Her tone lowered. "There's going to be a protest at City Hall about my shooting."

"Crap."

"Damn people eager to bitch about anything a cop does."

"Who would do that here?"

"Out-of-towners mostly. Captain said to keep a low profile. So, you just waiting here by the beans?"

Nick shrugged. "Why the grilling?"

Belinda cocked her head. "Because it looks like you're on a stake out."

"That's ridiculous." He tossed the beans in the air.

"That's Gavin Jones."

Nick turned. "Where?"

Belinda didn't point him out. She whispered. "Jesus Christ, Nick. How long are you going to deny it?"

"As long as it's not true." He fought against grabbing her by the shoulders and accusing her of tailing him. "He lives a mile from here. Uniforms see him skulking around all the time. He's a fixture. Chalk it up to a NOLA coincidence."

Belinda smirked. "Actually, I have seen him in here a couple times before with his old lady. Hard to miss that bastard"

"Yeah, he doesn't try to blend in." Nick put the beans down.

"What can I do to help?" Her attention stayed on Jones. "Distract him? Flatten his tire?"

"You can go finish your shopping."

She finally responded to Nick's expression. "Fine. Don't be mad. I'm sorry."

"Talk to you later? When we're cleared and back on the job?"

She hit his stomach. "Sure. Help time pass in the car."

He watched her travel down the bread aisle marveling at her baseball-sized calves. Was her being in the store also a NOLA coincidence? She *did* live right down the street. He dismissed her as a spy because Lou would never enlist her help. Also, she wouldn't be so blunt with a confrontation if that were the case. Even if she was tailing him, he was doing what was expected. Nick continued dogging his mark.

The checkout line Jones selected had an attractive redheaded cashier, very much like the woman he allegedly killed. Nick assumed a young, single man - or a married one for that matter - would seek out the pretty cashier. With a cocked head, he kept licking his lips, and running his hand over his crotch.

Belinda was still shopping when Gavin left the store. Nick spotted her car for good measure before exiting the parking lot. He didn't have to follow close, knowing where Jones was going. Chad Cooper, the cop that should've been doing the eradication, had done a good job on intel. The man kept a specific routine week by week as if he had OCD - as if he had never been accused of a single crime.

Nick parked a good distance away in order to watch the bare-bones structure. He would do the deed next week, if everything fell into place. He took the time to call Shelly to schedule a visit for the next day to find out what he was worried about. Whatever Shelly had to say, he couldn't back out now. Lou constantly preached about following the rules, but while growing up, disobeying minor orders had been the only way Nick could establish some form of independence. Lou had said that Nick was squirrelly when it came to eradications and wanted to make sure he still had what it took. He could back out to piss him off, but Lou would take that as an affront, if not the ultimate betrayal. Not to mention that sudden interest in vetting Cali again was strange. On the other hand, paranoia was the foundation of the Tribunal's success.

Chapter 12

Lou no longer had a wife or prospects for such. He had no kids to raise, not that he would entertain that endeavor again at sixty years of age. Nick's mother had done the hard part until her murder, and then he had to wing it. His own father's method of child rearing was barbaric, but Shelly had no other map. Children understood fear and pain, no disputing that. At least the watered-down version of corporal punishment had given his son enough direction in life to follow in his footsteps. And still, Nick had become a liability.

He tried to *court* the occasional broad, but it never worked out. Women's sensibilities tended to piss him off. They were either too timid or too bitchy, and always on the rag. Maybe he was just too old and selfish, but *he* wasn't the issue. Everyone carried baggage into a relationship. It was the eventual unpacking of that baggage that was the problem. And the younger girls, although easy to handle and manipulate, expected him to partake in their stupid activities like concerts or bar hopping. Instead, Lou enjoyed the occasional motel room *date* with the dancers from his favorite strip club, but otherwise, he had no one. He wanted no one.

No, that wasn't true. He had the Tribunal, and he had his father, and he had the bar. And now Nick's choices were risking it all.

As on most nights, Lou sat perched on his barstool. His glass of ice water added to the wet ring on the coaster. Marcus finished donating to the video poker machine and bellied up next to Lou. The young black man was the designated understudy of Lou's second in command, Gary Forche, but being Nick's best friend made the choice difficult. Lou realized those two were joined at the hip, and Marcus would either be better in the fold, or dead.

Shelly had been good friends with Marcus' grandfather. The only man of color Shelly ever got along with. And Lou hung out with Big Hoover in the good old days, sharing their love of cars at the junkyard, and now Nick had Marcus. Those two were sappy enough to think their future kids would be best friends, too. The optimistic, yet serious cop nursed a Coke as instructed. Seven other civilians were in the establishment, occupying tables and the video poker machines.

"I don't know if I've ever seen this place so busy." Marcus looked around. "What's the legal capacity here? Twenty people?" He chuckled.

"Makes me uncomfortable," Lou huffed.

"Shelly has to make money somehow." Marcus swirled the ice in his glass. "So, why aren't we drinking any of the good stuff?" He scoffed at his Coke.

"I'll tell you. Just relax. This place used to do major business when the camps were there." He pointed at the levee beyond door as if they were visible. "There used to be concrete steps every fifty yards or so leading up and down the other side of the levee. You walked across the railroad tracks and onto the piers to reach the camp."

"Yeah, I've been to your camp once or twice. Wiped out by a hurricane, right? My old man used to talk about it."

Lou cleared the condensation from his glass. "How's your *mom 'n em*? Big Hoover alright?"

"Mom is fine. Happy in Covington. She's dating a white dude. And my dad - the arthritis is pretty bad, his knees, he's so big, but the nursing home takes good care of him. He's completely blind now. Not even shadows."

"Ah, but, we knew it was coming."

"Yeah. He knows his way around that little room, though." Marcus' voice cracked. "He's so young to be there, but he doesn't want to live with me. He says he needs his independence, but he has to rely on a nursing staff."

"I think he just doesn't want to rely on his kid. It's supposed to be the other way around. Any way you slice it, it sucks."

"We appreciate your helping us with expenses. The bills are outrageous."

"That's exactly what our funds are for. Money put to good use. Your family and mine go way back to the days when black and whites didn't get along."

"Still that way in some cases. My dad liked you. You should visit more."

"I should. I met Big Hoover at the junk yard when I fourteen, cutting my teeth on a Chevy. Now, it's you and Nick, friends since birth. We're family. Only the best for Big Hoover."

"I'll tell him you asked about him."

Lou smiled. "Nick got pretty tight-lipped after he became a junior in high school. Never told me shit. He was always out the house doing stuff with you, from what he told me."

Marcus hesitated. "Yeah, he'd tell you he's sleeping at my house and I'd tell my dad we were sleeping at your house and we'd go out drinking, sneak in the window late at night."

"We both knew you did that."

"You did?"

"You think we weren't young?" Lou continued, "I had no idea what was going on in Nick's life. I tried to give him his space - his privacy, so I never pushed."

"Never had a spy on him?" Marcus looked away, then into his drink.

Lou allowed that comment. It was time to become vulnerable and sympathetic. "Never spied. Don't know if he even had a girlfriend 'cause he never introduced me to any. I thought he was a homo for a while."

A short burst of laughter. "Not gay." Marcus put his hand on Lou's back, but pulled it off a moment later. "He hooked up with girls, but nothing serious."

Lou almost pulled the kid's arm off at the shoulder to beat him with it, but he had steered the conversation that way, hadn't he? He needed Marcus to get comfortable. "Didn't you two have a falling out for a short time?"

"Nick would kill me if he knew we were talking about this." Marcus wiggled his finger at Lou.

"This isn't deep throat shit here, Marcus. We're just bullshitting."

"Right. There was a period between junior and senior year where we stopped hanging out as much. He never told me why."

"You think it was a girl? I heard rumblings about a pool party incident."

"Incident?" Marcus shrugged. "Don't remember much, Mr. Lou. There *was* this pool party where he hooked up with some fine-looking girl from the North Shore."

"Oh, yeah? What was her name? Describe her."

His eyes rolled back in his head. "Ah, don't remember the name. I was pretty drunk at the time. She was the hottest girl at the party, I remember that. Brunette."

"My boy got the hottest girl at the party, huh? Nice."

Lou waved Shelly over. Marcus inspected his empty glass. "Another Coke?"

"No. We may be up late. Shelly, get us both a coffee."
Lou pointed at the full pot. "So, it was a hook up. Not
really a girlfriend thing, right?" Lou asked.

Marcus curiously inspected the fresh cup of coffee
placed in front of him. "Well, I saw him with the same girl
one other time at the movies. I just caught a glimpse of her,
in the dark. He said they hooked up from time to time, but
she wasn't someone to bring around. I was like, *okay.*"

Lou waved his hand over his face. "What'd she look
like? She look like Cali at all? Was that his type?"

Marcus exhaled in thought. "No, didn't look like Cali.
I don't remember exactly. I probably couldn't pick her out
of a lineup. It's all a blur."

"Did she look like a particular movie star?" he
pushed.

The young cop took a careful sip and stared forward.
"No. Sorry, Mr. Lou. I don't know if I could describe my
first one-night stand, much less a girl I saw drunk at a party
when I was sixteen."

Lou assessed him. "You're a cop for Christ's sake."

"I was a kid."

"Ah," Lou faced forward, rotating the cup. "Just
wishing I had been more a part of Nick's life during that
time. Sorry."

Marcus sputtered air out his lips in dismissal.
"Whoever this girl was, didn't last that long. After
graduation, we started hanging out more again."

It was Lou's turn to put his hand on Marcus' back.
"Can you keep an eye on him? Let me know he's doing
okay from time to time. I'd consider it a personal favor."

Lou held up his coffee and Marcus toasted with him.
"I do that anyway, Mr. Lou."

They sat silent for a few moments. Lou looked around
the bar, then shouted, "Shelly! Closing time."

The old man's head perked up from cleaning glasses. He never hesitated. "We're closed! Everyone grab a *go cup* and exit, please."

Marcus looked around at the confused patrons. Lou expected them to be pissed, but he - nor they - didn't care. Everyone headed for the door with accepting faces, each pouring their alcohol into a clear plastic cup stacked at the exit. When the last straggler sashayed outside, Shelly locked the door and increased the music volume. He then took his bug detector and ran it over every inch of where the patrons had been until satisfied nothing had been planted.

Lou drank from his cup. "Shelly, top us off, will you?"

Shelly returned behind the bar and grabbed the pot. He consistently had coffee at the ready for the over-served.

Lou put his transmitter tracker on the bar. He waited for a negative reading. "I didn't invite you here to talk about Nick, although that was good."

"Why am I here, then?" Marcus watched Shelly add to the steaming cups with a steady hand.

"You remember Alex Weesham?" They turned to face each other.

Marcus paused, looking at the gadget, "I assume I can talk about it?"

Shelly held up a second T-9 device. "No transmissions here."

Lou nodded, using his hand to indicate a low volume.

"Alex Weesham. White dude, right? Two years ago, eradicated for a B&E where he put a sixteen-year-old girl in a coma – gave her brain damage. Actually, they never found Weesham's body."

"Because he was supposedly fed to the gators in Bayou St. John."

Marcus placed his hand over his mouth in surprise. "I figured that was done sometimes."

"Guess who was pinched for simple B&E in Tennessee with fake identification?"

"Weesham?"

Lou didn't answer.

"Who let him go?" Marcus asked, as only the cops with the *alibis* knew the eradicator.

Lou paused for effect. "Chad Cooper with the First," he choked on the name. "Weesham is Chad's cousin. He lied to me, to his mentor. To all of us."

Marcus looked confused. "You told Nick?"

"No, I'll leave that to you."

"Okay." Marcus gripped his coffee appearing more confused. "You want me and Nick to eradicate Weesham in Tennessee?"

"Not exactly." Lou finally let him off the hook. "What happens now is we deal with Cooper. This Weesham will no doubt offer up Cooper as a Tribunal member for a plea deal. The press will be all over it."

"You want us to… take care of Cooper?" Marcus still looked unsure. He took a bigger drink of the steaming brew, recoiling at the burn.

"Finish your coffee. Call Nick. Bring Cooper to this address for midnight tonight." Lou pushed a piece of paper toward him.

"Why not just have him meet you there?" Marcus inspected the address.

"He'll be suspicious about a meeting. Considering his betrayal, he might run or turn himself in to the feds. That would even be worse. Not sure if he's heard about Weesham's arrest yet. This is major, Marcus. *Big time fucking major*. He gets home from his bowling league around 11:30."

"You sure he's bowling?"

Lou nodded. "I have eyes in his bowling league. So far, he's unaware. Wait outside his house, but don't expose yourself to his family or neighbors. Don't knock on his door. If he doesn't show, text me with a simple *no*."

"Got it."

"I have to go to arrange things. Make this happen." Lou pointed at the paper. "Rip the address to shreds after you memorize it."

Marcus secured the paper without looking at it. "I'm on it."

Lou slid off his stool and walked toward the door, but stopped and turned. "Oh, and Marcus, I'd consider it a personal favor if you don't mention our conversation about Nick's dating life to him. He'd just think I was being nosy." Not that he truly cared.

"Got it."

The first number Lou called while in the Mustang was Gary Forche to make sure the members had been alerted. He surveyed the empty road, checking the set of headlights that appeared several blocks behind him. The headlights blinked twice, indicating his rear would be watched by a junior member for the journey.

Lou focused on the call. "On my way. Is everything set?"

Chapter 13

The nightly news started with a dramatic, over-the-top intro including a shot of Belinda leaving the station the day of the shooting. All they had to offer were the *expert's* opinions, and a few sound bites. A Black Lives Matter advocate went on about the injustice befalling black men and women across the country, and the New Orleans cops that twist justice.

Nick wouldn't be alarmed if the story gained traction. Anything happening outside of New Orleans didn't concern him. His eyes slowly closed while on the sofa. Cali's legs rested on his thighs, while she reclined on several large pillows. They would settle into bed when the news concluded, and the talk shows commenced.

A knock on the door startled Nick from a dream as his eyes had fully closed. "What the hell?"

Cali lifted her legs. "Maybe it's Jill next door."

"Yeah," Nick stood, almost stumbling. He caught his balance as he reached the window. "No, it's Marcus."

"Marcus?" Cali scooted to the edge of the sofa. "Did he try to call?"

"Maybe... I don't know. My phone didn't go off." Nick twisted the bolt and opened the door. "Is everything alright?"

"Hi, Cali." Marcus offered a slight wave, then addressed Nick. "Can we talk a second? Out here?"

Nick spoke over his shoulder to Cali. "I'll be back in a bit." He closed the door.

Marcus whispered, close to Nick's ear. "Lou needs us to pick up a cop, and bring him somewhere."

"Who? Did he say why?"

Marcus passed him a small note reading *Cooper* with the address. "He lied about a job. Job turned up in another state. The boys are waiting."

*This was why Lou had given him Cooper's eradication.*

Nick felt the blood drain from his face, recounting the conversation he and Cooper had about Alex Weesham years ago. Nick had told Cooper that if he trusted his cousin to go underground, he should let him go. Lou would be none the wiser. He slumped, and his knees buckled in an exaggerated show of frustration. "Okay, let me tell Cali something and I'll be right out."

Cali accepted that Marcus needed Nick, and it was of a personal nature. He told her not to wait up, giving her a gentle kiss. Once outside, he shot to his car to follow behind Marcus. After a fifteen-minute drive, Nick parked the Sonata on the curb in an open spot. Next to him was a chain link fence with barbed wire strung along the top. On the other side of the fence was a row of used cars with large, colorful sale prices on the windshields. Bright stadium lights kept the lot well lit. The gently-used vehicles were like sad orphans waiting for adoption.

The pair walked down a darkened alleyway to a respectable, well-kept doublewide with one bulb over the door for illumination. Nick stuck his hand under the top step and retrieved a key with a tag. He held it up to show Marcus. "A Toyota."

"Never a Ferrari." Marcus walked ahead of Nick to unlock the gate's padlock. They meandered on a path between rows of various models to the rear of the yard where a garage acted as a portal between the lot of cars and the alley behind the business. Inside the garage was their untraceable ride for any red light cameras or doorbell videos.

Nick drove the Toyota with a cap and glasses with fake lenses. Marcus pulled up his hoody up. They stayed silent under the weight of the impending meeting while listening to the radio. As usual, they were vigilant of the cars around them. Chad Cooper lived in Lakeview, on a nice white-bread block with beautiful houses and mowed lawns and flat, straight *banquettes*, what some locals called a sidewalk. They strategically parked under the cover of a large oak tree.

"Nice place." Marcus whistled with flourish.

"Wife's a banker."

"How you know that? You friends with him?"

"We crossed paths."

"I don't like this," Marcus stifled a belch, holding his stomach.

Nick hadn't told Marcus about his part in the Weesham pseudo-eradication. He could only pray that Cooper wouldn't offer that information, either. "This has to be for discipline. There's no way they would take out one of our own."

The chirping crickets were hypnotizing, but at least he hadn't been drinking with Cali, as he sometimes enjoyed a few beers. Several times, he had to force himself to stop thinking about the implications of Cooper ratting him out. The man had given his word; Nick had to trust him.

They watched for passing cars, as well as the porch of Chad Cooper's grand, Georgian home. Plants surrounded the white columns, and a rocking chair sat off to the side. Nick checked the time on his phone, glancing at Marcus with a shrug. His best friend adjusted the radio.

A set of headlights appeared around the corner. The car pulled onto the curb instead of the driveway, facing the duo. Nick and Marcus got out of the car, making their presence known from the shadows. Chad Cooper didn't register surprise from behind the Lexus' windshield. He stepped out with his hands in plain view. Despite the yellow, jovial bowling shirt, his body looked defeated.

"Give me a minute with my family." The sentence traveled the distance clearly.

Nick nodded. Cooper walked to his house while unbuttoning the shirt. Nick wouldn't want to confront Lou wearing that, either. *Maybe he'll run.*

"Think he'll run?" Marcus asked, "Or come out with guns blazing?"

"He might not know. Would you still go bowling if you expected this?" Nick walked to the front of the car. "He wouldn't put his family through a gunfight, either."

Marcus stepped up beside him, next to the bumper. "Chad Cooper has a wife and two kids. We take out criminals. Not our own. Not the brotherhood."

Nick folded his arms and stared at the house. "I couldn't tell you what goes on in Lou's mind. I only know it's a very dark place."

"If Lou takes him out, then that changes everything."

"I think it's a scare tactic. Lou has these psychological tests he likes to put people through. He tests loyalty. I told you about how I almost shit my pants when I was eleven."

"Sanders," he whispered. "I think I would've shit my pants."

"Above all, we protect each other." Nick rubbed between his eyes.

"Then, why aren't we taking him to Shelly's? No one gets whacked at Shelly's."

"Quiet. Lou told me about this bionic ear thing that can pick up whispers from three hundred yards."

The front door opened. Chad Cooper slowly traversed the sidewalk wearing a new blue T-shirt over his small pot belly. His eyes were red. When Chad reached the car, Nick blocked his progress, staring at a man that had lost hope. Cooper spread his arms out and Marcus patted him down.

"Sorry, Chad," Nick said.

"Clean." Marcus opened the back door for him.

"What'd you tell your wife?" Nick asked.

"That I was going back out for drinks. She was half asleep, so she didn't argue. I kissed my kids. There were sleeping." His voice broke.

Nick drove toward the destination with a country station playing on the radio. Marcus turned down the volume and positioned his torso to speak to Cooper in the back.

"So, I guess you know?" Marcus asked.

"A lawyer called me an hour ago. My cousin was trying to keep me out of it. He hasn't said a word since they got him."

"What were you thinking letting an eradication go?" Marcus asked, strained, "You could have backed out when they first approached you."

"I have no issue with taking scum of the streets." Cooper shot him a look, then gazed out the window. "Weesham's my cousin. I should never have been asked."

"You were asked because Lou wanted to see if you would. He thinks a few of us new guys are still suspect." Nick felt bile rising up from his stomach.

"Why didn't you tell Lou you couldn't kill your cousin?" Marcus asked.

"I did."

Nick tilted his head to the rearview mirror, playing dumb. "What did Lou say?"

Chad caught Nick's eyes for a knowing second. "He said he'd get someone else to do it. And promised me

whoever they chose to kill my cousin wouldn't be…
humane about it. As if to punish me for declining."

"So, you said you'd do it." Nick finished.

Chad nodded. "I convinced him that we weren't close
and I'd take him out quick. Which we weren't really, but
we grew up together. Played at each other's houses. I told
him I'd give him proof of death."

"The picture?" Marcus asked.

"Yeah, floating in the bayou. Should have known I
couldn't trust the bastard to stay hidden." He laughed, and
choked a bit. "I mean, if you see this choice on a stupid cop
show, you'd scream at the screen not to do it. Don't trust
the criminal. Don't trust the junkie. Don't trust family with
a history of screwing up." His fist slammed against the side
of the door.

"You think this is a *judgment*?" Nick said.

Chad's voice cracked. "Yes."

"If this is, they're going to give you an opportunity to
state your case." Nick gauged his reaction.

"I acted on my own." His eyes locked on Nick's in
the mirror. "I couldn't kill family. If I have to die, I'll die
with my honor intact. I'll die with my secrets, but you have
to promise me something, Nick."

Nick swallowed a lump. "What's that?"

"My wife makes good money. I'm not worried about
that. She's smart. She figured things out, even though we
never talked about it. But, my kids. I want to be cremated
with my kids believing I was a good guy."

"I'm sure they do."

"Look in on my kids from time to time?"

"I promise."

Cooper's intent to keep silent about Nick was
courageous sitting in the back seat, but that sentiment could
dissolve under torture or impending death. "Good," Chad
said.

"Just remember the tactics we use during interrogations. He'll smell bullshit, so it's okay to admit you thought you'd get away with it. You'll piss him off if you don't show remorse. He doesn't want you defiant, he wants you belly up. And he'll say shit to bait you, too. Don't fall for his bullshit," Nick said. "I was just telling that to Marcus. He'll push you, and then let you off."

Cooper's eyes darted out the window. "Honestly, when I heard about my cousin coming back to life, I considered packing everyone up and running." He suffered through one hard laugh.

"You can't be sure how it's going to go down," Marcus chimed in.

"Really?" Chad cackled maniacally. "What Tribunal are *you* in?"

The decade old mistreated Tercel drove past a perimeter squad car of a young member who immediately spoke into a phone. There would be one at each corner, fanning outward, waiting to report unwanted guests. They soon pulled into the fenced-in parking lot of the abandoned industrial building. Delta Printing was still on the sign. The streetlight offered little visibility. They parked in the closest spot to the warped door. Nick left the engine running, just staring at the crumbling, boarded up structure.

"Guess this is it." Chad sat still.

"We'll have to go in with you," Marcus said.

Nick didn't say anything as he exited the car. Cooper's fingers shook while gently closing the door. Could he trust the condemned man to stay quiet? A man facing death will bargain for every second of life. The threesome checked their surroundings, not seeing any other vehicle, nor soul. Nick rapped with his knuckles.

The door opened, as if by non-existent wind. Nick cautiously stuck his head in the entrance, smelling dust and oil. The cavernous space was black inside, as the windows had been painted over just like Shelly's bar. As soon as the threesome was inside, an intense floodlight hit their eyes. Nick covered his brow, but the initial blast of light had blinded him.

"Turn that shit off," Nick blurted.

Someone pulled Nick's hands down from his face, and a sack swallowed his head. More hands dragged him farther into the building. His feet stumbled forward until he finally stopped, kicking what seemed like a chair. He heard the sounds of furniture scraping along the floor. Shoes tapped, and muffled whispers mixed together. Fabric whipped like curtains in the wind. Then it all ceased, like they were in the eye of the storm.

No one said a word.

Chapter 14

Nick balanced on strained legs while murmurs floated around him. His senses were erratic, overly stimulated with panic. Two hands on his shoulders forced him to descend into a chair, almost rocking it backwards. The sack vanished from his head, and the piercing light was gone. When Nick's eyes focused in the bleak darkness, he saw nine men in Mardi Gras masks and drab clothing seated in a semi-circle. To his left, Chad Cooper and Marcus each were relegated to their own chair.

The narrow room extended into the distance. Ancient, dusty printing contraptions had been abandoned, left to rust and degrade amongst rats, spiders, and roaches. One of the Tribunal could possibly own the land at this point. Fat exhaust pipes ran the length of the ceiling along with iron beams and drooping cables. None of the overhead lights were on.

Nick focused to the right to see one masked man, obviously Lou due to his size, standing off to the side, also in a beige outfit.

"Welcome boys," Lou said, "You've come on a very rare and special day. Never do we allow our junior members to partake in a judgment. And never has the subject of a judgment been present… or been a fellow officer."

"You can't put Chad on trial." Nick demanded, almost jumping from his seat.

"I'd be more concerned with what's going to happen to you."

Nick blinked hard. "Me?"

Lou paced in front of the silent Tribunal members while speaking. The green feathers on his mask bent from his sweeping motions. "Anything you want to explain?"

Nick glanced at Cooper whose head twitched slightly. He lost his breath. "What the hell are you talking about?"

"Last chance to clear your name." He stopped at Nick's feet like a big shot lawyer.

Nick dug in. "How can I defend something I didn't do? Or know about? I've met Chad, but I've never seen Alex Weesham before."

"There was no conspiracy," Cooper stated.

"Shut up!" Lou demanded, swinging a pointed finger. Birds would have flown from the rafters if there were any. "You'll have your turn."

"This is bullshit." Nick stood. "Just what do think happened?"

"No questions from you." Lou paced in front of him. "Was there conspiracy?"

Nick spoke through his teeth. "I told you, I don't know anything about Weesham. This is ridiculous."

Lou glared through the purple, green, and gold mask. He pointed at the chair until Nick sat again. "I know that you urged Cooper to let his cousin go. If denial is all you have, then I call for a vote. How does the Tribunal vote?"

The other nine turned to each other rigidly. In unison, the nine men offered a thumbs down. Lou clenched his fists, then gazed up to the ceiling as if accepting the answer. Was this part of the show? He couldn't know anything, unless Cooper had been lying this whole time.

Nick instantly became queasy. "Wait, just like that? In a matter of five minutes, you've decided to eradicate me?"

Lou summoned Marcus. "Hoover, front and center, son."

*Son?* Lou had to be angry about something, or maybe hurt. The man had never referred to anyone as *son*. The fact he didn't want to dissect the offending issue was clue one to his duplicity.

Marcus took small steps to Lou's side. He glanced at the members as well as Nick. He wiped his palms on his shirt. Sweat appeared on his face like condensation from a cold beer. Lou dramatically checked the gun, spun the revolver's cylinder, and then handed him the weapon.

"How can I do this not knowing what he did wrong?"

Lou slapped his shoulder. "We have audio of Cooper admitting it. *We* know. That's all that matters."

"You want me to kill your son? I - I - I - can't."

"You need to do this," Lou commanded, "Nick betrayed the Tribunal. This is bigger than your friendship. Bigger than any of us."

His voice rose. "He's blood."

"No." Lou slammed his fist into his palm. "No son of mine would betray me, or the Tribunal with a co-conspirator." Lou put his hand on Marcus' shoulder.

"I meant *my* blood," Marcus said.

Lou huffed, but lowered his voice. "This is a choice that will change the course of your life. You're either with us, or not with us. If you choose not to be, then we part ways. On the honor of the Tribunal."

Nick almost laughed. He and Marcus actually had this discussion to the contrary. Once you're in the Tribunal, you don't leave, although no one has ever tried. The rules of mafia applied here.

The voice of Gary Forche penetrated the air. "Nick Rush's actions have put the Tribunal in jeopardy. The needs of the many outweigh the needs of the few. He must be eradicated."

*Star Trek quotes.* Nick bit his lip to avoid mocking him. *Just do it, Marcus,* he thought. *It'll be okay.*

"I can't." Marcus held the gun like it was contagious.

Nick said, "If you don't pull that trigger, they'll kill both of us."

"Not another word," Lou commanded.

Tears mixed with his perspiration. "Don't make me do this."

Nick didn't speak, but he and Marcus entered that silent plane, communicating through their eyes like twins might do. There had been many occasions where they had to read each other without speaking. Nick wasn't showing panic. He gave an inkling of a nod.

Marcus turned his head slightly, as if he understood. But, did he? Nick thought it might've registered.

Lou pushed him forward. "Carry out the Tribunal's orders… now."

Marcus raised the trembling gun.

Nick mouthed the words *do it* like a bad ventriloquist.

Had Lou found out about Nick consulting Cooper about his cousin's escape? His gut told him no, but then he had hit the nail on the head with a guess. Could there really be a bullet in the chamber? Marcus lowered the gun, and with swollen eyes, he pressed it against Nick's heart. The weapon stopped shaking. Marcus sniffed hard, sucking it up. He opened his eyes wide and blinked hard, releasing a tear.

Lou and Nick found each other. Even in the dark, through the mask, he could see the vacant and hallow depths of Lou's soul.

"You're my brother," Marcus whispered, and like ripping off a bandage, he pulled the trigger.

The firing pin hitting an empty chamber was the most beautiful sound he had ever heard. Nick flinched with an adrenaline push, but only because of natural, human uncertainty. His heart sped up and thumped at it slowed. Both shooter and victim let out an exasperating gasp, as if suddenly there was oxygen.

"Oh, God." Marcus bent at the waist.

Nick finally extended a wink at his best friend, but will never admit he peed a little. Marcus received the same test as Nick, and with the same result. But in the eyes of the Tribunal, Marcus pulled the trigger on a fellow cop. That was sure to exalt him to a higher status.

Lou, however, didn't seem to have caught on that Nick had warned him. "Good job, Hoover. Good to know you have it when it counts." He took the gun. "Pull yourself together. Have a seat. Cooper, right here." Lou pointed at the chair. He proceeded to load bullets into the revolver.

Nick took Marcus by the arm, squeezing cognition back into him. He finally accepted that nothing happened. But, the reality of another life at stake replaced his relief. Nick gently pulled Marcus until his feet responded, and their found their chairs.

"How did you know?" Marcus asked without volume.

Once in their seats, Nick whispered, "A lifetime of Lou."

"Right." Marcus wiped his face with his shirt.

Nick patted his shoulder. "It's not over."

Lou clasped his hands behind his back, extending his belly. "Nick's guidance in the Weesham debacle is inconsequential. His actions give pause, but they will be dealt with at a later date. Officer Cooper is responsible no matter who suggested what. He alone made the decision. He will state his case. The Tribunal will decide his fate. Pay attention, Nick, because you might be in charge one day."

"Not likely," mumbled Mr. Gary.

Nick set his jaw. "If I was in charge, I wouldn't let two members risk leading the FBI to a location that has every elder member present."

Lou looked to the silent, generic members. "I told you he has a hard on for the feds." He stepped up to Nick. "So opinionated, and yet, so naive. Unfortunately, your help has brought this upon Cooper."

"It was the right decision."

Lou spoke volumes with a mere look. He cleared his throat. "Time to begin."

The masked men stiffened. They looked more like a cult than the saviors of New Orleans. Lou pulled his chair to the side of the accused. Cooper's breathing was labored, but under control.

"State your case." Lou didn't check a watch or any timer.

Cooper cleared his throat. His voice shook. "Alex Weesham is my cousin. Family. I know you gave me a choice, and I thought I could go through with it, but I grew up with that guy." He waited through the silence. "I had every intention of doing it. Other criminals left town to avoid us, right? I figured it was just like that. He's been silent for years. He'll be okay."

"Your time's not up," Lou prompted. "Details. Did anyone see you that day?"

"No. I brought Weesham to a tributary off Lake Maurepas, near a dark stretch of I-55," he said, offhandedly. "I grew up in Manchac. I knew the area well. There was no one around for miles. I was going to do it, but the mosquitos and bugs kept attacking us. Like a sign."

"Bugs?" Lou questioned.

"Yeah. There was something about us fending off the bugs… it delayed the decision."

"Don't blame the mosquitos." Lou folded his arms.

"I told my cousin what was happening, and he begged for his life. He cried. What was I to do?"

Lou put his face in the condemned man's face. "You knew the risks."

"How could I know the risks when it's never happened before?"

Lou almost gave him that argument. "But, you know *us*."

"I know the Tribunal is on the side of right." No one spoke. He continued, "What he did to that girl. An accidental coma and brain damage isn't the usual eradication material."

Lou shook his head, slowly. "He didn't do time. A member knows the father. He gave the daughter brain damage. Weesham *is* eradiation material."

Cooper's eyes grew wet. "I had the gun to his head. One more second. Just one more... the damn bugs." Cooper haphazardly slapped at his arm and cheek as if reliving the moment. "He promised me he'd leave town and change his identity. One I'd provide, so I knew it'd be legit. I told him to get in the water and I took his picture to prove I did it."

"And that is a betrayal."

"That's loyalty. To both my families." Cooper shrugged. A tear ran down his face. "We're bulletproof, damnit. Bulletproof."

"We'll finish the job for you. It'll be done before he's released." Lou summoned fake sympathy. "Why not just tell us you couldn't do it?"

His sniffled. "I thought you might freeze me out, or worse. Marcus had no other choice but to pull the trigger just now. I know my cousin. He'll keep quiet."

"He'll name you," Lou countered.

"What can he say? I'm not connected to you guys. You made sure of that. I'm on an island. We all are."

"Is that all?" Lou asked.

"I have a wife and two kids. Please. You know I won't say a word. You know it."

Lou looked to the attentive Tribunal. They were like Dobermans waiting for a robber to try to leave before attacking. Lou said, "You'd turn in a heartbeat once they offered you witness protection."

"I would have done that already. We can work this out within the Tribunal. I messed up, but I'm loyal. You can kill me anytime you want if I don't come through."

"You'll run, Chad." Lou placed his hand gently on the man's shoulder. "And then, you'll talk. Plus, we let you slide, other members might think no consequences will befall them." Lou faced the elders once again. They were old-school and hardened, yet hiding behind the ceremony.

One by one, they each gave a thumbs up or a thumbs down. Cooper's mentor didn't get a vote. It was seven for eradication and zero against. Lou nodded and presented the gun and a blindfold to the one man whose vote held no weight. Cooper's mentor had chosen him and would decommission him, too.

Cooper's body bucked. He didn't try to run, nor fight. His body stopped trembling. His chin rose. In the final seconds left on earth, Chad would leave with dignity.

Lou motioned with a flip of his hand. "You two boys can leave now."

Nick put his face an inch away from his father's. "He's one of us."

His father whispered. "We're certainly going to kill Weesham, but Cooper is one of ours. He won't be killed."

*Won't be killed?* Nick couldn't tell through the mask if he meant it. There was no precedent to compare this to. He had to accept Lou's proclamation. He had to believe it, or be complicit in a good man's murder. Or even be eradicated himself.

"Lou…" Marcus interrupted.

"Don't," Nick barked at Marcus.

Lou pointed to one of the elder members. "Escort them out and make sure they leave."

The man stood without hesitation.

Nick began walking. "Let's just go."

Without looking back, they wasted no time heading to the door. Like leaving the portal from another dimension, they were back on earth again – back in reality. The masked figure stood in the door with his arms folded. Nick and Marcus slowly walked to the car and drove away in silence.

A few blocks away, Marcus wiped at new tears. "He's one of us."

"Lou said they weren't going to kill him."

"You believe him?"

"I don't know. Lou gave me Gavin Jones. It was supposed to be Cooper's."

"Jesus. Sorry.'

Nick stopped at a light on an empty road. "If we tried to physically stop Lou tonight, they would have killed us, too. We can't speak of this again."

"You can't be okay with this."

Nick dabbed at his eyes. "What you said in there. I feel the same way. You're my brother you know that? My *real* brother." Marcus didn't reply. "I'm going to see Shelly early tomorrow. After that, let's go see your dad at the nursing home. We need this."

"Yeah, I think I need that, too." Marcus calmed. "I can't imagine the new crop will accept this."

"They'll be too scared to revolt." Nick almost laughed through the stress of the night.

Marcus wrung his hands. "One day we were kids and the next, we're killers. How did we get here?"

"I miss being a kid." He drove slowly, carefully. "This is like the wasps."

Marcus choked on a laugh. "Man, I haven't thought of that in a while. You think this is like the wasps we found when we were seven?"

"Just like that. We found that junked yellow school bus in the junk yard that Mr. Mike said not to go into."

"But, we did." Marcus nodded in remembrance.

"I closed the bus door so that they wouldn't hear us laughing and screaming inside, sealing our fate."

A sullen smile grew on Marcus' lips. "We started jumping up and down on the seats, having a grand old time."

"Until the family of wasps scattered from under the seat to see what the disturbance was."

They both succumbed to reluctant laughter. Marcus said, "We beat on that door like we were in the gas chamber. Thank God, my grandpa was looking for us."

"We were so swollen from stings. We looked like Rocky and Apollo at the end of the movie."

"Yeah," Marcus' voice drifted, and the smile left. "Never been so scared in my life. Don't know if it was from the wasps or our dads finding out."

"Both." The laughter subsided. Nick finally turned to him. "How do you feel about jumping on some more seats…?"

Chapter 15

Nick felt unsure about leaving Marcus on his apartment doorstep while each in their fragile condition. Kareena had been waiting up for him. He took solace in Marcus' girlfriend taking over support. Nick could only hope she didn't know anything about the extracurricular activities. It was much safer that way. He wanted to tell Cali countless times, to confess the whole rotten deal. Going to visit Mr. Mike at the nursing home would give him and Marcus a moral boost.

The night wasn't quite over for Nick. He took a direct route back to Chad Cooper's house in a haze, thinking about happier times spent at Marcus' house as kids. Mr. Mike, or Big Hoover as some called him, loved to perform in their fake concerts. He would hold wrestling matches in the living room. Mr. Mike roughhoused as if he was still a teenager. Nick remembered the anticipation of riding his bike up to their gate, and the depressed feeling when he left.

One night when they were about ten-years old while having a pizza-eating contest at the kitchen table, Mr. Mike leaned into Marcus with a toothy smile while pulling his son into a full-on hug. They laughed in unison. Nick realized Lou was seriously broken at that point. He so envied that kind of life.

He could never tell Lou he'd wished Mr. Mike were his real father. But, having a brother was the next best thing. Marcus would be his best man at his wedding and eventually they'd raise their kids together. If he was able, Mr. Mike could walk Cali down the aisle. Nick pulled onto Cooper's street, drifting back into the present. Memories were all Chad's children would have left of their father.

Once parked near Cooper's house, he impatiently waited for a car to drop off the Tribunal member, possibly toss him out the back seat tied up or something of the sort. They wouldn't just release him at the state line. They'd let him say goodbye to his family.

*Jesus Christ, no they wouldn't.*

Nick was so *stupid*. There was no way in hell Lou was letting Cooper go, but he needed to believe it so badly. He gave thought to knocking on Chad's door and telling his family exactly what was going on. But, what if he was wrong? What if this was another test, and Cooper would make it home safely in just a few minutes, or by morning?

After sitting for an hour, fatigued from an adrenaline dump, it wasn't sleep that took hold, but anger. Did the bond of the boys and girls in blue not mean anything? Sweat seeped through his clothes, despite the air conditioning. Chad Cooper was certainly dead, and Nick had failed to act. He was complicit.

Despite everything Lou had drilled into his head about discretion, Nick floated above his body as it stepped out of the car and approached Cooper's home. His mind screamed at his physical form to turn around and leave this place forever, but his feet continued on. With a gigantic leap in time, he watched his knuckles rapping on the front door.

Eventually, a wide-eyed woman wrapped tightly in a flower-patterned robe appeared in the threshold. The space between them was charged, almost electric. She waited for him to say something. Her face was red and splotchy. New tears welled in her irritated eyes.

Nick stepped just inside the foyer. He faced her, looking around the room and up the stairs. The kids were asleep. They stared at each other in silence. Finally, with a mere tilting of his head, she faltered, putting her face in her hands in full sob.

Without warning, her hand swung out, smacking his face with full force. Her fists beat at his chest, eventually losing power until he was able to hold her. She fought against his embrace at first, but gave in, sliding down until she was sitting on the floor, sucking in air.

"I'm so sorry," he whispered, kneeling at her side.

His widow slapped a piece of paper against his chest. Nick took the note and read it.

*Do what they say. I will always love you.*

"What do I do now?" She asked, looking up at him.

"You need to file a missing person's report. You need stay quiet, and go along with the investigation for your children's sake. It's the only way."

"That's not what I meant." She seethed with clenched teeth. "Get out, you bastard. Get the fuck out of my house." She pointed without looking at him. "You're worse than the criminals."

Nick spotted two children at the top of the stairs. He turned away quickly, lest he break down, also. The image of Cooper's crumpled, grieving wife imprinted behind his eyes. He left her curled up on the floor, heavy in her pain. His mind afforded another leap in time, suddenly aware he was in the car. The inside seemed pressurized like an airplane, with his ears needing to pop. His heart needed a rest. A wave washed over him, clouding his vision.

Once the car accelerated, his mind disconnected. Autopilot clicked on. He drove with his windows rolled down, but didn't remember arriving home or parking. He couldn't recall the route, pulling onto his street, or stopping just inches from the wall under his carport.

It took several minutes for Nick to exit the car. The symptoms of a fever overtook his body, but the back of his hand to his forehead indicated nothing of the sort. As if working on instinct, he dragged his feet into the side entrance of his house, bypassing the normal check of the street.

He pulled his shirt off immediately after entering the kitchen. His shoes fell hapless in the hallway and his shorts and underwear dropped just before the bedroom. Sweat burned on his skin. The compression behind his eyes mounted.

Cali was snuggled under the blanket as the window unit hummed a grating tune. Nick turned on the cold water in the shower, leaving the hot untouched. His breathing eased as heat radiated off his skin like the sun on black asphalt. He positioned his neck under the jets of cold water, cringing at the sting of conflicting temperatures, psychosomatic as they were. The water acted as a distraction, something to focus on. It put out the fire that threatened to reduce him to ash.

*The Tribunal killed a fellow cop, leaving his wife a widow with children.*

He cried as quietly as possible. After a number of minutes, he shut off the shower. Rivers of water diminished as they merged and flowed to the drain. Nick shivered. His mind returned and connected with this body. Had he finally broke?

Muscle memory allowed him to blindly reach for a towel. Not bothering to comb his hair or put on clothes, his stiff gait struggled to the dresser in order to pull out the new Spiderman sweatpants. He brought them to the bed and he sat on the edge, facing the window that housed the air conditioner.

Goose bumps along with little tremors came and went, but he couldn't put the sweatpants on. Something prevented it. He couldn't find his way to slide under the covers. He stared forward as if looking out the window past the air unit. If it was an anxiety attack, he didn't know how to fix it. His fingers pinched and pulled at the sweatpants.

A voice came to life in his ears, but it wasn't Cali. It was his mother. *It will be okay.*

He answered his mom in thought. *I want out. I want out. I want out.*

"Nick, what are you doing?" Cali asked, lifting herself upright.

His mouth opened, but he couldn't speak. The bed shook as she moved closer. Her face appeared in his peripheral with her body pressing against his backside. Leaning on an extended arm, she used her other hand to caress his face. He must have looked ridiculous to be sitting there naked, holding the sweatpants in his lap.

She spoke lightly into his ear. "You're scaring me. What's going on? What did you and Marcus do?"

Nick turned to her. His voice barely registered any sound. "Nothing."

"Talk to me."

"Just sit with me." He spoke as if out of breath.

Cali rubbed his back. "I'm here. I'm not going anywhere."

"I'm just tired. So tired." Nick let his body lean toward his pillow, or Cali had possibly guided him that way. Her warm body kept to his side, spooning him as he curled into the fetal position. He laid his head on the sweatpants.

"You want covers?" she asked.

Nick nodded, turning to face her as the blanket came up to their necks. He smiled, touching her face. "I love you so much."

"I love you, too." Her voice soothed the fire. Her fingers mingled with his. Her lips touched his earlobe. "We're going to be okay."

Chad Cooper had his wife to confide in. Marcus had Kareena. Nick had no one intimate to share with. Where was his support – his *other*? It as an impossibility. That knowledge could put loved ones at risk, but keeping it bottled up couldn't be good for anyone involved.

Nick didn't realize he had been holding his breath. He filled his lungs, then closed his eyes, releasing two streams of tears. "Cali, I'm Tribunal. And we did something so bad tonight."

## Chapter 16

His entire body hurt with fatigue. But, as cliché as it sounded, he felt lighter. Cali had taken it all in, listening without judgement. She never ran, nor tried to call the FBI. It was as if she suspected all along, which didn't surprise him. She offered no solutions, and never faltered. It was everything he could wish for. She had wanted to sit with his confession for a while, and then they'd discuss it further. Nick had no issues with that.

That morning, Nick had found it hard to get out of bed. Thankfully, Cali didn't push. With multiple reassurances, and a Mr. Mike visit on the agenda, Cali left for work with noted apprehension. A promise of frequent texts got her out the door. He spent a half hour sitting in the quiet with a coffee, debating his role in all this.

Before the morning sun had gained strength, Nick pulled up to the rear entrance of Shelly's knowing Lou would be at work. He parked in an isolated spot between the garage and a privacy fence that served as a barrier to the neighborhood. He rang the bell on the back door. His grandfather answered wearing a Saints cap, dark glasses, a Hawaiian shirt and khaki shorts. His socks were almost to his knees.

"Let's do it," Shelly said. He turned back inside.

Nick followed him into the back of the bar, then into the musty side garage. Tools, paint cans, boxes, and shelving units filled with miscellaneous crap surrounded the covered vehicle in the center. They each positioned themselves on opposite sides next to a tarp covering the car, simultaneously pulling the thick material back to reveal an immaculate black 1975 Camaro.

Nick took a moment. "Never gets old."

Shelly dropped into the driver's side. "You're a fool not to drive it."

"Fuck Lou." Nick slid in and shut the passenger door.

The engine purred to life, just aggressive enough not to be distracting. Shelly smiled, slowing pulling out onto the street. "I like this time we have, you and me."

"If Lou knew you toured the neighborhood every week or two with me, he'd have an aneurism." Nick watched the joy on the old man's face as he checked the surroundings. He was like a flower that only bloomed when they drove around. "Amazing you can do this."

"This car is an extension to the house. I feel safe."

"That feeling's a commodity, nowadays."

"Something's wrong. I can tell." Shelly rolled the window down to let the breeze in.

"It's nothing."

"Cooper?"

Nick glanced at him, never knowing just how much Shelly was involved. "Let's not talk about it. Unless that's what you wanted to talk about."

"Partly."

Nick tuned the original radio, keeping it low. "You have the floor."

"Not sure if you should do this one." His voice was a low whisper. He turned the corner to circle back toward the bar.

"And end up like Cooper?" Nick was also unsure just how much he could confide in his pawpaw.

"I don't like it." It was a simple statement, but if Shelly said it, it held a lot of weight.

"What don't you like?"

"Why he chose you after your counseling of the Weesham incident. It doesn't add up. Something is going on."

Nick rubbed his lip, easing back in the seat. "Yeah, but Lou wouldn't do anything to hurt the Tribunal."

"*I don't like it.*" It was a hammer.

Nick changed the subject as that uneasy feeling returned. "What triggered your agoraphobia?"

"You haven't asked me that in months."

"I'm hoping you'll tell me one day before you die."

"I promise I'll tell you before I die." He stopped on the side of the road, under a blooming magnolia tree. "Looks good since the reupholstering, right?"

"They did a great job." Nick admired the brand-new cloth seats in the back that just been installed after the feds had ripped the insides to pieces ten years earlier. Or at least they guessed it was the feds having found no signs of a break in. They were looking for something, and without a warrant. So, Nick and Shelly had to start the interior from scratch. Once or twice a month, they repaired something. That was the beauty of an ongoing project.

"Grab the humidor back there."

Nick reached over to secure a cigar box. "This thing is awesome."

Shelly opened the laminated box in his lap and pulled out a giant Cuban stogie. "Join an old man in an indulgence, won't you?"

\#

Nick felt his energy returning. He called Marcus to make sure the Big Hoover visit was still on the agenda. It was an abbreviated *yes-and-no* phone call, avoiding any conversation about the night before. They decided to ride together.

Marcus picked Nick up ten minutes later. They listened to a playlist of Hip Hop on Bluetooth to fill the silence. Besides asking how each other was doing, they hadn't said anything meaningful until pulling into the nursing home parking lot. Silence between them was never awkward. If anything, they communicated just as well without saying a word. Marcus told Nick that his dad was going to be happy to see him.

The Brightstar was the best nursing home New Orleans had to offer. It was complete with sprawling grounds, smooth paths with the occasional bench or handrail, and gardens of colorful flowers. Its biggest selling point was the round-the-clock nursing care. The building itself was white, flat, with numerous windows, looking much like a small hospital from the street. The leather, marbled, and mirrored lobby could be in any four-star hotel brochure, assuring family that their loved ones were cared for. They even had a guard.

Mr. Mike sat in his cushy recliner with a large pair of black sunglasses, the kind that looked like welder goggles. Marcus and Nick took position on the fairly comfortable sofa. There was a faint scent of bleach as if someone had just cleaned. On the opposite side of the recliner was a walker with tennis balls on the front legs. The room was like a small *staged-for-sale* studio with a bathroom. A vase of real flowers sat on the coffee table. For the moment, the television was off. Mr. Mike said he could listen to reruns he had seen, and visualize the scenes very well. Most visits were spent recalling better days.

"Remember all those comics we used to collect, Dad?" Marcus asked.

Mr. Mike's head kicked back in a laugh. He had lost about a hundred pounds since the arthritis took hold, weighing about two hundred at the moment. His full beard started going gray. Back in the day, Nick considered him the black version of Lou, only with compassion and minus the intimidation. "Yeah, you two were always saying how much money you'd get for them one day. Shit, you sold all yours for what? A couple hundred dollars?"

"Three hundred," Marcus said.

"About four for me," Nick added. "I was just telling Cali about the day my head went into the ceiling fan during one of our famous wrestling matches."

Marcus cackled. "That was hysterical. That ceiling fan stopped dead in its tracks, yo!"

Mr. Mike offered a sympathetic grin. "Sorry about that, Nick. I thought I could spin you over my head. Can barely stand with knees now. My dancing days are over."

"Miss Brandy thought we were going to put another hole in the wall."

"Yeah, Mom liked our lip-synching contests better than our wrestling matches." Marcus consumed his tea in one gulp.

Mr. Mike continued to stare forward. "Right – right, I remember. You'd bet comic books that you wouldn't miss any words of the songs. But, what I really want to know is what you did with all those girlie magazines you used to have."

Nick and Marcus glanced at each other. Nick said, "You found those? They were so well hidden."

"Shit." Mr. Mike wiped at his nose. "There ain't no place in that house that was a hiding spot. I knew every inch. That hole in the drywall of your closet was a little suspicious to me."

"Damn, Dad. And you didn't say anything?"

"That's normal for young boys. I made sure the magazines didn't get too racy. Now, your dad Lou knew how to hide his porn. Shelly was never going to find his stash, or drugs or whatever he wanted to hide."

"Lou and you became friends at your dad's auto yard, right?" Nick asked Mr. Mike.

"We met at the auto yard, but friends is a stretch." He pointed toward Nick. "Your pawpaw Shelly bought that piece of shit Chevy to work on with Lou. Can't believe got it running."

"Sold it to get the Mustang," Nick added.

Mr. Mike nodded. "Shelly and my dad had that secret friendship – one that they didn't advertise. Shelly paid my dad monthly to let Lou work in the garage. That's when Lou and I met."

"Lou got free parts from the yard," Marcus said. "Put it together like that Stephen King movie Christine."

Mr. Mike continued, "I worked there part-time. Lou was always there under a hood, but he loved to talk with me about what he was doing to the Mustang." He looked in Marcus' direction, then to Nick, despite not being able to see them.

Nick said, "My dad did the same thing with my Camaro. I was only twelve when he bought it for us to fix up."

"Your father wasn't always such a hard ass." He retreated into his own thoughts. "Sorry."

"Don't be." Nick stood and bent down next to the recliner, taking Mr. Mike's arm. "You were like a second father to me. I don't know what I would've done without you and Miss Brandy, and Marcus. I don't know who I'd be."

Mr. Mike put his hand on Nick's shoulder, then his cheek. "You were our second child. Still are. You knew that."

"I did." Nick stood, finding his way to the small refrigerator for a water. He wiped his eyes nonchalantly before returning. "I used to pretend you were my real father."

Marcus smiled. "The neighborhood kids knew it wasn't true."

"I can't pass for black?" Nick laughed.

"Not with that dick." Marcus pulled his father's arm in the air to give him a high-five.

#

Nick and Marcus decided to walk the grounds of Brightstar after Mr. Mike took an array of medication and fell asleep in his recliner. The flower-lined path led them to a large, no-frills fountain surrounded by benches and a circle of bushes. No residents were out in the early afternoon sun, despite the tolerable humidity.

Marcus collapsed on a concrete bench, deflating with his hands on his face. Nick sat next to him, leaning back against wooden slats. The fountain had a steady push of water, streaming down three tiers into the base with a carpet of coins at the bottom. Birds appeared out of nowhere, expecting a donation of bread, but they had none.

"He's doing great, yeah?" Nick slapped his back.

"Today." Marcus took a breath and straightened up. "It's getting harder for him to walk and get around. He's in so much pain from the arthritis. And blind? I don't know if I can handle seeing him that way."

"He's a tough man. He's proud of you."

Marcus' mouth quivered in a smile. He looked at the fountain. "Lou was grilling me about your high school dating life last night, before I came and got you."

"What?"

"Specifically, the year you were seeing Tanya Sanders." Marcus looked around.

"What'd you tell him?"

"I told him everything." Marcus couldn't hold a straight face. "I told him nothing, dude."

"Don't friggin' scare me like that." Nick held his heart. "Don't know what he's digging for. He's been like a dog with a bone about Cali."

"He knows about the pool party."

"Figures he would. I was just thinking about the *church slap* the other day."

"Can't believe you met his daughter at the funeral, then ran into her again a few years later."

They each leaned back in silence as if both remembering that day. Marcus and Nick had attended a high school pool party hosted by Jessica Robicheaux, one of Kramer's most popular students. She had a built-in pool, which was rare in the East, with young, hip, enabling parents that were rumored to have met as teens while modeling.

Nick had sat poolside on a lounge chair that was covered by a damp beach towel. He wore a pair of long, faded green swim trunks and dark sunglasses hanging from a rope around his neck. At fifteen, he hadn't considered himself a pro at drinking, but thanks to Lou's poker games and Marcus' stealth at swiping Mr. Mike's beer, he wasn't a novice, either. He tended to be invited to most parties, from the freshmen to the seniors. An event with underage drinking wouldn't get busted while Nick Rush was there.

Over the blasting music, someone had yelled the name *Tanya* from the backyard entrance. Nick twisted to see a toned brunette wearing a gripping tee-shirt down to her waist. A girl hugged Tanya and began introducing her with each step, like a reception line. He put his hand over his eyes to deflect glare. It all came back to him.

*Tanya Sanders.*

Nick faced the pool again, leaning back against the chair. His head swiveled slightly, just enough to see Tanya making rounds. She had lost the bangs. Her hair was pulled back into a ponytail, showcasing perfect facial symmetry. Her body had filled in from what he remembered, most prominently the parts a boy his age would notice first. The guys were falling over themselves trying to catch a peek at the hot girl that no one knew.

Transfixed, like the very first time they had met, he couldn't look away. Her eyes scanned the pool area, locking on his for just a moment before he spun away. He quickly put his sunglasses on, but it had been too late. *She could never recognize an eleven-year-old kid from four years ago*, he had thought. After all, he had the advantage of hearing her name called out.

"Nick, isn't it?" Tanya had said from behind the chair, over his shoulder.

He looked up, swinging his legs over the lounger to stand. They faced each other, both having grown, but he had gained three inches on her. "That's right. I'm surprised you remember."

"You left an impression." She smiled, but her eyes didn't.

"So did you." He touched his cheek with a full grin. "I'm sorry about what I said. That was stupid." He took off the sunglasses, leaving them dangle at his chest.

She shifted her weight, staying in his personal space. "We were kids. We say stupid things."

He looked around. "Who do you know here?"

"Polly. She's my only friend here in NOLA." She pointed at a girl that looked familiar to him.

"Only friend in New Orleans? I find that hard to believe."

"Me and my mom moved to Slidell a few months after my dad's funeral. Polly has relatives she visits in Slidell, so we stayed in touch. It's only about a half hour drive across the lake to get here."

"That's cool."

"Polly likes this guy who goes to Brother Martin. Marcus something. He's around here somewhere."

Nick nodded. "Yeah, he's here. Can I get you a beer? Jessica's parents are inside. They let us drink, but no one is allowed to drive home."

"That's trust."

"Yeah, we either walk or call parents. I could have driven my Camaro, but my dad doesn't like me driving it without him 'cause I don't have a permit." He had tried to impress her.

"How's the water?" Tanya hadn't waited for an answer. She grabbed her shirt at the waist and pulled up. As if in slow motion, her mid-drift stole his attention. His eyes absorbed perfectly sculpted curves, and a flat stomach with a cute belly button. Her bikini top lifted and fell as the shirt flew off her head. If that wasn't enough, she released her ponytail, unleashing a majestic plume of hair that fell behind her shoulders. She handed the discarded items to Nick, then turned and dove between two kids in the deep end.

Nick told himself to take a breath, inhaling the Chlorine. *Okay, so... Okay.*

Tanya had climbed out of the pool like a slow-motion bikini model. She deftly used her hands to wring out her hair, walking back to Nick as he opened a towel big enough to swallow her. After drying, she bent to retrieve a tube and handed it to him. Without any words, she presented her back, moving her hair over her front shoulder. Nick fumbled to pop the cap off and squeezed a dollop of sunscreen into his hand. He spread the lotion over every inch, slowly and deliberately.

"Looks like you can use some, too," she finally said, answering his prayers.

During that next hour, Nick and Tanya had spent equal time talking with other kids, as well as each other. Marcus and Polly connected and disappeared, but Nick didn't care about that. Every time he and Tanya were fortunate enough to be one on one, they would find something new they had in common, like their taste in music, movies, and easy conversation.

Late afternoon had crept in. Nick nursed his beer as drinking games commenced around them. Most of the teens were happily buzzed, still swimming and eating from a mountain of McDonald's hamburgers Jessica's father had purchased. There wasn't any childish drama, crying or throwing up just yet. Every now and again, Jessica's dad could be seen making rounds. The kids respected the house, and kept it from turning into a stereotypical teen movie party.

Nick monitored Tanya, but without crowding her, either. Her father had killed his mother - *allegedly,* and yet, she was the most beautiful thing he'd ever seen. *The sins of the parents shouldn't be handed down*, he thought.

Still, despite Harold Sanders having been a suspected murderer, Tanya was innocent and pure… an angel. She had only been twelve when *Slimeball* Harry strangled his mother weeks after having worked on their plumbing. But, Tanya believed her father was innocent. In the eyes of the law, he was. *Forget her,* he had thought. Like Romeo and Juliet, their houses were divided. Lou would have an aneurism. They could never be together. But, maybe sticking it to Lou was part of the reason he had been drawn to her.

As the sun set, and gas lamps were lit, Nick took his fourth beer to his favorite lounge chair and sat back on the gigantic towel, half reclined, like a hospital bed. Couples had paired to make out in the pool, and the other kids collected on the patio, drinking from a garbage can of Jungle Juice. An upbeat Beatles song played in the background.

After a few minutes, a hand slapped his shoulder from the side. "Move over."

Still in her bikini, Tanya had stood by his legs looking down at him, expectedly. Nick edged over, exposing the left half of the lounger. Careful not to spill beer, she took a close position next to him. The chair sank slightly in the grass, but otherwise supported their combined weight without issue.

He blushed. "Funny to see you again after all these years."

"I never forgot you. Weird as it sounds, I think you might've been my first crush."

"And your first slap?"

This time, she grew crimson. "I wasn't sorry about it then, but I am now."

"Actually, you were my first crush, too." He laughed, taking in some warm beer. "I looked you up on Facebook last year, but I never had the courage to friend you."

"You should have. I'll admit, I thought about you for months after." She placed her hand on his neck.

Nick locked eyes with her, unsure what was happening, but allowed his lips to touch hers. While *One* by U2 carried across the party, they kissed like their lives depended on it. As if sensing Nick's exposure, Tanya's leg covered the bulge in his swimsuit. His hand stayed on her rib cage, occasionally running his thumb under her bikini, testing his boundaries.

Someone kicked the lounge chair and they stopped to look at the culprit. Polly hovered over them with a beer, swaying with a surprised expression. Marcus had his arms wrapped around her waist to hold her steady, looking over her shoulder.

"Go away," Tanya pleaded.

"I can't believe this," Polly giggled. She swatted at bugs flying around her head, and her beer spilled as she struggled.

"What's so funny?" Tanya asked.

It took a second for Polly to find her slurring voice. "I can't believe you two are kissing. Do you know who this is?"

"Nick." Tanya looked at him, confused. "What's your last name?"

"Let's go somewhere and talk," Nick said.

"Rush," Polly pushed through her lips. "Nick *Rush*. Father is one Lou *Rush*. Married to one Alison Campbell *Rush*." Polly stopped as if over-acting. She broke from Marcus to whisper loudly in Tanya's ear. "This is Alison Rush's kid." She sucked her lips in with exaggerated surprise.

Nick dipped his head, squeezing his eyes shut. He felt Tanya staring at him. The entire pool party seemed have gone on pause. She waited for an explanation.

"Tanya…"

She had slapped him across the face… much harder that time, then jumped off the lounge chair. "Wait – the funeral? You knew who I was all along? What kind of freak are you?"

"Your father was innocent. I believe that now." Blood rushed to his head. He yelled to her while as she stormed out, "I don't know who killed my mother."

Polly left also, shaking her head at him, but fell to her knees into the grass. "Marcus, help me up!" Her hands swatted the ground. When Marcus didn't leave Nick's side, two other kids helped her to stumble on, but not without shooting him the bird.

Nick put his hands over his glowing face, feeling the chair bend as Marcus sat beside him. He glanced through his fingers at his friend, and shook his head with a groan.

"Women," Marcus bluntly stated, and the night ended there.


#


A passing Brightstar resident snapped Nick from his memories. He stood from the bench and approached the fountain. The hungry birds on the ground scattered. Marcus said, "Funny how life takes twists and turns you'd never expect."

Nick cracked his neck in a stretch. "How could Lou have found out about that party?"

Marcus, put his hands over his eyes to block glare. "Maybe he had you followed back then and he always knew. He was just fishing. Got pretty specific, though, like he suspects something."

Nick took a penny from his pocket and flipped it behind his back and into the water. "I never told you how me and Tanya hooked up again a few days later."

"Never told me the details. Spill it. Get my mind off everything."

Nick returned to his side and spoke low, a habit that formed with everyone in the Tribunal. "Three days after the pool party incident, the entire school was buzzing"

"A few guys knew about it at Brother Martin, too."

"Girls I never spoke to fixed their hair and giggled as they walked by. Guys nodded and offered high-fives."

"Nothing like a girl being pissed at you to boost popularity."

"Right. Anyway, that day I didn't want to ride the bus home and put up with the bullshit, so I walked home. I just cleared the I-10 overpass and was at the service road when her SUV pulled up."

"She came over from Slidell on a school day just to find you?"

"Yeah, she did. I didn't know what the hell to expect when she ordered me to get in. She was dressed in a white blouse, a green plaid skirt, and knee-high socks.

"Ah, Catholic school uniform. Sexy. Wrong to say at this age, but sexy."

Nick nodded. "She had a cute ponytail sprouting from the top of her head, too. I got in and didn't say anything as we drove around. We ended up at the Lakefront – right by

West End. She backed into a spot where instead of facing the lake, we had a view of the street and the picnic area."

"Interesting. That is about the time you started avoiding me."

He smiled. "Sorry. We started talking about what happened. The slap. She asked if I really thought her father was innocent of killing my mom."

"And?"

"I told her that I was kid and believed everything Lou told me. She reached into a little cooler in the back seat and pulled out two bottles of water and I knew we'd be okay. She said I embarrassed her and hurt her. I told her I lied because I didn't want to ruin what we started. Because I liked her."

"Aww. Sweet."

"She said I shouldn't like her. But, then I told her something… it was like a line straight out of a rom-com."

"What, dude?"

He smiled, feeling himself flush. "I told her that from that first day I saw her, I felt like the void my mother left wasn't so big anymore."

"Wow. What a line."

"Wasn't a line. I asked if she still had that crush. She said driving a half hour over the Twin Span should prove she did."

"Right."

"We kissed, and I didn't get slapped. But, then the weirdness started."

"How so?"

"We had to make ground rules. First, her mother was making her move out of state after she graduated high school, so no matter what, it wasn't going to last. I didn't care."

"Obviously."

"Then, I told her Lou can never know about us. Never. I waited for her to slap me again. But, she agreed because her mom couldn't know about us either. No social media, no pictures, no nothing."

"That's rough for kids that age."

"That's what happened with me and you. If anyone saw us together, we just say it's a blind date or not serious," Nick added. "No one knew her in New Orleans, and no one knew me over in Slidell. We had dedicated email addresses. Pre-paid phones. A meeting place that only we knew about in both cities. I learned how to be a spy."

Marcus shook his head. "Secrecy keeps the romance hot. And then when she left, it ended. Sent you into a spiral."

"Yeah. It practically killed me. The hardest part was acting normal in front of Lou." Nick checked his cell phone. "Speaking of which, he wants me at Shelly's this afternoon for some damn reason. I gotta roll. You ready? I could Uber if you want to go back in."

Marcus sighed, coming back to reality. He looked up at the building. "Old man will be sleeping for hours, let's go."

Chapter 17

After Nick was dropped off home, he made a quick turkey sandwich with a glass of sweet tea. The visit to the two elder influences in his life didn't relieve him of the dark mood created by the Cooper situation. It only made him sad for Mr. Mike and wistful for the late Tanya Sanders. He thought about skipping his meeting with Lou, but that would only make things worse.

The slow drive to Shelly's was spent fantasizing about his Gavin Jones plans coming to fruition. He dragged his feet from the parking lot into the bar, and then to his stool at Lou's side. The contrast of feelings between seeing Mr. Mike and Lou was like a warm and fuzzy blanket to a bed of tacks.

"I'm here. What's so important?" Nick shoved the stool under his butt. Shelly watched curiously, but from a distance.

"Good evening to you, too," Lou grumbled.

Nick stared at him. "Don't expect me to be pleasant."

"Cooper will turn up. Don't worry."

"Bastard," he whispered.

"You need to get over it, and fast."

"Why am I here?"

He shrugged. "Why didn't you ever tell me you had a secret girlfriend in high school?" His voice indicated actual interest, like he simply flipped a switch.

Nick's thoughts scrambled in low gear for an ulterior motive. "I never dated anyone in high school – not seriously. You would have met them."

Lou rested his hands on the bar. "Relax. Marcus and I were just shooting the shit and he mentioned it. I was going to let it slide, but it's bugging me."

"Your psychosis isn't my problem." Nick took a hard drink from his afternoon beer. "I was searching for my individualism. For privacy. For a life outside of your reach."

"I gave you freedom in spades. And what did you give me in return? Nothing."

"You gave me every reason to take whatever freedom I could."

His face softened. "You might not appreciate the way I disciplined you, but I tried to bond with you after your mother died."

"The Camaro?" Nick pointed beyond the wall to the garage and laughed.

"Yes, the one your refuse to drive – out of spite."

"Damn right, out of spite." It came out louder than he wanted to. "You instigated that."

"That lesson was for your own good."

"Were you tired of putting your ring impression in my face? You want to know why we didn't bond?"

Lou perked up. "I do. I really do."

Nick hissed, "I saw you kill Harry Sanders."

Lou didn't flinch, giving a quick glance to his bug detector on the bar. "I suspected you did."

"Some days I think I needed to see that. It made me see you for what you are."

"And what am I?"

"You're the man that raised me to be a killer."

Lou looked at Shelly for just a moment. The *killer* comment wasn't a big deal to them. What Nick didn't say was more powerful. He omitted the word *father*. Nick thought he saw his eyes glimmer. Lou admitted, "Fair enough."

"You told me to call you Lou for Christ's sake. Like you wanted to erase the father-son boundaries and have us just be boss and worker. What did you expect?"

Lou poked Nick with a hard finger. "I expect loyalty and respect. I may not be the hippie, coddling, father you wanted, but I raised a man, not an ungrateful whiney pussy. Shelly raised me way harder than I raised you. You want to know what the difference between us is?"

"Tell me."

"The day I was medically discharged from the Marines for a heart murmur, Shelly let me know how disappointed he was – and not with words."

Nick glanced at Shelly, who stared at the floor. "You beat him up for a medical condition?" He looked back to Lou. "That wasn't your fault."

"Damn right, it wasn't my fault. For the first time in my life, I fought back. Shelly's a tough bastard, but he was no match for me – for my training. I almost killed him. It was the last time he ever laid a hand on me. The power shifted that day."

"Power. Of course." Nick held back saying more. "Thanks for sharing that."

"Don't get no ideas. You're not ready to take the power from me."

Nick hesitated. "If asking about a girl I might've dated in high school is the reason you had me come, it wasn't a good one. I gotta go. Cali will be pissed if I'm out late three nights in a row."

"That's not why you're here." Lou stared forward. "Following Gavin Jones?"

"Gathering intel. What about it?" Nick grudgingly rested a butt cheek on the stool.

"Cooper already established the routine. You didn't have to go in the store where security cameras are."

"We were both shopping," Nick sucked in breath, remaining calm. "Coincidence. Belinda showed up for Christ's sake. It happens. She tell you I was following Jones?"

Lou slammed his empty bottle of beer down. "I don't talk to that bitch, and she's getting on my last nerve, too. I have my sources."

"I'm ready. It's going to happen next week."

Lou spoke normally again. "I want to know exactly when and where. Marcus your second?"

"Of course." Nick slowly rose. "Next week. His house. I know what I'm doing."

"You want to know why the Tribunal never got caught in twenty years?"

*Here we go again.* "Because nothing is ever said outside of this bar."

"Because no one ever questioned me. And I'm always right. The Tribunal only works if you follow orders. Otherwise, all we're left with is a house of cards – cards and egos." Lou sipped at his new beer, sitting back on his stool. "How's Big Hoover, by the way. You and Marcus have a good visit?" Lou's eyes swept over Nick and Shelly before returning to the television.

Chapter 18

The night before, Nick had told Cali about the three eradications he had committed, and how he had regret for each one. And how he felt justified for each one, also. However, he wouldn't go into detail about anyone else in the Tribunal, and she accepted that.

Nick's administrative leave officially ended. Cali had left early for her shift as Nick showered. She had changed subtly since he confessed. Her comments were more weighted, and she held her gaze a moment longer. He hoped it was a good thing, otherwise she could be planning her escape.

He was due into the station after roll call to talk to Sergeant Mary-Ann Bagley, who was making a special trip out to deliver her findings. He supposed it was a positive outcome, or Lou would have informed him otherwise.

While eating his cereal, he flipped through the news stations several times as they were having an eventful news cycle. The lead story was Chad Cooper's family having a press conference in search for their patriarch. Many things happened to New Orleans police officers, but how many just vanish? Nick thought Chad's wife did a spectacular job at pretending her husband would be found alive. Police

Superintendent Harrison vowed to use every resource to locate him.

A short segment was dedicated to the national groups condemning Belinda's shooting of a black man. The protest on the steps of City Hall was sparse, to say the least. Was it due to support or fear? That was the major argument. Would they be there with the signs and chants if the rapist was white? Same circumstances, different opinions. Nick stayed away from those conversations.

CNN continued to play the sound bite of one New Orleanian, a confident forty-something African American lady who said, "The only thing black and white here is that a rapist is off the street." She had that no-nonsense tone and scowl of a serious woman.

One advocate interviewed said that they'd have to wait to see what the investigation into the Goodman shooting determined, but to this point, proper use of force was used. That enraged over-dramatic politicians and civic leaders in other cities fighting for airtime, but they could only speculate that the investigation was being guided by like-minded individuals.

Nick's morning had barely started when he turned the television off. He found himself separating his role in the Tribunal and his work as a beat officer. Nick portrayed two different people, much like Jekyll and Hyde. But, having Cali know had released so much pressure.

He wore his civvies into the station, arriving just after first watch started their day. Other cops regulated to desk duty greeted him with optimism. It seemed everyone knew what the outcome would be, except Nick. Whether or not it was wishful thinking, they could be putting on a brave face before his dismissal. Marcus had even texted, wanting to be constantly updated.

Nick found himself waiting in the empty war room playing a trivia game on his cell. After twenty minutes with a cooling cup of coffee, Sergeant Mary-Ann Bagley entered with a chipper smile and sat opposite him, placing a laptop on the table. A sweet fragrance had entered with her.

She bounced into her chair, then hunched forward. "How are you this morning?"

"Anxious. Just spit it out." Nick let his arms dangle between his legs.

"In time. I want to show you something." There was no hint of impending doom, or a *we got you* expression. She hadn't a care in the world.

He leaned over the table to get a good look as she positioned the laptop sideways on the table. They each had a decent view, albeit at an angle. Mary Ann hummed, having the personality of a kindergarten teacher working with a child. She clicked a file and a video started. Nick recognized the scene of Belinda's shooting, having been recorded from the window above. Latavious Washington was attacking the female viciously.

"Who filmed this?" Nick held back the impending doom.

Bagley pointed, actually smiling. "Oh, look. There you are arriving at the scene. That Goodman is so aggressive. Does she have something to prove, you think?"

Nick closed the laptop, but Bagley didn't argue or bat an eyelash. He said, "I was there. I don't need to see it. So, I suppose this means I'm done - Belinda and me. Will there be charges?"

Bagley reached into the front of her satchel and pulled out something round. It flipped open like a clamshell. He couldn't believe she was checking her make up in a compact mirror. Her eyes darted to him. "Your memory apparently doesn't match the video."

"My memory is spot on."

"You really don't get it, do you?"

Nick's fingers combed through his hair. "You have the proof you need. What are you waiting for?"

She placed the compact back. "The man that shot this video brought it straight to Superintendent Harrison at Headquarters. Harrison called me into the meeting. We asked the man if he posted the video to any social media sights. The man said no. The man said the only copy was on the phone that was in his possession."

"You know he made copies. Who is this man? What was he doing filming instead of calling 9-1-1 or stopping the rape?"

"His wife called while he filmed. He's a proud, *black* New Orleanian." Bagley opened up the laptop again and the video was still playing. "He told us how his son used to run with a drug dealer that mysteriously died, drowning in the river just blocks away. His son turned his life around."

"Yeah?"

"He said that victim could have easily been his wife." Bagley remained silent until the video ended. "I saw the man resisting arrest – clearly struggling. But, I might see where others would think the opposite." She selected the red X in the corner and made a show of right clicking on the file to delete it. "The gentleman handed over his phone and let me download it to show you."

"I still don't see what this achieves."

She shrugged. "Nothing really. Thought you might be curious."

"I'm not. What does he want? Money?"

"We had a tech look at the phone and his social media. He didn't make a copy or send it to anyone else. Harrison allowed me to delete the video off his phone while he and the owner watched. That was truly the only copy before I made this one."

"Why didn't he just delete it himself? Why'd he even come into the Headquarters?"

"To thank Harrison personally. In essence, to thank you."

"That's just unreal. So, what now?"

Bagley cleared her throat and straightened up. Her business face was back. "We've investigated and reviewed your case thoroughly, Officer Rush. You should be happy to hear you've been cleared of any wrong-doing in the shooting death of Latavious Washington."

"Amazing. What about Officer Goodman?" His hands clasped.

"She, as well." Bagley smiled. "She had a lengthy session with the department psychiatrist and has been cleared. She's lucky she was with you."

"I'm not so sure anymore. Are there going to be any protesters waiting for us outside those doors? Once the public hears we're cleared..."

"No protests. Speaking as a black citizen living in today's New Orleans, I understand the high percentage of black crime given the economic status of our majority. I won't dispute it. The percentages correctly reflect the white and Hispanic criminals, too. The Tribunal doesn't discriminate, and I think that's a major reason the public is on board."

"I wouldn't know,"

"That's good, officer. Tow the line."

Nick said, weakly. "Just worried about Belinda."

She gave him a sideways eye. Her tone was assuring. "With you, she falls under the umbrella. Without you, she gets wet."

"Have you told her any of this?" He pointed at the laptop.

"No one knows, except Harrison, me, and you." Her eyes rolled. "And I'm sure your father Captain Rush will find out. Goodman knows she's cleared. I did that by phone. This - this was much more enjoyable."

"You're kind of twisted, aren't you?"

Her head bobbed back in a silent laugh. "I wouldn't mention the video in the ranks, but I'm sure you're well versed with your parameters."

"And you have a way with words."

"You can claim your firearm and rejoin your classmates. I have to prepare for the press conference. I'm sure the public will be relieved to know two of its finest officers will be back on the street to protect them." She presented a lazy salute.

Nick watched her leave the room with her shoulders pinned back. He sat with his hands wrapped around his coffee to keep from biting his nails. After getting the feeling back in his legs, he stood and left the room.

The men and women roaming the main room clapped as he traversed the desks and chairs. Belinda appeared from the adjoining hallway and enthusiastically embraced him. She laughed in his ear. "I can't believe this. It's such a relief. I knew we'd be okay."

"We're lucky, Belinda."

She turned to give a passing cop a high five. Another officer approached and she mimicked a flurry of kicks and blows as if sparring for the MMA.

Nick wanted to scold her, but bit his tongue. "Get in uniform. I'll meet you at the car."

As Belinda left for the locker room, Nick stuck his head in his captain's office. "Guess we're all good. I'm back."

Captain Gains shuffled papers on his cluttered desk. "Get changed and get out there. We have a large influx of tourists with this medical convention. Try not to shoot anyone."

"Did you talk to Lou?" His captain glanced at him without acknowledgement. "Of course, you did."

"Put this behind you. You and Goodman need to get back into the routine and I'll tell you what I told Goodman – let this go. The more you talk about it, the bigger the chance you say the wrong thing. It's done."

"Yes, sir." Nick left the room, feeling just a touch more invincible than he ever had before.

Chapter 19

Nick fiddled with the radar mount and keypad that sat between him and Belinda in the blue and white. He drove the squad car away from the Eighth District toward Bourbon Street as his partner sounded the siren in celebration. Business owners hosed off sidewalks. Food and beverage trucks hugged the curbs while making deliveries. The sparse tourists observed the squad car in curiosity, waiting to see if some crime had been committed nearby. First stop was to get Belinda's late morning bagel and coffee from a corner shop.

They settled at the entrance of the French Market where fruits and vegetables were on display. Walk farther in, and one would find every hot sauce made by man and womankind. Past that, in the belly of the beast, were an eclectic hodge-podge of knick-knacks, shirts, signs and tourist trinkets. Real shoppers would be able to find the *cool* stuff amongst the crap that would soon find a landfill.

Nick turned on the air-conditioning. He watched a sampling of middle-America walking by, wondering about their lives. He hoped they were really as carefree as they appeared. People-watching was one of the best parts of patrolling the Quarter.

Belinda finally burst. "What did Bagley tell you?"

He took his time. "Only that we used necessary force and it was a justified shooting. Very professional. Weird and professional."

Belinda flashed her large smile. "And no backlash from the public. No angry people on my doorstep with torches and pitchforks. I feel like a new person, Nick. Reborn."

"We got lucky, Belinda. That can't ever happen again."

She sipped her coffee. "That was my first kill. Person, I mean. The guys want to take me out for a kill party. Pat O'Briens, baby."

"Kill parties. I never liked those."

"I've killed rats, and a nutria once." She wiped her bottom lip after a short laugh. "Not much of a difference sometimes."

"Big difference." Nick finally let sympathy seep in. "How are you really?"

"You mean, am I *changed*? Maybe, but for the better. I mean, I've discharged my weapon three other times, and that was exciting in itself, but actually taking a criminal off the street..." she stopped.

"It affects people in different ways. You seem to see it as a good thing."

"That's bad?"

"I'm not telling you how to feel, whether its remorse or jubilation..."

"Jubilation?" she mumbled to herself.

Nick ignored her. "It's our job to arrest the alleged criminals and let the court system decide their fate. We don't decide anything. We don't judge or impose their punishment."

Belinda squinted, as if she couldn't compute. She gazed at him, incredulously. An explosion of laughter shot out her mouth and she covered the sound with her hand. "That's rich, Nick. Fucking rich coming from you."

A sudden whumping on the driver's side window caught their attention. An over-weight man holding a very large green drink in one hand pressed his bare belly against the glass. He let out one long scream. "Whoooooaaaaah!" And then he moved on, staggering over the curb.

"He'll probably be getting a tour of O.P.P. later." Belinda mused.

Nick continued, letting the man have his fun. "All I'm saying is that it seems the Tribunal acts after the court system fails."

"Whatever." She collected herself.

"Don't *whatever* me. It's disrespectful and not a good look."

"Alright, *dad*." She danced with her arms as she sat. "It's like a drug. Like I woke up from a deep sleep."

"Jesus, Belinda. Did you tell the department psychiatrist that?"

"No. I said I was sorry for what had to be done, and I've come to terms with it. He put himself in that position. I'm not haunted. Yadda yadda."

"How would you feel if a report came back that the man was mentally retarded? What if he had the I.Q. of a four-year old and had just wandered away from his caregivers?"

"He wasn't!"

"See? You can't even face that possibility. That shit can't happen again. Not with me."

"You telling me not to shoot anyone in self-defense?"

"Now, you're lying to yourself."

She finally frowned, putting down her coffee. "You need to let me be happy about this."

"I need you to feel the weight of it. You didn't get away with littering."

"Funny how you equate him with garbage." She took a breath. "I need to talk to Lou about this." She bit into her bagel.

"Why in the hell would you want to talk to Lou?"

She chewed and talked. "I just proved I can do it."

"That wasn't an audition. Get out of the car, Belinda."
Nick didn't wait for her to respond. He stepped onto the
sidewalk near Margaritaville. Colorful beads hung in
nearby trees growing from patches of dirt in concrete cut-
outs.

Belinda was slow to get out, having to situate her
breakfast. "Why are we getting out of the car?"

Nick distanced himself behind the squad about ten
yards, waiting for his partner to catch up. "You're being
careless."

Belinda's head reared back. "How do you figure?"

"Do you think I'm Tribunal?"

"I know you are." Her arms folded.

"And yet, you fucking speak your mind in the car?
What if the dash cam audio was on?"

"It wasn't."

"We're in a car full of surveillance equipment."

"Alright, maybe you have a point." She tightened the
squeeze on her torso.

"And you can't pester Lou."

"I don't pester him. Only you, really."

He watched two men dressed as vampires pass. "And
yet, you don't listen to me." Nick's face turned hard along
with his tone. "Everybody knows you want in. And if they
wanted you in, you'd *be* in. You getting cleared of this
shooting doesn't change shit. If anything, it makes it worse.
They see you as a loose cannon."

"You're against me, aren't you? Is it because I'm a
woman? I'll bet there's not one woman in it."

"You're grasping at every excuse and avoiding the
real reason. They don't want you."

"I thought you'd help me, but I can do this without
you." She turned back for the car.

Nick ran to her side. "He'll kill you."

She stopped, just feet from the hood. "Why would you say that?"

"Because it's true. Doesn't matter that you're a cop. That you were an MMA fighter. That you're probably in better shape than any cop on the force. The fact that you want it, is exactly why you won't be approached."

"That doesn't make sense."

"The original ten formed reluctantly, as a *necessity*. There was no bloodlust. They were cautious, and careful who they targeted. No one enjoyed it. Even now, no one enjoys it."

Belinda contemplated that. "I see it as either having the balls or not having the balls."

Nick put his hand over his heart. "You have to trust me on this."

"I do trust you. But, you don't make those decisions, and you don't speak for Lou."

Nick turned away from the sun's glare. "What do you think happened to Chad Cooper?"

She hesitated. "He disappeared. You know what happened?"

"No, I don't. And no one ever will." He stared her down.

"Jesus, Nick. Really?"

"You're dancing around bear traps."

"Cooper is one of us," she said in thought.

"*Was*. So, you have to drop it." Nick felt the beads of sweat forming. He was saying way too much.

Belinda nodded. "I won't mention it again. Let's get back to the air conditioning, please."

Nick watched her get into the car with a sad expression. Time would tell if she was serious, but for today, he wanted to get through the shift without any more drama.

Chapter 20

Cali had made it home from an uneventful shift at the hospital with more energy than usual. She and Nick ate Chinese, but her future husband only consumed a quarter of his usual order. He never lost his appetite, no matter what kind of day he had. She asked if he was feeling okay, and he gave a short answer, which she accepted for the moment.

They settled into the sofa for a few hours of mind-numbing television. Cali thought it might be a relaxing night, but she couldn't help but worry. Despite not saying anything, the shaking of the couch with his fidgeting was magnified in her mind. She had to remember he had gone through something the other night with Marcus that affected him to the bone.

"What's going on?" She put the volume on mute. "You said your first day back went fine."

His eyes darted to her before his head could turn. "Huh, oh, Yeah, it was good."

"You're twitchy over there."

"It's the Jones thing."

"You want to back out? Would Lou let you?"

He leaned back into the sofa, but kept looking at her. "I don't know. He'd question it. Then, he'd stop trusting me. And if I couldn't perform my duties... I fear what the Tribunal vote would be... son or no son. What would we do then?"

"It doesn't matter, as long as we're together. Oh, man, did that sound as sappy to you?" She propped herself up against a large, velvety pillow. "But, cheat on me, and we're done."

He smiled. "Then, I have no worries. Could you do a Tribunal murder? Morally or ethically speaking."

"I couldn't kill anyone, I don't think... unless they attacked me."

"Belinda wants to, given her recent shooting. We argued this morning." He smirked.

"And what did she say?" She watched him, curling her hair with her finger. "She has a taste for it now?"

"Bloodlust? Yeah, something like that." He thought a moment. "It's one thing to kill someone while defending yourself, but to set out and take a life... I don't know. Do you mean it... that you'd run away with me?"

"I would."

"To Europe? To never come back here again. You'd do that? At a drop of the hat?"

"Give me a hat." She grinned with closed lips.

He nodded, looking far off. "After this Jones thing. Let's do it."

"What?" Cali stiffened.

"Not at a drop of a hat, but without anyone knowing...especially Lou. We'll abandon the house. It was paid for with Tribunal money anyway, and we'll get two tickets to Paris and start fresh."

"Seems like you thought about it very seriously." Cali had to keep even. "Okay."

Nick stood. "We're doing this?"

Cali was unsure, but answered anyway. "We're doing this." A nervous smile appeared.

"I think I need a beer to even out. You want a beer?"

"Yeah, I'll take a beer."

Nick leaned in and gave her a kiss, but with the implications of the sudden change of plans, she couldn't put anything behind it.

Chapter 21

Eradication day had finally arrived.

Nick settled into a state of calm. Having Cali on board was a stabilizing factor. Marcus was his brother, but Cali was his everything. If she agreed with the process, then it must be the right thing. And the fact that moving Europe was on the table made him optimistic for the future. She wasn't tethered to family, which made the decision easy.

The unmarked police car guided by Marcus eased through Gavin Jones' neighborhood. Long-suffered, sporadic ranch houses lined the pothole-ravaged streets. Most had an attempted refurbishing by residents who moved back after *the storm*, but in the decade since then, additional repairs have mostly been ignored. Bulldozed lots were common from those that sold their uninhabitable homes back to the state.

The right-side tires nudged the curb a block away from the address. Marcus huffed and slapped the wheel. "Here we go. You got this?"

"I got this." Nick told him.

"After pulling that trigger against your heart, I'll never doubt you." Marcus forced his attention to the neighborhood. "I thought you and I were, I don't know, simpatico on eradications. Never thought you'd *want* to do one."

Nick gave him the most serious look he could. "I don't want to do it. But, he's a murderer. He's an abuser. Probably rapes women, too."

Marcus laughed with troubled overtones. "Oh, I don't care about that scum inside. Make him suffer. I'm just worried about you."

"And I love you for it."

Marcus held up his hand for Nick to take in a strong grip. "Love you, too."

"Think we'd be together if we were gay?" Nick asked.

"Probably." They laughed, breaking up the tension.

"Okay, remember, after you see Jones come back from the store and enter his house, drive out to my place, grab my phone off the table and text Cali to establish my alibi. It'll ping off the right tower. A few hearts with the lips emoji. Type *miss you*."

"Aw, that's sweet." Marcus blew a kiss.

"It's our thing. Listen, I'm going to try to get his girlfriend's location out of him. So, it might be awhile."

"Remember there may be more than one he's killed. Lou would shit if you can solve some missing persons cases along the way."

"I'll make him think he can save his life by confessing. Once he's dead, they might never find her."

"Got it. I'll wait for your burner call. You ready?"

"Suddenly, I'm not sure." Nick spun a soccer ball in his lap. It bounced against the thin Kevlar vest under his baggy sweatshirt.

Marcus adjusted the music to a lower volume. "See you on the other side." He slapped Nick's head in a playful manner.

Nick got out feeling like an Airborne Ranger landing behind enemy lines. Marcus raised a stupid thumbs-up to get a smile, ready to park somewhere nearby until he spotted Jones. If anyone reported Nick breaking and entering, Marcus could head it off at the pass.

The soccer ball bounced while navigating the sidewalk toward Jones' house. He wore cargo shorts, a thin Chicago Fire hooded sweatshirt, and the vest for protection. The ball rolled forward at his feet while his hands were protected by flesh colored surgical gloves. He didn't expect anyone to question the odd get-up. No tattoos were visible, and a Saint's cap was pulled low over his brow in case someone had a video camera doorbell. Big, cheap sunglasses and a dark, unshaven scruff completed the ensemble.

The temperature hung in the upper sixties and cloudy. Being a weekday, no kids were playing, no lawns were being mowed, or joggers jogging. People were at work, such as it was in the area. Nick had scouted three unsecured houses to choose from for entry. He remembered his days as a kid, when he and his friends would cut through people's yards to shorten their journey. Neighbors accepted that young boys jumped their fences, and most didn't care or even noticed.

The house with the chain link fence would be easiest, but the taller, wooden fence would offer the best concealment. He paused under the shade of a large tree to practice a few tricks with the ball, just fifteen feet from a gate extending from the side of the house. There wasn't an obvious security camera in sight.

With confidence, he kicked the ball into the yard. His acting skills came into play as he slumped in disappointment. He trotted up to the fence and peered over it. All was clear, on both sides. No dogs. He pressed the handle on the gate. It opened without protest. First obstacle was conquered.

Seconds later, after passing a barbecue pit, a clothesline, and a swing set, Nick tossed the ball into Jones' yard. He hopped over the fence dividing the two properties and soon found himself hugging the bricks in the back of Jones' house. Around his neck was a bandana, which he pulled over his mouth and nose for entry. The nearest window was open, as it was typical for residents to get all the free air-conditioning they could. He slid out the flimsy, aluminum screen and shimmied inside, careful to be stealthy.

Once he collected himself off the floor, he waited, sweating heavily under the vest and sweatshirt.

Nick decided not to leave Jones' bedroom until he arrived. The less he disturbed, the better. Air pulled at the bandana as he inhaled. There was no particular smell as fresh, cool air had been ventilating through the window, but he caught a whiff of tuna. The bed against the cracked wall was a simple queen frame, unmade. The foundation was sinking. A plain lamp sat on two stacked crates used as a nightstand. The green carpet was much darker where foot-traffic existed. Dirty clothes littered the floor. He didn't see any framed pictures of friends or family, or even the girl Gavin allegedly killed.

A beat-up dresser and mirror were positioned against the opposite discolored wall. Nick's reflection looked like the Unabomber, with his shady hood and menacing sunglasses. His conversation with Cali came back to him. Doubt about killing again festered. What was he doing?

He waited at the entrance of the bedroom, holding an unregistered gun near his chest. Not long after, the lock on the front door clicked over, resonating like an explosion. Nick peered down the hallway to see a shadow bouncing around the kitchen. Jones was putting away his single-man groceries. Each sound amplified his solitude. He heard cabinets opening and the knocking around of items, as well as the suction of the refrigerator door.

*Europe was a plane ride away.*

Nick lightly stepped into the hallway, creeping ever closer. Did he really want to commit to this plan? He could climb right back out the window, grab their passports and head for the airport. Suddenly, having it be in front of him, he didn't want to kill this man.

He pressed his back against the wall. The sounds from the kitchen stopped. Nick finally saw Jones' backside. This man got away with murder. He put away the last item and sat at the kitchen table, a tiny circle that would barely fit four. He hunched there, looking at nothing, as if waiting for the slaughter. No television was on, nor music played. No alcohol rested in front of him. Would anyone in Jones' situation not drink? Light up a joint or do drugs?

Cooper's decision to exile his cousin was the right one. He told Cali he would do this job, but the nausea grew in his belly. Faced with death, would Gavin Jones flee town? If Nick just made the offer, would this career criminal agree?

*What if he killed again?*

Nick leaned forward, surprised that Jones didn't catch any micron of movement. He stepped fully into view and stood there, not even raising his weapon at the man. *Look at me.*

Finally, Jones did see him. *Was that a smirk?* The man casually produced a gun from under the table. Nick's reflexes kicked in just as Jones fired. An immediate jolt to his ribs forced him to the floor. He was hit. He checked for a hole in the vest where the intense pain was, but it had held. Jones had been waiting for him.

"FBI! Freeze!" boomed from a headless voice.

All he saw was the cracked ceiling. There were no busted doors or glass breaking. Nick heard footsteps filling the house. Two men at the end of the hall pointed automatic weapons at his chest. FBI was scrawled along their tac vests. They had been in the other bedrooms the entire time, waiting for him to make a move. Nick dropped his gun to the floor.

Gavin Jones yelled, "Don't move."

One of the agents straightened up, facing Jones. "Holster your weapon and go wait in the bedroom."

"I had to fire. He was going to kill me," Jones argued.

"I said, go wait in the bedroom," the agent repeated in a voice not to be ignored. The same agent knelt at Nick's side. "Lucky you had a vest. You okay?"

He didn't answer. While Jones retreated, Nick was turned onto his stomach and his hands secured with plastic zip ties. His side was burning.

"Don't struggle," the agent said.

A classic rock song by Styx suddenly played in Nick's head. *The jig is up. The news is out. They finally found me.*

## Chapter 22

Thankfully, Marcus hadn't been parked by Jones' house when the feds discretely walked Nick out to their waiting black SUV. He still wore the vest. His ribs ached where the bullet hit. They placed him in the back seat - no fuss, nor spectacle. Ten minutes after Jones had arrived home, Nick found himself being transported in an expansive, Ford Club Wagon to the FBI building located on Leon C. Simon at the Lakefront.

Gavin Jones was an *agent*, not a criminal. And that agent tried to kill him. The man in charge, called *Fizz* by his partner, kept watch on the right side of Nick, weapon pointed in a casual manner. Nick considered Jones during the journey, the man who played the role of petty criminal for six years, just to lure the Tribunal into a hit.

*Could Lou have sent him into a trap?*

With Jones nowhere in sight, the feds had regarded his injury when strapping him into the seat. They were cordial about the arrest, which meant they wanted him on their side. And that was probably why *Fizz* was so pissed that Jones fired off a round. Was Jones a scared agent, or what Shelly suspected?

He pictured Lou sitting at Shelly's with other cops, unaware of the time bomb about to go off. Cali came to mind, making her rounds at the hospital, getting a visit from two sharply dressed agents. They wouldn't offer any information as they left together under the stares of her coworkers, but she'd know things went sideways. Would the feds be able to contain his arrest from the press? That was the question.

The SUV pulled into a secured area with designated parking spots for the transport vehicles. The key-coded, reinforced doubled doors led directly into the detention rooms and the processing room. Everyone in the detention hallway had a badge around their neck to allow them to enter or exit, otherwise, there was no getting out.

As they trudged on, Nick noticed little boxes set in the wall next to the detention rooms, much like apartment mailboxes. One agent slid his gun into the cubby and closed it with a key. Obviously, no firearms were allowed in with the prisoners. That agent entered one of the rooms and closed the door.

Nick's ties were cut, and two agents helped as he gingerly raised his arms to remove the sweatshirt. The vest came off next, and then they allowed him to put the sweatshirt back on. A nice bruise had already started where the bullet hit. He was escorted into a different interview room that was about eight by ten feet, with a table and three chairs. They let him face the entrance, cuffing him again to an embedded loop in the tabletop.

He noticed recording equipment was set up against the wall along with security bars for additional handcuffing options. He also noticed a phone on the wall and a large button near the door - a panic button.

The feds had thoroughly searched him, procuring his surgical gloves. Nothing else had been on his person. Making someone wait was an excellent tool in letting a criminal sweat it out. A guilty person could get pretty rattled in the quiet. Except, Nick didn't get the time to rehearse a confession or denial. The door opened and a humorless balding man in a white shirt and blue tie stepped inside with a stuffed folder. The senior agent kept a permanent squint and the tip of his nose pointed upwards. His expression lent to that of a task master.

He placed the folder down with ease. "You want water? A Coke?"

"I'm good."

"I'm Agent Charles Long." He extended his hand far enough for Nick to shake.

His bruised ribs ached. The plastic tie dug into his skin. "Nick Rush, but I'm sure you know that." He looked at the folder.

Agent Long took his time in positioning the chair in order to sit, as if at dinner. Nick imagined the man nimbly placing a napkin in his lap while dining with his mother. He opened the folder like a menu, looking up at him a couple of times.

"Stellar career so far, Officer Rush. Thirty-one years of age. Graduated the academy ten years ago. Joined young. That's good."

"I always knew."

"Nice recommendation letter from your father Captain Louis Rush."

"You gonna get me for nepotism, too?"

Long's lips thinned in a smile, his eyes disappeared. "Pissed about your father getting you on the force instead of your own merits?"

Silence.

"Sorry about your mother. Truly." He stared at Nick, unblinking. "Must've been difficult."

"I was ten." As if that explained everything.

"And she was killed by an unknown assailant. Add that with Lou Rush as a role model, your career path was pretty much set."

"Is this my therapy session?"

Long brightened. "Just want to understand you better. You want to be on the side of right, don't you? I mean, that's what the Tribunal is all about."

"Tribunal?"

"Were you happy when the only person of interest in your mom's death was murdered shortly after the trial? Roughly the same time the Tribunal was suspected of forming. Did your father convince you that justice was served?"

"Don't know anything about that."

"I can see why you might want to become a policeman. You saw the respect your father commanded."

"Do we have to do this back and forth? Why not just get to the nuts and bolts?"

Long's finger scratched his cheek. He suddenly looked sleepy. "Sure, we can skip the dog and pony show. It's simple. How much jail time you do depends on your cooperation."

"Jail time for what? B and E? That's all you got."

"Did you know that Gavin Jones isn't an asset? He's not a criminal. He's a federal agent."

*No shit, Long.* "And this woman he supposedly murdered?" *Assigned to another case by now,* he thought.

"Alive and well back at Quantico." He leaned forward, resting his arms on the table.

Nick stayed even. "Your operation has been in effect all this time?"

"It was the only way to establish the agents. When we set up store fronts, like dry cleaners for example, they stay open for years to get established. Many cases take years for trust to take root within a community or with certain factions."

"Impressive." Nick pulled at his plastic ties, shifting the table slightly. "What happens now?"

"You're being arrested under a federal warrant. When we're done with you, you'll be processed, taken to the federal courthouse. The US Marshals Service for the Eastern District of Louisiana will take you to a holding cell to await your appearance before a magistrate judge."

"Maybe it's time for a lawyer."

"Fine. We know you went there to kill Agent Jones; under orders from Lou Rush, leader of the Tribunal."

"Why don't law enforcement types say *allegedly*? I have no part in what those cops are doing." Nick made fists. "I went there to rob that guy. Have you seen a NOPD paycheck?"

"I thought you didn't want to play games. I'm being straight with you. You either help us nail your father and the Tribunal, or you go to federal prison."

"At least I'll have a life."

"A cop in prison? Yeah, you'll have a nice, relaxing life."

Nick withdrew. "I have nothing to say. Aren't you supposed to stop questioning when I ask for a lawyer?"

Long sighed and stood. "That's fine. We have everything we need without your assistance. Someone will be in shortly to take you through processing. I'm sure you're familiar with it."

Nick thought twice about it. "You screwed yourself. You're forcing them to close ranks."

He stopped at the door. "You think this is all we have? We have people in places you could never imagine."

"You guys have been after the Tribunal for-*ever*. And you got something now because I broke into a house?" His chuckle built into a laugh that abruptly stopped.

Long shrugged, but he still wasn't leaving. "Do you know that Officer Chad Cooper's body was found by a hunter in Southwest Louisiana? Just got the identification this morning. He's been a suspected Tribunal member for years."

Nick felt himself lose color. "That's horrible."

"His kid was looking out his window the night he went missing. Said he left with two men. A black man and a white man, but he couldn't give a good description. Said his dad was acting very strange. Your best friend is Marcus Hoover, isn't it? Fellow African American member."

"Sounds like you need to find these two men."

"In the meantime, we're going to charge you with the attempted murder of a federal agent, breaking and entering, conspiracy to commit murder."

"Conspiracy? Where you get that?"

The agent finally showed a twinge of emotion. "We have a nice little recording that you'll eventually hear." He hiked an eyebrow.

"Bullshit, or you would have used it already."

"Agent Jones and his girlfriend weren't the only agents with established roles in this operation."

The door opened and a woman walked past Long. His world stopped spinning. Still wearing her hospital scrubs, Cali glided in as if she belonged there, but she didn't resemble his fiancé at all. His eyes dropped to a Bureau security badge hanging around her neck.

"Nick, I'm so sorry." She barely looked at him.

Long smiled smugly. "Let me formally introduce you to Special Agent Maddox.

Chapter 23

"What the hell is going on?" Nick couldn't look away from the female impersonating his fiancé. The room swayed at the sudden disconnect from this impossibility.

Agent Long kept his mouth shut, letting the explosive realization settle into resignation. Nick shook his head and blinked incessantly. He brought his face to his hands, wiping at his forehead. When he peeked at her, she was still there with the same expression of concern.

Cali stood rigid near the door; her shoulders back. "I'm not a nurse, Nick. I'm a federal agent."

"Did the FBI put you up to this? You're not in trouble, Cali. They have nothing on me."

She took a step farther inside. "They're not using me. I am a real FBI agent."

Nick clenched his fists. "No, you're a nurse. I've seen you go to work every day for seven years." He swallowed hard. "How do you fake being a nurse? You treat people at the hospital. Can I get some water, please?"

"And someone cut his cuffs," Long yelled at no one in particular.

Cali continued, "I am a registered nurse, too. The Bureau thought it would be the perfect cover to use my education. Our meeting up again was meticulously planned."

A redheaded, freckled agent entered the room and placed an open bottle of water on the table. Long gestured to Nick's hands and the agent cut the restraints with gardening shears. Nick rubbed his wrists before taking a long gulp of water. "Quantico? You got your nursing degree *and* completed training at Quantico?"

"Not so surprising." Cali gave into a slow blink. When Nick didn't respond, She filled the silence with footsteps to the empty chair. She comfortably sat next to Agent Long, looking at Nick like PETA looks at an animal in the zoo.

Nick continued, "That's why the agents were already in place at Jones' house. I told you... trusted you... and you used me. Almost got me killed."

Cali didn't have a response.

Nick's attention fell on Long. "Jones was here five years." His eyes darted to Cali. "We've been together six..." He let out a breath and squeezed his eyes shut as if it would all go away. "How could I be so blind?"

Cali placed her hands on the table, palms down. "Because we gave you no reason so suspect anything. Normally, we'd work in conjunction with law enforcement. Well, in this case... we had to skirt around that courtesy."

"How... how could you do this? You have no heart... no... soul." Nick fought hard to keep tears from falling. "If you loved me, you could have stopped this. You could have stopped me when I told you."

"If I had told you I was an agent, how would you have reacted to that?" Cali kept her gaze. "And any answer you give would be hypothetical. My best chance to get you from under Lou's thumb was to get you here." She pointed straight down at the table.

"I'm not Tribunal."

"Oh, Nick." She said with sympathy.

He glared at her. "You should take off your engagement ring." Nick pointed.

Cali covered it with her other hand.

"We have an out for you," Long suggested.

"I can't believe this is happening." He tried to stand, but fell flat in the chair. "It was fake. All fake."

"Nick..."

"Fake!" he shouted.

Cali took his outburst calmly. "I do love you, Nick. But, I have to think of the bigger picture."

"Bullshit! Having sex with me was part of the assignment?"

She cleared her throat and took interest in her lap. "I wrestled with that. The Bureau gave me every opportunity to refuse the assignment."

Nick scowled. "You were very convincing in bed. You'd be surprised, Long. The positions she could get in. The faces she made. Or maybe you wouldn't be surprised. How the hell do I know?"

Cali's cheeks turned red. "You're angry and that's understandable."

"Well, thanks for understanding," He blurted.

"This is more important than hurt feelings."

"Hurt feelings? How about you putting me away for life in the process? Maybe I need a lawyer." Nick looked at Long.

Long took his opportunity. "A lawyer isn't a good idea. You have to get over your anger and think about yourself right now."

Cali finished her thought. "If it wasn't me, Agent Long would have found someone else. This was the only way."

"Lou suspected you all along. I loved you. *I loved you.*"

"I'm sorry."

"Shut up. Stop it. Just stop it." He brought his face down to his hands.

Cali said, "You need time to let it sink in."

"Stop fucking trying to placate me. This is over, Cali. You have no right to speak like you know me. Don't explain. Don't justify. Just get on with charging me with *breaking and entering*. I want my lawyer."

Cali continued, "You need to deal with the truth, Nick. Your father is the leader of the Tribunal. The fact that you could lie to my face for all these years proves you're no different than me. You've been hiding your own secret all this time."

"My secret wasn't about hurting you." *Shit, he was faltering.* He still needed to start denying everything.

She wiped the corner of her eye. "Oh, so if you went to prison for being a vigilante assassin, that wouldn't hurt me?"

"Not the same," he said with less conviction.

"I guess we both pretended to be somebody else."

"What if I wouldn't have gone after Jones? Would you have married me in the hopes I'd slip up at some point?"

"Your eradications have gotten so few and far between… yes, I would have married you just so I could start chipping away at Lou." She finally let go of her shame. "All or nothing."

"You stole six years from my life." He raised his head in defiance. "Fuck both of you."

Cali reached out and put her hand on his. Nick pulled back his arm as if riding a bucking bronco. The chair threatened to slide from under him. Long needlessly prepared for action.

"It's fine, Agent Long," Cali said in a whisper.

"Fine," Long held his hands up in a calming manner.

"I think I'm going to throw up. Get her out of here," he yelled.

Cali ignored the outburst. "We have an offer, Nick. And it's time sensitive."

He laughed, but quickly calmed himself. "You want to turn me against Lou. I know how you operate. How you use people."

"We want the head of the snake." Cali put the burner they secured at the raid on the table. "I don't want you to go to jail… and you will, Nick. Believe me, we got you dead to rights. But if you testify, we can arrange witness protection…"

"No WITSEC," Long interrupted.

Cali seemed to do a double-take. "What, but we discussed…"

"That is no longer feasible." Long stared at Nick, as if assessing his reaction.

Nick jumped at the offer, despite himself, "Wait, I'd consider witness protection. Wouldn't my testimony be enough?"

"I'm glad you finally recognize your predicament." Long exhaled. "No, your testimony wouldn't be enough," Long said with a glance at Cali. "You're too far removed from all the earlier murders and it's your word against theirs. These cops cleaned up their own crime scenes. No physical evidence left behind at all."

Nick slowly nodded. "What if I testify about Lou's involvement in the three murders I committed?"

Long shook his head. "Your three murders could be prosecuted, but the jurors might turn against you when they learn of your immunity. Any trial will be moved to an out of state venue. You won't have New Orleanians as jurors. And they'd be faced with charging the man that told you to kill while you, the man that did the actual killing, would go free."

Cali cautiously added, "Not to mention Lou would flip it all back on you. Say it was your idea."

Long folded his arms. "If I was a juror, it would leave a sour taste in *my* mouth, I know. And without any evidence, it's could go sideways."

"You want me back in. With a wire. That won't work."

"We know a wire would be discovered." Long admitted.

"Lou fucking checks himself from time to time."

"We'll circumvent the wire. Make the call to your father. Tell him it took longer than you thought, but the job is done. You have some kind of code to convey that, right?"

"I'd never say that over the phone." Nick's heart hammered, deep and visceral. "He'll know the job is done when I show my face."

Cali said, "We can put Jones back in that house and you can tell Lou something prevented the job."

Long grimaced. "Unfortunately, Agent Winger – Jones - has recused himself from the operation. He's ranting and raving that he's done. Done with the Bureau."

Nick wasn't surprised. "He seemed a little off."

Long shrugged. "After six years, he'd rather quit than go back in. But, that's not your concern."

Cali explained, "Fortunately, our agents were there since the morning. There was no outside activity for anyone to report back. Lou is still at Shelly's as we speak. Marcus is still waiting for you. Tell Lou the eradication was a success. Our agents will take care of the crime scene."

Nick looked at her incredulously. "There needs to be a body."

Long said, "Quantico Body Farm cadaver, matching our agent's height and weight. He was donated after being burned in an arson case. It's been here since you told Agent Maddox about the eradication."

"Burned. You want to stage a fire?" Nick stated, again seeing Cali's confusion. Long hadn't included her in the decision.

Long reached out to stop Cali from speaking. "Tell Lou you set the house on fire. We'll swoop in soon after, and claim the body before the autopsy is done."

Cali added, "Lou knows the FBI investigates every suspicious death of any criminal in this city. This is just one more. He'll believe us stealing the corpse is business as usual."

Nick couldn't argue that point.

"This will be over before anyone figures out it's not Jones," Long agreed.

"The fire is a stupid move. I'd never do that. They don't risk harming other people."

Long coughed. "Except other cops."

Cali stressed. "The house is empty. It would be a controlled burn and the fire department will get there before it spreads."

"And if I don't agree to do this?"

"Attempted murder of a federal agent alone will put you in prison." Cali pushed his phone a little closer. "And the Tribunal will go on as usual – without you."

"And if I agree?"

Long said, "We won't risk bugging Shelly's again. We haven't ever recorded anything of use there, anyway. What we want – what gets you federal protection – is his *ledger*."

"Ledger?" Nick always imaged there *was* one.

"A ledger listing every murder the Tribunal has ever committed and the person who committed them. It contains details to revisit because there is no way he can remember the hundreds of murders and alibis."

Nick gave a deep nod. "I'm not sure where it is, but I can deliver it. Shelly loves to keep track of things – like some kind of bookkeeper. I'll bet he knows. Lou's grooming me to take over. He'll give it to me if push for it." Nick waited through the silence. "For full immunity."

"We can arrange that," Cali said.

Long smiled. "You give us this ledger, I can guarantee full immunity."

"Marcus gets it, too."

"If he cooperates when the time comes, I don't see it as being a problem."

"I want it in writing."

"We'll add Marcus as an addendum, but we've already drawn up the agreement." Long seemed pleased.

Nick couldn't get comfortable in his chair. "If I get the ledger or I don't, my career, my life is over." He looked at the woman he thought was his soul mate. "Can you give me a few minutes to think about this?"

"Minutes are all you have. The offer is time sensitive, and that is not a cliché." Cali said, as she and Long left the room.

Chapter 24

Nick sat perfectly still at the table, knowing he was on closed-circuit monitors. Cali's betrayal seemed to have sucked all the energy from him. He would have given his life in any circumstance to save hers. But, she let him waltz into the Jones gauntlet, just to use him for her vendetta against Lou. Agent Charles Long was correct, at this critical point and time, he couldn't sit and analyze her actions. He needed to save himself. It was all he had.

Agent Long and Cali had never once mentioned Tanya Sanders. It was as if she had disappeared off the face of the earth. By all accounts, *she had*. Tanya had become a missing person that wasn't missing at all. He recounted the day he had last seen the daughter of Harry Sanders, and met Cali Maddox all within the very same moment.

It had been six years ago. At Lou's urging after graduating the academy, Nick had begun to give blood every three months, as most law enforcement did. At first, he thought choosing Ochsner Hospital was random, but now he knew better. The entire encounter played in his head like a scene in a movie.

Nick had gripped the armrests in a less than comfortable chair while waiting for the nurse. He remembered a poster of a little boy smiling after hitting a tee-ball, advertising the benefits of saving a life with a donation.

While he had waited to be siphoned, Nick snagged a dated *Time* magazine that had an article on the NOPD's exploits during Hurricane Katrina. He almost threw it in the trash, but someone at the hospital held onto it for a reason. Directly after Hurricane Katrina, the NOPD's reputation had taken a big hit by killing looters as well as innocent residents that stayed during the flooding. The crime rate just started taking a significant plunge when the storm hit, and those rogue cops gave the department a black eye. Most of the offending officers had gone to trial or had been pled out, but the nation still saw the stain on the city.

When Nick had become an officer, Lou said those undisciplined, hair-trigger cops were the reason the Tribunal was so choosey with new members. Nick argued that the psychological trauma experienced during those days were enough to push the most sane over the edge. Not that he condoned their actions, but without law, he likened those days to the Lord of the Flies.

Shelly's became legendary for staying open after the flooding. Hayne Boulevard along the levee only sustained a foot or less of water. However, if you traveled just two blocks away from the lake, Nick's block as an example, you'd find yourself in five feet of water. With the help of generators, a steady stream of cops, and creative food and beverage acquisition, Shelly's could serve the public that stayed.

Directly after the storm, the police needed to turn around public opinion, and the Tribunal had righted the ship by doing what it did best. Granted, the FBI was still investigating the NOPD for crimes during the flooding, but they became less newsworthy. There were jokes going around that *every* cop was a Tribunal member during the time of Martial Law. And oddly enough, Lou had said that none of the Tribunal members took part in shooting looters because they were disciplined.

While he had skimmed the articles, a familiar voice greeted him. "Hi, Nick."

When the nurse walked in, Nick froze in the moment. Tanya's hair had been dyed blonde and was pulled back into a ponytail and she wore studious-looking glasses, but the face was indisputable. "Oh, my God."

She smiled wide, holding up an iPad. "I saw your name on my schedule. So good to see you."

He leapt from the chair and gave her a warm embrace. They laughed and rocked back and forth. He asked, "What are you doing here?"

"I just moved back a month ago after Ochsner offered me a job."

"Your hair is so blonde. Natural looking. I like it." He almost ran his fingers through her ponytail, but pulled back. His lips wanted to kiss her, like they did in the last moments before they had said goodbye forever.

"Thanks, all part of the new me." She spun in a quick circle with her arms extended.

"You should have called. Why didn't you call me?"

She looked down. "It's complicated. I wasn't sure I should. Things have changed."

An older, male nurse stuck his head in the door. "Cali, you got the labs from that work accident earlier?"

"They haven't come up yet. Give me a minute, Jeff," Tanya answered.

*Cali?* Nick ignored what the nurse called his ex-girlfriend for the moment. "We talked about how to handle your leaving. We decided not to stay in contact, not to drag anything out. And you move back after five years? Just like that?"

"It wasn't planned, Nick."

He finally looked at her name badge. "Cali Maddox? That's not your name. Are you married?"

"No, nothing like that."

Nick's brow furrowed. "Is that a nickname? Cause *Bama* would be more appropriate since that's where you moved."

"No," she laughed. She held both his hands, looking into his eyes. "I legally changed my name after I moved. Changed my hair. Stopped plucking my eyebrows." She popped them up and down.

"Why Cali?"

She blushed, looking down at her feet. "Going Back to Cali was playing on the day I decided to change my name."

"L.L. Cool J? Really?"

"No. I've always liked the traditional Callie." She spelled it out for him. "But, then I wanted to be more original."

Nick's eyes narrowed. "Why the new identity? You thought I might come find you?"

"No, so the *world* couldn't find me. It wasn't about you, Nick. You were the only bright spot in a miserable life. I needed to shed my old self. I needed to start fresh, and I did."

"Okay. Okay, I get that you're not as excited about seeing me again as I am about you."

"Stop it, Nick. It's everything I have not to burst out of my skin. But, I don't want to set myself up for disappointment. I want to be happy again."

"You think I wouldn't want that for you… for us? A lot has changed here since you left, too."

She ran her hand down his chest. "You became a cop, I see. Good for you. New Orleans is on the rise since the storm."

"There's still so much that never came back."

"It killed me seeing what was happening here."

"My house was flooded. Lou had flood insurance and rebuilt, but I got my own place now."

"I would hope so." She hiked a thick, dyed eyebrow.

"I kept trying to look you up. Facebook and stuff. See how you were doing. That's why I couldn't find anything. You were in hiding."

"You might leave New Orleans, but New Orleans never leaves you." She stifled a laugh. "I always hated Slidell. I'm back, but as a new person."

Nick finally sat. "You could have been here for years before we ran into each other."

"My mom always said you can't live your life going backwards. What we had was special, but we're two different people now. What if we ruin that memory?"

"What if we make better ones? Would you want to die with the regret of missing out on something special?"

"We should start. Give me your arm." Tanya - or Cali, sat beside Nick and prepared his skin with antiseptic, then opened the donation kit. "I'm glad you feel that way. I was scared you wouldn't." She looked around before planting a soft kiss on his lips. She slapped his cheek lightly for good measure.

"Let's meet out for a drink, *Cali*." He gave a lopsided smile, letting her hand slip out of his. "And catch up on our lives properly over beers."

"I'd like that."

He watched the needle enter his arm with none of the previous apprehension, wincing at the pinch, but not feeling any pain. "You have to promise me one thing, though."

"What is it?" Cali checked that the line had no kinks. The tube quickly filled with blood.

"Lou never found out about us. He's bound to meet you at some point. Whatever happens from here on out, Lou can never learn about our past history."

"Deja vu. Well, my new name works out." She held up her nametag.

"With your new hair color and style, I doubt anyone from here or Slidell would recognize you."

"No one here in New Orleans. Not even Polly." She stood as the bag filled with blood. "Why keep it a secret? We're adults now, what do you care what he thinks?"

"He wouldn't understand. It would wreck our relationship, such as it is."

"So, we're starting fresh? Just casually dating for now?"

"Sure. We'll take it slow."

Cali stood, checked the room, then leaned over and planted another gentle kiss on his lips. "Wasn't ever going to mention Tanya Sanders again, anyway."

Chapter 25

Special Agent Cali Maddox had never been to the New Orleans FBI office. In fact, no one there knew she was living in the city in an undercover operation. It had been just under an hour since arresting Nick. She and Agent Long sat at the empty desk in the open floor plan, two flights above their potential asset. With curious stares, several agents introduced themselves as they walked by the temporary cubicle Agent Long assigned to her. They said nothing of the arrest.

Cali leaned back in the unfamiliar space. A decade-old computer hummed with life under the desk, like a purring cat. Soon, the other agents left them alone while scurrying nearby, taking phone calls or tapping on their computers. The walls were lined with filing cabinets and tasteful works of art, some New Orleans themed.

When they conceived the operation six years ago, Cali had no idea it would go on for so long. She learned about how the FBI set up fake businesses like sporting goods stores that stayed open for years to fool their targets, but assumed Lou Rush would figure out who she was at some point. If anyone looked past the faked surface history of Cali Maddox, they'd find that her relatives were deceased. She doubted Lou had ever seen herself as Tanya, much less would remember her face.

And just like that, the all-consuming operation was over. She likened it to living under the earth's crust like a mole-person, and finally climbing out to the surface. There was bright sun and fresh air to take in.

"What happened to instructing your agents not to use deadly force?" Cali asked.

"Everyone had rubber bullets and tasers… except Winger. Somehow, he didn't get the memo, or ignored the instructions. We're going to question him and Agent Fizz."

"I would have appreciated a heads up in there." Cali moved on. "You pull witness protection off the table and make me look foolish."

Long tilted his head with a sigh. "Sorry, the Director gave me pause for thought. I was actually debating it up to that point."

"Has nothing to do with my caring for him."

"You love him." He didn't appear to enjoy saying that.

"I did at one time. A long time ago. I do care for him, but I don't love him the same way." Cali pointed at the dossier resting near Charles' arm. "Where is Agent Winger, our *Gavin Jones*?"

Long glanced at the folder. "He's derailed to put it mildly. Hence the unnecessary shot at Rush. If it wasn't for the vest… he's being brought to Virginia."

"Why not here?"

"According to the agent in charge, Winger didn't need to fire his weapon. He cracked. The Director doesn't want him anywhere near this case until they interview him."

She gave into a nod. "I suppose we can't be too careful."

"You know, I expected this operation would implode within the first few months. I thought it was improbable that anything would come from you dating your childhood sweetheart."

"You make it sound like a Hallmark card. Lou Rush is our guy, Nick his son and protégé. Stroke of luck that we had a history. It was a perfect *in*." She watched his feet as they nervously tapped.

"May I be blunt?"

"Please."

"I know it's none of my business, and I shouldn't ask. How *did* you feel about… the relations?"

She glanced at him with a quick smile. "He really wanted to hurt me in there."

"I get that. But, the sacrifice."

"Not a hardship." She left it there.

"Well, we can finally see the light at the end of the tunnel. I was hoping when this was all over, you might want to stay here at the field office. Nothing like an agent that's a local."

"I never really gave much thought to my assignment after this."

"Maybe we can have a nice celebratory dinner and talk about your future. Your career. The whole team, of course."

*The whole team*? Cali's response didn't come out immediately, but she hoped it sounded convincing. "I'd like that."

Long smirked, breaking into a short laugh. "I thought of you as a Cold War Russian spy. An embedded asset living a normal life, to be activated at any moment. Like Agent Winger."

"Now, it's coming to a head." Cali's personal cell phone chimed. She looked at the screen and huffed with a laugh. "It seems Nick sent me a text. I'll bet his GPS puts him at home."

Long whistled. "They are good, I'll give them that."

"Alibi established." Cali texted a kiss emoji for the person actually texting. She put the phone down. She understood that this was a make or break scenario - feast or famine. If they came away with nothing, it could mean the end of her career or being exiled to a remote location like North Dakota. "Can I ask you something?" Cali faced Long.

"Of course."

"What if we're successful?"

"I don't understand the question." His eyes narrowed.

She slumped in the chair. "Things were bad before Katrina, but in the aftermath, the Tribunal kept things from going to shit."

"You can't know that. The city could have recovered on its own."

"What if we break up this ring of vigilante cops? And things slide back to the way they used to be? What if tourists can't walk the Quarter again without the fear of getting mugged or killed? Are we to think that the blood of the next murder in the Quarter isn't on our hands?"

"No. Certainly not. You break the law, you are a criminal. We will always be in the right and the criminal will always be to blame."

"I don't agree with that. If a judge lets a known murderer free on a technicality, and he murders again... then, the system is to blame as much as the killer. When we choose to follow the law instead of what is right, *we* – Charles – *we* are to blame."

"I see what you're saying, but you're talking about a human being with choices. You're taking the blame away from the person with the choice to kill or not to kill. Your argument holds water if a Pit Bull kills a dog and the owner lets the Pit off his leash a second time and it kills another animal." He pointed at his head. "A Pit can't think about the choice."

"I get that."

"You're conflicted."

"And you're not? Twenty years ago, New Orleans was the murder capital of the world. Ever since these known offenders started getting mysteriously murdered, the city turned around. It's a virtual Utopia compared to how it used to be."

"Is it Nick? Is he getting to you?"

"No, of course not, but have we really considered public opinion in all this? The backlash of dismantling a group considered to be heroes?"

He leaned forward, elbows on his knees, looking quickly at his watch. "I ever tell you about my interview with the mother of Tyrone Macrone, the gang leader that was found in the Mississippi?"

"Happened three months before Katrina. I remember hearing about that."

Long steepled his fingers. "Macrone was estimated to be victim number one hundred forty-three by our count. I was younger, frustrated, to say the least. The family was poor, living in Bywater. The house was falling apart, but she invited me inside. The furniture was old, damaged, cushions had duct tape, the whole sha-bang." His face darkened. "She proceeds to tell me how wonderful her Tyrone was as a child and how he fell in with the wrong people and how he began his life of crime."

"Typical story."

"Typical story," he repeated. "She told me how he had robbed a friend of hers. She told me how he sold drugs to kids. How he robbed tourists on the outskirts of the Quarter. She said he killed rival gang members. He told me how her own son had beat her."

"Let me guess, she wasn't a cooperative witness."

"A hostile one. She wouldn't have told me who killed her son if she knew his name. She told me she felt safe going to the corner store, something she's never experienced her entire life. She said her son was a lost cause, and New Orleans was a better place without him."

"Sounds like an argument for vigilantism." Cali tossed a balled-up piece of paper back forth in her hands.

"She was lying." He paused for effect. "She was too scared to say anything different. What she wanted to say was the cops executed her son without a trial. Without giving him a chance to rehabilitate in prison. Those words of NOPD support must have been torturous coming from her mouth. Like poison." Long seemed sympathetic. "She loved her son and couldn't even express it for fear of retaliation."

"You know this how?"

"My training. I excel in reading people. Body language. Her inflections. I even saw it in her eyes. Just like I know you're unsure about my intentions with the dinner invitation."

"No. It's just... I just didn't expect it. I'm back in the real world and I feel a bit unbalanced. Tunnel vision. I want this to be over."

"The ledger is our Grail. We found nothing after a complete search of Shelly's before his agoraphobia took hold, upstairs and down. Even in that Camaro. I pretty much suspended the investigation at that point to fall back and regroup. Come up with a better plan."

"This plan."

"We have to remember the collateral damage around the country. Are you forgetting the major cities that tried to emulate their model? No one has been able to recreate the secrecy. A lot of good cops in those cities had their careers ruined, their lives lost to prison. These New Orleans cops are criminals, but smart ones. The law is being broken. The results of those broken laws are inconsequential. You can't have second thoughts."

Cali gave in to a long blink. "Never. But, I wouldn't be a good agent if I didn't consider every ramification, right?" She finished her water. "There's the law, and then there's justice."

"Was your father's murder justice?"

Cali dipped her head. "No. Of course not. Ironic that the first Tribunal murder was of an innocent man. And I go and find the proof of that *after* he had been murdered."

"We can't be sure he wasn't the only innocent one, either."

"I think Nick believes honestly that my father didn't kill his mother. He wouldn't have been with me, otherwise."

Long folded his arms, glancing at his watch. "His pal Marcus Hoover is going to start getting antsy."

"Let's go see if he decided." Cali threw a ball of paper into the wastebasket.

## Chapter 26

Nick's eyes were closed in concentration. Other agents had to be curious as to why an NOPD cop was being questioned. Was there still a smokescreen, or did the entire building know? How many other agents must there be watching this scene go down? If they've kept this under wraps for six years, it was very likely no one else knew the real reason yet; not with the chance of them having to continue the charade.

He likened this to a volcano eruption or a total eclipse. After six years in the making, you can't help but bear witness. The entire Bureau and law enforcement world would blow up once this came to light. That was why he had to disappear once this ended. Now, without Cali. He never thought he could see himself living anywhere other than NOLA. In any other city, he might shrivel up and die.

The door of the interview room finally opened, jolting him from his trance. Nick watched with more composure as Cali entered with Agent Long. Was that man a replacement for Harry, her father? A plug-in parent? No, he didn't get that sense. Could there be more between them? *They weren't screwing,* he thought with confidence. When Nick had mentioned their sex life, Long's expression revealed a hidden jealousy. He could imagine Agent Long taking her under his wing, while harboring a deep-seeded lust for his protégée. Cali would never let herself be seduced. She probably *did* use the old man's desire for her own benefit in green-lighting this operation.

"The clock's ticking," Cali said to Nick, almost blocking his view of Long.

Nick took a deep breath. That woman had to be the best actress in the world, because either she faked loving him this entire time, or she really did in an abnormal kind of way. *No, stop it.*

"Nick?" Cali asked.

"Who else knows about what went down today?" Nick addressed Long.

Long stepped to the side holding a paper in his hand, staying behind Cali. "Just the agents that arrested you. And they are sworn to secrecy."

"Did they twist the lock on their lips and throw away the key, too?"

"They did," Long quipped.

Nick asked. "So, there's no rogue agent here in this building that's going to call the Picayune and sell a story? Harry Sander's daughter becomes FBI to solve her father's murder?"

Cali jumped in. "No one knows, and those who do are on board. You're safe to return." She pulled down on her hospital top as if they just had a quickie.

Her scrubs looked like a costume, now. The clothes didn't fit her new personality. It was as if she was the cause of the chilly temperature in the room. He sensed a wall had been erected around her, a force-field of sorts. She had lived through the ultimate undercover operation. Any hint of impropriety and Lou would have taken her out. She would have been a hell of a cop.

"I imagine you have eyes on Shelly's," Nick stated.

Cali properly sat with an arched back. The harsh light brought out the imperfections in her skin, but her green eyes still commanded attention. "Your father is still at Shelly's. Marcus has returned in an unmarked cop car to Gavin's neighborhood. It can still work. Tell me you've made the right decision."

Nick forced his neck to crack. His shoulders ached. He had to piss, but wouldn't give them the satisfaction. "If I agree, what happens now?"

She gave a single nod at the burner phone Long placed on the table. "We drop you off near Jones' house. You call Marcus. Tell him the deal is done. Go to Shelly's. Get the ledger."

He mocked, "Yeah, I'll just ask for it. The book that would take down the whole Tribunal." Nick couldn't get his arms in a relaxed position. "It's my only shot, right? Because nobody talks. There's nothing digital. Eradications are set with initials and numbers on a piece of paper and passed on to be shredded. If anything is said, precautions are taken. How many agents posing as cops have rotated in and out of the ranks without a clue? Cali couldn't even get anything from me and God knows she tried."

"Ease into it." Long nodded, fiddling with the paper he held. "He's eluded us for over a decade. Last thing we want is for him to suspect something on this first meeting. We'll let you settle back into your life." Long looked between them.

"Our life, you mean," Nick blurted with a sour face.

"Yes, we'll have to carry on as if nothing's happened," she said, meekly.

"I don't know if I can do that given how much I hate you right now."

Cali's expression never softened. "With what you've been doing for the past ten years? I know you can."

"From here on out, I only care about myself. And Marcus gets full immunity as well for anything I say or have done? In writing?"

Long slapped the paper down on the table with a pen. "We kept it short. No fancy wording. Already signed by the judge."

He inhaled deeply, scanning the document, notarized with a federal seal. "And I'll be allowed to live anywhere? I can't stay here after this. No probation or any shit like that?"

"It's there in the terms. We'll fly you anywhere in the country. You won't be allowed to leave the US airspace for ten years past the first day of the first trial." Long nodded. "But, you'll need to be available for testimony in subsequent trials. No Skype or video. You come back here under federal protection."

He gave in to a long pause. "Even if I don't flip, Lou would find a way to have me killed in prison, possibly before my own trial." His eyes darted between them, thinking about Chad Cooper's eradication. "What the hell? I have no other family. No one to fight for." He settled a hard stare on Cali.

"Then, you'll do it?" Cali asked.

Nick searched the pocked ceiling tiles as if the tears collecting in his eyes would evaporate. Going back into that world wasn't a good idea. He finally blinked, letting a single tear fall. His body bucked and kicked out in a frustrated decision. His head shook up and down in agreement. Cali turned to the video camera in the corner, giving the signal that it was a go.

He stared at the document. "I can't call him from here. I need to do it at the house and then get picked up right away. Give me my vest back, and I'll need a straight blade, too."

"What for?"

"It's my reason for setting the fire. And where's the bathroom?" He really needed to vomit.

Chapter 27

The sun's descent beat on the west side of the FBI
building. Nick remained in a daze, climbing into the
passenger seat of a maroon Impala with Agent Long as the
driver. The fed didn't expand on Cali's involvement, nor
tried to explain her deception. He was in charge and didn't
have to fill the silence.

Nick almost expected an ambush from the Tribunal,
possibly a single gunshot from somewhere in the distance.
Or maybe Long would whack him right there to keep the
Tribunal afloat, if that was his agenda. The way he hi-
jacked the witness protection decision led Nick to believe
Long could be holding out even more information from
Cali.

Despite Cali's personal intentions of revenge toward
Lou, Nick had put himself in this quagmire. He didn't have
to become a cop. Avoiding that profession would have
solved *everything*. All his young life, he wanted to distance
himself from Lou, yet there he was, still under his vulture
wing. He had been born on the perimeter of a black hole,
and was sucked in when his mother died. Lou made him
believe there were no other stars or planets to reach for.

Just before arriving at their destination, Long spoke, "Bringing Cali on board was the best and worst decision of my career."

Nick turned to him, but didn't ask why. He knew an explanation was coming.

"The *best* because without her, we wouldn't be here now, so close to putting an end to this."

"And the worst?"

His jaw clenched. "The worst because she loved you going in, and she still loves you now... and I ignored it."

"Love and trust... two different things. Seems we both can't trust her true intentions."

"I don't like you." He waited a few seconds. "But, she's special. You know it."

"Who's really biased here?"

"This operation and her love for you is like one octopus fighting with another, their tentacles all knotted up, not knowing where one tentacle begins or ends. You're pissed now, but this is a way out for both of you. Don't fuck it up."

"Great advice. Thanks." Nick nodded.

"Just get that fucking ledger, and one of those octopi goes away."

The timing worked out as smoke rose in the distance. Long dropped off Nick two blocks away from Jones' house. With the straight blade, Nick sliced a tiny cut onto the top of his hand. Blood dripped on the ground like candle wax. He called the number and a minute later, the same unmarked car pulled to the curb with Marcus at the wheel.

Nick climbed in with his hand pressed against his sweatshirt just as he heard an approaching fire engine. "Done."

"Took long enough. You get him to give up his girlfriend's location?"

"No. Don't expect me to talk about it."

"What's that? Blood?" Marcus knew not to say anything incriminating as he inspected Nick up and down, focusing on his blotchy, crimson sweatshirt.

"Drive."

He then stared toward Jones' house. "Is that a fire?"

"Had to." Nick looked out the passenger window. "My blood was in the house."

"So, you did that?"

"Would you prefer I hire a maid service? What if forensics got a hold of it? Let's just go."

Marcus' face grew dark. "What if neighbors…? What if a responder…? You really think that was the best decision?"

"Had to think on my feet."

"You have your burner. You could have called and asked what to do. Anything left behind would get *lost*." Marcus slammed the wheel.

"What if the suits showed up and took over with some kind of jurisdiction bullshit. Would *they* lose my DNA?" This was good practice for facing Lou. "Just bring me to my house, please."

His best friend softened. "Check the glove box. Put something on that."

Nick found a first aid kit. "Thanks."

Once Nick was dropped off on the curb of his house, Marcus left for Shelly's. The routine of evidence disposal had to remain the same. Any change would signal a red flag. So, before going inside, Nick popped his trunk and pulled out a black trash bag. He stood at his side door, under the carport, hidden from curious eyes. He took off the vest and clothes he wore in Jones' house and stuffed them into the trash bag, leaving the evidence just outside the door. Marcus would have another member drive by and collect it for proper disposal.

After a quick shower, he dressed in jeans and a tee-shirt. The left side of his ribs were bruised and tender. The quiet house amplified his doubts, but he also couldn't deny a twinge of relief. He was on the *other side* now. However, he was still with – and without Cali. Before leaving, he ate a handful of pecans to quell his hunger. He headed straight to Shelly's, a four-minute ride.

Nick parked next to Lou's Mustang and sat there a moment. Three other cars were there, any of which could be his hearse. He watched the closed sign on the front door until it vibrated behind his eyes. If Lou knew anything at all, if he suspected betrayal, there would be a bullet waiting for him on the inside. He imagined the scene in *Goodfellas* when Joe Pesci got it in the back of the head, thinking he was being *made*. Nick would be the first murder victim ever at Shelly's. The surface of the concrete-like oyster shell lot pushed back on his heels while approaching the screen door. He took a relaxing breath as he stepped inside, disturbing the darkness.

Mr. Gary was laughing with Tom Chipolee, called *Chipotle* by close friends, another one of Lou's poker players. Lou chatted with a surprisingly relaxed Marcus. The television silently played on the wall behind the bar. Shelly wasn't anywhere in sight, probably doing something upstairs. He tried not to walk into the bar with FBI stink on him.

Lou said, "Marcus, get Nick a beer." Rock music filled the small space, bouncing off the close walls. He leaned into his son. "So, you chickened out? Didn't do it?"

Nick tried to speak a hair louder than usual, not bothering to warn Lou to check for transmitters. "No, I did it. Jones is dead."

Lou froze. His entire body slowly turned to Nick. "He's dead?"

"You act like I wasn't supposed to do it."

"No. No. I just thought you'd abort."

"He's dead. I took care of him. Just now." Nick used his bandaged hand to take the beer from Marcus.

Lou's face registered fear, then went pale. "Good. I knew you had it in you." The nervous man scrambled for his T-9 transmitter detector.

Nick took the device and scanned himself. "It didn't go quite as planned, though."

Lou put the device on the bar, then scratched at his nose. If Nick didn't know better, he'd say that Lou was visibly scared. His father cleared his throat. The words came out like a child. "Tell me what happened. The whole story. Now."

"I thought we don't talk…"

"Now!"

Nick's face twitched. "I got dropped off a block away, disguised myself. Went in through the neighbor's yard. Climbed in through the window and killed him. One shot to the head."

Both of Lou's hands slammed onto the bar causing everyone to flinch. Sweat formed on his brow. "Cut and dry. No complications?"

Nick looked at his self-inflicted wound. "I cut my hand climbing through the window. I got blood in his bedroom." He showed the bandage. "There was a gas can by his mower, so I improvised. Fire."

Lou's jaw clenched, and his temple pulsed. He got off the stool and paced. "You set fire to his house?"

"I don't know where I dripped. I absolutely had to. After that, I needed to get home and clean up."

Lou clenched his teeth. "Did you know about this, Marcus?"

"Not the fire. But, I probably would have done the same thing."

"Bullshit. I asked you to look out for him." Lou deflated. "Tell me again what happened."

## Chapter 28

No one other than Tribunal occupied the bar. Father and son hadn't spoken for a half hour, facing forward, sitting close. The fact that Lou hadn't exploded meant he was beyond angry, and didn't know what to do about it. There wasn't a word that could encapsulate what Lou was feeling. It meant a beating wasn't good enough. But, was a simple fire worth the rage?

Lou finally pointed to Marcus. "Turn the music back down. I got a fucking headache."

A set of headlights barely flashed in the black-painted window. Despite the closed sign, someone was coming inside. The non-conversation would have to continue at another time.

"It's Goodman," Chipotle said from the door. "I'll get rid of her."

"No." Lou exhaled, exasperated. He motioned to let her in. He didn't hesitate or send her away, which confused, if not scared Nick. His father wanted this confrontation.

The door creaked open, and the fellow cop invaded their sanctuary. She looked around skittishly, yet determined. Nick, as well as the others, greeted her with forced cheer. As if anything else could go wrong today.

Needing to protect her from Lou, Nick met her halfway inside.

"Belinda, is everything alright?" He tried to shoo her back to the door.

"No, everything isn't okay, Nick. I need to talk to Lou."

Nick sniffed near her mouth. "I smell whiskey on you."

"I did a shot of courage… or two. Who are you? My mom? Let me see Lou." Her powerful arms almost pushed Nick aside.

"No. You have to avoid Lou right now. He's not in a good mood."

"Is he ever?" Belinda broke from his grasp with a face he'd seen just before one of her MMA fights. She approached Lou who eyed her suspiciously. Her arm rested on the bar, just a foot away from him. "What do I have to do, captain? I'll do anything."

Lou scratched at his nose. "You need to keep your yap shut, that's what you need to do."

She shifted her weight, looking around at the other policeman who kept eyeing her. "You need a replacement for Cooper, right? I want in. How do I get… in?"

Nick had no idea how Lou was keeping it together. He said, "Cooper? Sad what happened. But, I have no idea what you mean."

"I get it, Lou. I get it. You won't be sorry if you let me in."

"You're in." Lou straightened, waving his arms around the bar. His voice was hard, rising ever so slightly. "You're *in* Shelly's. Now, you order a beer and stare at the television, play video poker, or tell sob stories about the tragic end to your cage fighting – or leave."

"Captain…"

"You need to listen to your partner Nicky here. If you're not going to order a beer, you need to get out of this bar."

"I'll kill anyone you want. Didn't I just prove that? I practically helped Nick track Gavin Jones the other day."

"Okay, no more warnings." Lou snapped his fingers.

Nick tried to pull her away from Lou, but Mr. Gary already had her wrapped up with a hand over her mouth. She struggled and tried to scream, but only made muffled noises. It required some effort for Mr. Gary to drag her to the other side of the room.

"Lou, she doesn't know what she'd doing. She's drunk and confused. Let her go. I'll talk to her."

He poked his finger in a scolding manner. "She's a time bomb. Never thought I'd get this much dissention in my own ranks. Cooper... her."

"You can't mean... you'd never be that reckless."

"*Reckless* coming from the fire-starter? You no longer have any say in anything."

"Lou, you can't."

He took pleasure in his protests. "She is no longer your concern. What if the feds approach her about watching Jones? She's a problem. A big fucking one."

While Belinda struggled, Lou gave Marcus a nod, like they had discussed this option already. Marcus blinked away brief shock. He left the bar with worry written on his face. Lou had planned on this contingency. Did Marcus have to pull the trigger for real?

Lou summoned Belinda with a flip of his fingers, but she had to be carried to Lou's side, still wrapped in Mr. Gary's arms. *Rebel Yell* by Billy Idol pounded out the speakers, matching the hardcore scene transpiring before their eyes. Nick was close enough to make out Lou's words hissing into Belinda's ear. "This place could be bugged. The wrong word out of you and we all go down. If we let you go, will you say anything else?"

Belinda shook her head, tears collecting.

"Will you sit at this bar, drink with us like normal people?"

Belinda nodded with glassy eyes.

Lou lowered his hand at Mr. Gary and he slowly released Belinda, freeing her mouth. She wiped her eyes with a napkin that Lou graciously offered. Mr. Gary cleaned his hand of Belinda's saliva and lip gloss on his pants. Shelly brought everyone a fresh beer and shot of Tequila, on the house.

"Don't you have somewhere to be, Nick?" Lou asked. "You had a long day."

Nick looked at Belinda. "I can stay."

"No, you better get back to that little lady of yours." Lou tapped Belinda's bottle with his. She smiled in relief. "Spend some quality time with Cali, because who knows how much time we all have left on this earth."

Nick swallowed as much beer as he could while staring at Lou. He gave Belinda a prolonged embrace. "See you later."

"Bye, Nick." Her voice was the softest he'd ever heard.

Nick charged from the bar, getting hit by a blanket of humidity. Evening had settled in and the crickets made it known in song. He stepped in small circles outside of the front door, trying to decide if he should go back inside. The feds wouldn't have picked up conversation from inside, not that any confessions were made. He pulled out his cell to call Marcus, but that would be a mistake. *Should he contact the feds*? No, that could expose the entire plan if they attempted to save Belinda. He could do this on his own.

Without being followed, he drove his car a short distance into the neighborhood and parked. The Tribunal had eradicated one of its own, and now Lou ordered a hit on an over-zealous cop. This couldn't keep happening.

He walked back toward Hayne Boulevard under the emerging stars. For the best vantage point to watch Shelly's front door, his feet carried him across the four lanes of spotty traffic to the levee where he climbed to the top, stopping to rest against the fence. The ripples of the lake's surface glimmered.

Once settled at the peak, he stretched his arms out to cling onto the chain link, letting his body sag reminiscent of Jesus on the cross. The lake breeze cooled his heated skin. He silently asked his mom for strength, if not spiritual guidance. Saving Belinda could jeopardize his own freedom.

Chapter 29

Nick reflected on his choices while on top of the levee with his back to the lake, watching Shelly's front door. Finding the ledger seemed impossible at this point. If the supposed Holy Grail was anywhere, it was in that establishment. Maybe upstairs? In the wall? None of the second-floor windows were lit up, so Shelly probably had returned downstairs to the bar. Every so often, he gazed at the clear sky, the moon and stars in full view.

That test for Marcus to pull the trigger on him was a precursor to taking out Belinda. Lou probably had it planned for weeks. Marcus should have challenged Lou's decision. *Yeah, right. What was he thinking?* No one could ever challenge Lou's decisions.

Nick's arrest and interrogation seemed surreal, like he imagined it. He looked at his cell, seeing Cali's response to Marcus' earlier text. Did Long just expect him to forgive Cali as if nothing happened? The old man was in love with her, that was obvious. Nick's heart broke all over again. *No, don't dwell or lament on her now.* While continuing to glance at Shelly's door, Nick shot another text that he would be a little late getting home and to eat without him, but then deleted it, realizing appearances didn't matter anymore. He eventually sat in the grass to give his legs a rest. Weariness caught up with him, and he had to fight not to close his eyes.

A little over an hour passed before Belinda stumbled out, searching the six-car lot for her vehicle. He didn't expect anyone to follow her from inside. Lou would never have anyone killed on that sacred ground. No, Marcus had been given his silent orders.

Nick started his descent down the levee while Belinda dug into her purse on side of the fender. With quick stepping feet, he carefully let gravity carry him to level ground. Belinda had only managed to open the driver's side door by the time Nick crossed the four barren lanes.

"Why don't you let me drive?" Nick asked, taking the key fob out of her hand. A sheen of sweat took hold on his brow.

"Partner!" Belinda exclaimed. She threw her arms around his neck and cackled. "You should have seen me in there. I think Lou's going to ask me. I think he trusts me."

"Shh. Quiet." Nick put a finger on her lips. She tried to lick at it.

He gently unwrapped her arms with a smile. She slurred, "But, I think they wanted a boy's night. Lou kicked me out. Enjoy your sausage fest." She stuck her tongue out at the door. "Let's go back to my place for a nightie-night cap."

"Okay." He took her purse and tossed it in the passenger seat. "Let's get you in the back seat."

"Back seat? Okay, I won't tell anyone. One last romp before marriage."

He opened the rear door. "Why don't we go back to your place, okay? Just lay down and we'll be there in no time."

She reached for the seat with her hands to crawl inside, not bothering to sit up. "Okay. I'll just relax back here for a little while."

"Okay." He closed the door, checking the bar's opaque window. Shelly didn't want anyone to be able to look inside, so the reverse was true, also.

Nick sat in the driver's seat, adjusting its position along with the mirrors. He took the gun from his ankle holster. He put it between his legs, upside down and pointed forward. Looking behind him, he backed out of the lot and drove past his car, taking a longer route Marcus wouldn't expect.

Belinda lived two miles away, in a house she bought after winning her first MMA fight. She secretly bet on herself to win and used the profits for a sizable down payment on a cheap, newly built house. Nick kept an eye out for an ambush, but Marcus wouldn't make a stupid mistake.

Belinda sang an unintelligible song from the back seat, however the song lyrics died out, and she started talking. In the rearview mirror, he saw her sitting up with her eyes closed. "I was going places, Nick," she moaned.

"Where?"

"I was a great MMA fighter. I used to train six hours a day. Muy Thai. Jiu Jitsu. Wrestling. I could kick any bitch's ass. Some dude's asses."

"I know. I saw you on Youtube."

She pouted. "Concussions. Quacks said if I kept on fighting, another big concussion could fuck me up for life. And just like that. Poof." She started crying.

"At least you had the shot, right? No regrets."

"No regrets," she said, and went quiet. "Why does it still hurt so much?"

"I don't know. Belinda, why do you want to be in the Tribunal so badly?"

"Can you keep a secret?"

"Of course."

"I don't know how I passed that psych exam. I'm fucked up." She laughed. "I liked to hurt other kids when I was a kid. My parents thought I was just evil. A judge let me see a therapist instead of going to juvie. Eventually, they got me into sports. I was a dirty player in whatever sport I played. I don't know why. I enjoy other people's pain. My own pain. It's like I'm broken, and don't care to fix it. If I wasn't a cop, I'd be in prison."

"That was a good choice," Nick capped off her monologue.

She yelped, turning it into a laugh. "Yes, it was!"

He pulled into her driveway and turned off the engine. It was dark, but not very late. No one roamed the street; a few of the houses had their lights on. He hadn't spotted Marcus' car, but the guy knew how to hide. Maybe they should just go to a hotel for the night.

Nick released his seat belt, then placed the fob in her purse while rooting around for her house keys. The designer bag contained a small revolver. A tap on the glass made his neck hairs stand on end. He turned to see a torso and a gun with a silencer pointed at him.

The window rolled down. "Was I speeding, officer?"

His muscular friend bent at the waist. The gun dropped. "You shouldn't be here."

"This is wrong, Marcus." Nick stared forward. "She's one of us. Cooper was one us."

"I wasn't going to kill her, Nick." But, Marcus still had the firearm ready.

"Could have fooled me."

"Get out the car." He backed away, stuck his gun in his waistband, and then pulled out a cell phone to obviously call Lou.

Nick slid from the car seat, pointing the barrel of his gun toward Marcus. His best friend lightly tossed the phone into the grass, but didn't bother to hand over his own firearm. "Really, Nick?" There was no panic or fear.

Nick dropped the gun to his side, then picked up Marcus' cell and gave it back to him. "What do we do?"

Marcus put the phone in his back pocket. "Lou wanted me to give her a DWI. He wanted to disgrace her and get her kicked off the force."

"Is that true?"

He shook his head. "That's not true, dude. I can't lie to you."

"Could you really kill her?"

"Yes. No. I have to. Probably not. I don't know." Marcus scratched his scalp. "Lou will flip out. There won't be any fake trial."

"Then, I'm taking the heat away from you." Nick put his personal sidearm in his waistband and casually pointed at Marcus' gun with the silencer, almost like an afterthought. "Gavin Jones shot me."

"What the fuck?"

Nick stood chest to chest with Marcus. "He had a gun and was ready for me." Nick left out the part about the FBI for now."

"Maybe Jones suspected an intruder."

"No. He came home, put up his groceries, then sat at his table and waited for me to make my move. He didn't call the cops or try to leave. Luckily, I got a shot off and killed him. Then set the fire."

"Yeah, but these criminals know we come after them, and they're ready for us. It's a lot more dangerous."

"I think Lou had something to do with it." He hoped Marcus couldn't see through the lie.

Confusion washed over Marcus' face. "Lou had something to do with Jones shooting you? Like he arranged it?"

"Gavin Jones was ready for me. He expected me." That was partially true.

"Christ, Nick." Marcus frowned. "If that's true… maybe it's time to disturb those wasps?"

Nick almost smiled. "It's time."

The back door of the car opened, and Belinda's head and shoulders fell out as she puked onto the driveway. Marcus said, "So, what do we do with her?"

"I'll handle that. But, in the meantime, we have to figure out what to do with you."

He shrugged. "I'll tell Lou neighbors were out. That I couldn't."

"I have a better plan." Nick put his hand on Marcus' shoulder, turning to see Belinda on all fours over a puddle of vomit, staring at them. She dry heaved as if her lungs were trying to escape her body.

Nick asked Marcus, "How's your right cross?"

Chapter 30


Nick entered his home just past midnight. The lights were on and Cali was sitting in the recliner, but her eyes were closed. The alien scene of her standing in the FBI interrogation room in her scrubs flashed. The most unnerving day of his life was finally over. His muscles relaxed involuntarily, contradicting his brain. As complicated as their relationship had always been, she was like a calming drug. Was she right about each of them betraying the other? They each had a secret life, and he would want to be forgiven, all things being equal.

He bypassed waking her and stood inside the bathroom door on a small rug to ease out of his shoes. After pulling off his socks, the rest of his attire followed, falling gently at his feet. He started the shower and waited for the hot water. His ribs were tender, lip was split, eye bruised, and his face scuffed. His body and mind were exhausted and defeated.

His fading adrenaline added extra weight onto his frame. He slapped the unmarked part of his face, feeling the sting from the cuts he suffered by the hands of Marcus. The Tribunal needed to be taken down and now Marcus was on board. Could they take down that powerhouse? What were the odds he and Marcus would escape alive, if not unscathed? He whisked away those thoughts, putting them aside to be dealt with later.

Satisfied with the water's heat, he positioned his back to the nozzle, closing his eyes and breathing heavily. The shower door opened, startling him.

Cali appeared, nude as well. "What happened to your face? Lou?"

Their naked bodies were inches apart. For the first time, he could see that she had aged. Bags had developed under her eyes. Worry lines popped from her delicate skin. "What are you doing in here?"

"I wouldn't put it past Lou to have the place bugged. You know this is the only place we can talk," she whispered as the water splashed against his back.

"I sweep the place regularly when you're not here." She didn't leave. "I don't have the ledger. So, what do you want me to tell you?" Nick reached past her to secure the shampoo. He squeezed a dollop in his hand. "I'm trying to stay calm. Get out, please."

She stayed planted. "I fought for WITSEC for just your testimony. I had no idea he'd change his mind."

Nick scrubbed the suds in his hair, eyes closed. "Yeah... appreciate the effort."

He wanted her to leave, but he hadn't the energy to get worked up over it. When the shampoo had rinsed from his hair, he opened his eyes to see her staring. Her expression was so earnest. He said, "It's all out in the open now. Neither of us have to pretend."

"I'm not pretending. If I didn't love you, I'd tell you point blank."

"Then, that makes it so much worse. You'll sacrifice everything we had to take Lou down."

"Seems we both want the same thing." She placed a bar of soap in one of his hands. "You're going to have a nice shiner. Marcus did this?"

"Lou put a hit on Belinda. Which I stopped."

"Shit." She gave it a quick consideration. "We kept a van parked near Shelly's with a bionic ear. The music was too loud and you spoke too low – too much interference. We didn't pick up anything at the bar except some scuffle with Belinda and we know you left early. And you weren't followed, don't worry."

"Yeah, Lou kicked me out." Nick kept his eyes on hers as he spun the soap.

She looked away first. "I want you to understand, when I took the assignment, I only had one mission – to bring Lou to justice for my father's death. Once you and me got going again, it just got too big. I got in too deep. I do love you. I do. You must feel that."

"I just don't know."

"Why would I try to convince you of that when I don't have to? I don't have to pretend jack shit." She touched his cheek. "I love you. What you asked me before… about Europe. Hell, if you wanted to run to Mexico tonight, I'd do it with you. I would."

Nick let that sink in. "Right now, these are all words."

"I don't want to be as petty as to say you kept a pretty big secret from me, too." She paused. "But, I will. A secret that you would want me to forgive if I was a normal nurse." She stood on her tip-toes to kiss his lips, but he didn't kiss her back.

"I'm upside-down right now. I need time." He stared past her vulnerability. "Why do you think Jones took a shot at me?"

She wiped the water from her eyes. "He was frayed. Long said so. Too much time playing that part. He had to constantly look over his shoulder for a kill shot. I can't imagine what that would do to a person."

"Could Jones have known anything about your part in this?"

"Long said he had no idea I'm embedded. But, they took him to Quantico for debriefing. He probably has no contact with the outside world."

"I hope you're right." Nick noticed the engagement ring was still on her finger.

"You need to find that ledger. You get your immunity and I'll quit the FBI."

"Stop it, Cali. Everything isn't fine. Not yet."

"With all the obstacles we've overcome, I can hope."

"I'm getting immunity for what I've done, but what about the things that happen *during* our deal?"

She squinted through the steam. "What did you do?"

"Nothing. You need deniability." He reached to turn the water off, but left his hand on the handle so they could continue to talk. "Marcus is going to turn up missing. He's working on something."

"*Something.*"

"That's all I'm going to say."

"So, he's going to become a missing person. The press is going to get squirrely about a second missing policeman."

"Better than a dead one." Nick tried not to look down at her body.

"Belinda must be scared."

"She's oblivious that anything happened. Lou got her drunk. I sobered her up with coffee and left her with a warning that she pissed Lou off. She can't be out there blind. Maybe she can leave town for a while, too."

Cali asked, "Will he go after her again?"

"Not right away. I messed up this perfect opportunity. And he's going to question me about why Belinda is still alive."

"And he'll think Marcus couldn't do it, and ran."

"Partly. I know how Lou's mind works. I can't tell him Marcus beat me up, but I want him to think it."

"Okay?" She was unsure.

"I'll blame his boys for this. But, he'll suspect me of lying. He'll come up with Marcus on his own and deduce that he ran and I'm covering for him."

"Why?"

"I'm not sure, yet. Some things have to come together."

"What does this mean for your safety?"

"I want him to get careless." He turned off the water. "Like I said, don't worry about bugs. I scanned."

Nick and Cali toweled off separately and dressed silently. They found themselves facing each other in the center of the room. He said, "Take the bed. I'll take the couch."

Cali sat on the edge of the mattress. "There's more. I need to tell you something."

Chapter 31

Nick was too exhausted to stand upright while Cali unloaded her story. He sat on the bed also, but a few feet away.

She started, staring into her lap. "My joining the Bureau wasn't a jump as much a gradual choice," Cali said.

"I don't care about…"

"You need to hear this."

"Okay." He exhaled, waiting.

"I found proof my father was innocent of killing your mom."

"You're kidding."

She barely smiled. "In the move to Alabama, I found letters my father hid. They were love letters from your mother to my father."

Nick's mouth opened, but nothing came out. His eyes narrowed instead.

"The letters were in an old children's lunchbox that my mom was going to throw away. I didn't tell her what I found. I didn't want to destroy her illusion of a faithful husband."

Nick shut his bloodshot eyes. "My mom and your dad exchanged love letters? You've known this all this time?"

"If I let you know, and it got back to Long... or worse yet, if you went after Lou because..."

"Because if your dad loved her, then Lou would be the primary suspect in my mom's murder. You think Lou killed my mother."

"I think on some level, you've suspected that, too. Is it that hard to believe?" She glanced up at him. "You had a mental block, put there by your father."

"Lou killed her." It came out as a revelation. He wiped at his eyes, fighting back the anger. "How did I not... stupid, I'm so stupid!"

"Shh, no. Don't do that. We have a plan, now. We're going to get him. Don't let this change anything."

"I hate him." Nick calmed himself. "So, they were in love. Makes sense, I guess. How happy my mom was after the first plumbing call."

"Her letters were amazing. They really loved each other." She placed her hand on his thigh. He let it sit for a moment, then gently brushed it off.

"Where are the letters?"

"In the case files. I'll get you copies."

They sat silent for a while.

"Are you alright?" Cali finally asked.

"Yeah. I'll be okay." Nick asked, "So, those letters made you want to be an agent?"

She wiped a tear. "So, I had this proof. Every time I visited mom from college, I passed by the FBI building in Montgomery. With my nursing degree in sight, I felt as if I was being pulled in another direction. So, one day, I went to the building with the letters, still not sure what I was doing. I took the lunchbox and entered the place scared shitless."

"Why?"

"Don't know, really. I think I knew my life was about to change. Stepping into that building was monumental. But, no alarms sounded, or armed agents descended from the ceiling. I ended up at the reception desk where a young man set me up to speak with a desk agent. This nice middle-aged lady. I told her I found evidence that could help a cold case in New Orleans. She asked why I didn't go to the NOPD first. I told her because I thought the police were involved."

"How'd she react to that?"

"Well, I showed her the letters, telling her how a cop's wife and my father were having an affair. She told me the letters didn't prove that my father didn't kill your mother. It just proved they were in love."

"I can see that conclusion. As a cop."

. "So, I told her my father was the first Tribunal murder, and the man that killed him was a police officer named Lou Rush. Her eyes lit up. That's when she put me in touch with Charles Long. He talked to me over the phone, and then flew out to interview me. By the end of the interview, I wanted to join."

"And that was that. He pulled strings and got you fast-tracked."

"Like a bullet-train. I had tunnel vision about Lou. You were on my mind, but not a consideration at that point."

Nick nodded. "I have a confession to make... as long as everything is out on the table."

"Please, tell me."

"I saw Lou kill your father."

Her expression didn't show shock or outrage. "I suspected."

His eyes widened. "And you didn't say anything?"

"And start a fight that we couldn't get past?"

"Yeah, you're right. It was the very start of my grooming." He wiped the memory away. "To think, my mom and your dad could still be together today if it weren't for him."

She let out a heavy breath, before scooting closer to him. She took his hand. "Searching out those Spiderman sweatpants wasn't part of my agenda. All those little moments where we shared a laugh. It was all real. I'll keep saying it until you believe me. I love you."

Chapter 32

During the early morning hours, Nick had stared at the ceiling while lying on the sofa. Sometime near four in the morning, he drifted off, but it wasn't a good sleep. A nagging pulled at his dreams, making them disjointed and shallow. He woke up just before ten that morning, still exhausted. The lack of sun coming through the window allowed the extra rest. It was storming outside, and a racket from the kitchen told him Cali was up and about.

Belinda instantly came to mind. He instinctively looked at the lamp beside the couch, which was still minus one listening device. When Nick had first bought the house, Lou and Mr. Gary performed a complete sweep of each room and deemed it clean. Lou promised he would sweep the house once a month – standard procedure for Tribunal members.

Without informing Lou, Nick performed his own sweep, finding a bug in each room of his house. Nick confronted Lou and destroyed the bugs. Lou played it off as caution, but eventually let it go. He thought about placing his own cameras, just to catch when Lou was inside his house, but those spy cameras were easily detected, and that back and forth was tiresome.

Cali entered the living room with a forlorn look on her face. "Bad news," she said.

"What?" Nick sat up.

"Gavin Jones – Winger – escaped from FBI custody this morning."

"Escaped? Was he under arrest?"

"He was being questioned because he shouldn't have had live ammo. From the brief message I got, there was a miscommunication. Winger wasn't put on full lockdown. He must've sensed what was happening and slipped away. He cracked, like we said. There's a manhunt."

Nick scratched at his head. "He's like a master of disguises. They need to find him."

"Long thinks he's heading to Canada. They'll get him." Cali looked down, then returned to the kitchen.

Nick got up and took his cell from the charger. He dialed Belinda's number.

"Hello?" Belinda answered in a breath.

*Still alive,* great. Nick didn't know if Lou had Belinda's place bugged, but considering her campaign to join the Tribunal over the years, she could have very well been an FBI asset. "How you feeling?"

"I feel like shit. After you left the bar, Lou kept setting up Tequila shots. You know how low my tolerance is. I lost count at six."

"Just wanted to make sure you were okay." He tried to fix his matted hair.

"Don't remember much after leaving, tell you the truth. How the hell I made it home is a mystery."

"You could have hurt someone, Belinda. You could have killed someone."

"I know. I never drink to that extent. You told me I have a hard head. I'm going to be avoiding alcohol for a long time."

"And you don't remember anything else?"

"Nope. Nothing. That's not unusual. I tend to black out."

Cali stood at the threshold between the kitchen and living room, watching him. He continued, "You ever remember things later. Days or weeks later?"

"No," she said with conviction, "Sometimes I get deja vu, but nothing solid. Why? Did I do something crazy?"

"Not that I know of." He paused. "You remember how you were told to be quiet at the bar when you first got there?"

"Yeah. One of the scariest *oh-shit* moments of my life."

Nick propped himself up on the sofa cushion. "Belinda, I'm scared for you. Drop it." If ever Lou was listening in, that'd be good for him to hear.

"I get that now. I have this aggressive nature and when I want what I want, things can get intense."

"That cannot happen again."

"Understood. From now on, my head will stay down. Lou won't have to worry about me anymore."

"Good. Okay, I gotta go."

Nick pulled the phone away from his ear and dialed a second number. Cali kept her position near the kitchen. It rang four times. He peered out of window to see a downpour.

"Yeah," Lou answered.

"Why'd you sic your goons on me?" he asked with urgency. "For going against your wishes?"

That threw him. "What the hell you talking about?"

"Don't pretend. My face looks like a car accident. You scare the shit out of me with Belinda, and decide to order a good old-fashioned beating instead?"

"What are you talking about? You get beat up?"

"I figured you'd deny it." He thought back to Marcus' fist contacting his face. "I conveniently get beat up Tribunal-style by three guys outside my house. Didn't rob me. Didn't say a word. Just kicked my ass. And Belinda is fine. Okay."

"I'll talk with the boys. I didn't order that."

"Mr. Gary has always had it out for me. Whatever. Look, I called to check up on her this morning not expecting to get an answer, but she's fine."

"Why wouldn't she be?"

"That was just a scare tactic for my benefit?" Nick bit at his nails in concentration.

"Listen to yourself. Maybe you should be checking in on Marcus. He's not answering."

"He's not? Did your *boys* pay him a visit, too?"

A heavy breath came over the speaker. "You're trying my patience."

"I'll try him myself. You're going to let Belinda slide, right? We can't have two cops… you know what I'm saying."

His voice tightened. "You don't decide what's good."

"Beat the shit of me all you want. You go after her, and I'm out. How's that?"

"Shut your trap." The phone call dropped.

Cali didn't say anything, retreating back into the kitchen. It was all such a chess match. Lou didn't accuse him of interfering with Belinda, and Nick hadn't claimed innocence. Their first face-to-face would be interesting. Whenever it went down, Nick couldn't show weakness. He'd convince Lou that the fire was a mistake, yes, but he was ready to take over. Lou would pretend all was forgiven, but another hit would be in the works. Nick could push for the secret ledger at that point. A leader would need that.

Nick padded into the kitchen in his boxers and frayed Saint's tee-shirt to see Cali preparing a spread to barbecue, ironically while lightning flashed in the kitchen window. Things seemed to be back to normal – but, considering the past few weeks, normalcy was out the window.

"Sleep good? Any pain?" She fiddled with a pack of hamburgers on the counter.

"Not really. Belinda's going to lay low."

"The feds thought about using her, but her psych profile... well, we decided not. The NOPD doesn't seem to check the results."

"What's all this?" Nick asked, stepping up behind her.

"I wanted to grill today before the burgers go bad, but it's supposed to rain all day. So, I thought we'd grill tomorrow when you get home from work. We got charcoal, lighter fluid, food, and a sunny day."

"Are we really back to normal here?"

"What are we supposed to do? Sit next to each other on the sofa staring forward until something happens? Any normalcy is good for us." She smiled. "I'll pick up beer later," she said as incentive. "As for today, I figured we can have turkey sandwiches."

"I thought you had to work." He reached for the coffee.

Cali stopped seasoning the burgers and cleaned off her hands in the sink. "I took off to spend the day here, but the weather doesn't want to cooperate." She wiped her hands dry, then stepped up to Nick, inviting him to reciprocate with her eyes.

"I need to run an errand."

"No problem." She rubbed at his crotch over his boxers, lips on his ear. "Ssh. Don't say anything."

He put the cup down and closed his eyes while she caressed him to arousal. For those few seconds, he was ready to let go – to let this happen. He backed away, pushing her shoulders at the same time. "No, you can't manipulate me that way."

"I'm not manipulating..."

"Damn it, just yesterday I learned you were an FBI agent looking to take down the Tribunal with me in it. I

believe you when you said you don't have to keep
pretending, but I'm still raw here. Let me sit with it."

"Okay." She turned back to the counter. "I'll give you
all the time you need."

He stood there for a moment, trying to stay strong,
but feeling himself weaken. *Christ, what he wouldn't do for
her.*

## Chapter 33

At the station that morning, Captain Lou Rush pressed the burner phone to his ear. He stared at a rookie's ass as she nursed a coffee. It had been a while since he'd reached out for companionship. His libido usually reminded him when he needed a temporary fix to set his mind straight. However, the curvy policewoman resembled Belinda, and he lost the mood.

Marcus had run into a problem, he thought, and failed to report back. Or maybe Marcus couldn't go through pull the trigger for real, and decided to leave town. Nick's mysterious beating could have something to do with it. He continued to refresh the NOLA and CNN websites, waiting for the feds to report a Tribunal murder with Gavin Jones, but the story never broke. The NOLA website contained a buried story of a fire that killed a New Orleans East resident. That was all.

He pulled the phone from his ear and looked at its screen. The call dropped without offering Marcus' voicemail. He dialed the dedicated number for Marcus' Q-Bug planted on his coffee table the night of Cooper's eradication, but only heard a television. Lou shoved the phone into his pocket, closed his eyes and considered his options. Whatever they were, they wouldn't get done sitting at a desk.

Lou bolted out of the office, speaking loudly to the uniformed officer sitting at a computer. "Simms, I'm heading out. Godcheaux can handle things. Don't know when I'll be back." He didn't wait for a response.

Steady drizzle helped sour his mood. However, sweat collected under his clothes the minute he stepped outside. Lou put on a NOPD windbreaker and threw his XL tweed jacket in his back seat. He drove to Marcus' apartment trying to remain calm. Renovated after the storm, the complex still looked dilapidated, but Marcus and his girlfriend suffered with it while house hunting. Despite not seeing his car, Lou pounded on the door. He peeked in the window while shaking out his umbrella.

A muffled female voice came from the other side. "Who is it?"

"It's Lou, Kareena. Open up." He assumed it was actually Kareena, or it could be a very awkward moment, but that was the least of his concerns. The door slowly opened. An anxious, mocha skinned face with light brown eyes appeared. Her long curls cascaded down onto her bare shoulders. Lou had never gone for black women, but had to admit she was nice piece.

"Lou, are you looking for Marcus, too? He's not answering his phone."

Lou peered inside. "Yeah, I'm looking for him. When was the last time you spoke with your beaux?"

"Yesterday, before he went to Shelly's. I fell asleep waiting for him, which isn't that unusual. But when he wasn't here this morning, I called Nick and everyone I could think of."

"Except me."

Kareena stammered, "You're right... I should have."

He placed the umbrella outside the door. "Can I come in?"

She backed away, opening the door wide. Lou filled a large portion of the space. He scanned the room trying to remember how it looked when he was there last. Nothing was out of the ordinary. No new pieces of furniture and nothing seemed missing. He caught the faint aroma of weed.

Lou spoke while slowly taking inventory. "Would you know if he came home after you were asleep and then left again?"

"That's possible, but these walls are thin. You hear everything." She followed him around the small apartment and into the bedroom.

"You'll have your new house soon." Lou was unapologetic in his inspection of the closet and the dresser drawers. He fell just short of tossing the place.

"What are you doing?" she asked.

"Seeing if he packed anything for a trip. No one can find him, so I need to know if he didn't go to Vegas or the casinos on the Gulf Shore. You know how he likes to gamble."

"He would have told me."

"Like he tells you everything?" Lou looked at her out the corner of his eye. "Well, let me know immediately if you hear from him. He could just be sleeping it off somewhere."

"I hope so." She walked ahead of him to the door.

"Did Nick try calling for him?"

"Yeah, several times."

"Don't worry, Kareena. I'm sure he's fine."

After settling back into his car, Lou opened a hidden compartment under his seat and pulled out another burner phone with red tape on it. He used so many, he wondered how he managed to keep track of them. He watched water cascade down his windshield as it rang. Still, no answer. He shoved the phone back into its hidden home. He dabbed the moisture from his face. The returning tightness caused him to massage his sternum.

Lou put Marcus on the back burner. He used his regular cell to make a call to the fire chief for a quick meeting. Ten minutes later, Lou pulled up to Gavin Jones' charred address where a makeshift chain link fence guarded the house with *no entry* signs. He parked behind a running sprint vehicle and approached the driver's side under his umbrella. The faint smell of wet, burnt wood occasionally wafted past.

The window rolled down on approach. "Who's in charge here?" Lou asked with a forced smile.

"I think we all know who." Jason Breaux stuck his hand out of the window in greeting. The man's hair stuck up like a rooster. "How's things at the Fifth?"

"Like a sideshow. How's Pooty? Still doing the oil painting?"

"Poot's fine. Painting keeps her busy. She's looking to show her collection on Jackson Square." The fire chief rolled his eyes.

"She should."

Lou expected him to denounce his wife's talent, however Jason closed his mouth with a smile. "So, Lou, how can I help you?"

"What can you tell me about the blaze."

Jason's wrinkles deepened as he appraised the house. "Don't know much yet until the investigator submits his report. What do you need to know?"

"I think I'll know when I hear it. When I learned it was Gavin Jones, my ears perked, you know?"

"The guy who got away with killing his girlfriend." Jason nodded with a slight smile. "Shame." He took one final look and adjusted the air vent. "You're getting wet. You want to climb in for this?"

"No thanks. Was he home at the time?" Lou shot his thumb over his shoulder.

"We have one fatality. He's at the coroner. The fire was contained before it could spread to the neighbors. Actually, I find it strange how isolated the fire was – just to the room the body was in." Jason wiped down the top of his head. His hair continued to reach skyward.

"Do you know if it was him? Jones?"

"Could be 'cause only one body was found. Supposedly, the resident." He hesitated, lowering his voice. "Should I keep tabs on the arson investigation?"

"Could you?"

Jason nodded. "The body had a bullet in his head. That wasn't released to the press. I know that much. Someone torched it to cover up the murder. No way around that."

Lou patted his shoulder. "No reason to go around *that*, my friend. The truth, either way."

Jason slumped and let out a breath. "Whew, good. That's a tough one to doctor up on my end. I heard Debrow has the body. Good man, that one."

"That he is." With a pat on the wet hood, Lou thanked Jason and returned to his car. He pulled out the blue-tape burner and called a dedicated number, where an answer should be guaranteed. Seems no one is available these days.

His palm smashed the dashboard as he cursed. The whole eradication scenario stank like canal water. He drove to the medical examiner's on Earhart Boulevard, a fifteen million dollar building newly separate from the coroner's office on Rampart. Up until recently, dead bodies had been stored in refrigerated trucks behind a temporary facility, which started after Hurricane Katrina. Back then, there weren't even offices or private areas for grieving family members. Now, they were state of the art.

He entered the cool reception area where a young, black lady manned the counter. "Hello, can I help you?"

"Yes, you can, dahlin'. I'm Captain Rush - Lou. Is Dr. Debrow in?"

"He sure is, Captain." She looked him up and down with a flirty smile.

"Can you let him know I'm here?" Lou asked, flourished with a wink.

"Sure, hold on." The lady got on the phone.

Moments later, Coroner Winston Dubrow opened the door. He was a young man with an old man's name. He looked like he should be running for mayor, with perfectly swept hair and smart glasses. "Lou, what can I do for you?"

"I understand you have a recent arrival from a fire?"

"We *had* a recent arrival from a fire. Two hours after he came in, so did the feds. They took him." Debrow motioned for Lou to follow.

"They just came in a got him?" Lou and the receptionist exchanged a final glance.

"They had a warrant, and I had no one here to stop them." The pair traveled down a hall with intermittent doors on each side. "Just said it part of a federal investigation. This isn't the first autopsy they high-jacked. You know that."

"Right." He marveled at how everything was new and smelled like antiseptic. They entered a thick, steel door into a walk-in cooler with several bodies in black bags lining the wall.

"We had him right here," he presented a table bolted into the wall about waist high. "I did a visual and took some pictures just before they got him. Want to see them?"

"Sure. What could you tell from a visual?"

"Not much." Debrow walked out of the room to the hallway, which reminded Lou of his high school days. He let Debrow offer information voluntarily. "There was a GSW to the head. This would be the obvious cause of death. Why shoot someone who was already dead, right?"

"Right, unless it's a ruse."

"I suppose." Debrow waved his hand. "You like the new digs?"

"Sure. I've been here a couple of times. Never had the tour, though."

Winston proudly opened the door to a pristine autopsy room, furnished with new equipment, in a sterile, temperature-regulated room. The wall tiles were blue at the bottom, sporadically changing to white as if floating toward the ceiling. Classical music flowed from a wireless speaker in the corner.

"I absolutely love this place." Winston spun in a circle. "We have twenty-three thousand square feet. We can store over a hundred bodies. We have five autopsy stations." He pointed at the ceiling. "A mental health suite and an entire floor for toxicology and histological labs, although we don't have the money to staff it. I'm sending my samples to St. Louis and have to wait up to six weeks for the results."

"I know. That doesn't help the boys in blue."

"Shit, I'm happy to finally have this place."

"In the meantime, Headquarters is falling apart."

"The city can only afford one project at a time, my friend." Debrow led Lou to a desk in an adjacent office. There were shelves with books and binders and file cabinets with long, narrow drawers. A Blue Dog painting hung prominently on the wall facing the desk. He pulled out a very expensive looking camera.

"Nice contraption."

"Canon EOS 5D. Twenty-three megapixel. Incredible shots." Debrow searched the screen on the camera. "Haven't downloaded the Jones shots yet." He handed it to Lou.

"Feels expensive." Lou scrolled with the proper button.

"About three grand. So, as you can see, all we have is a completely crispy criminal."

"Looks like a burnt mannequin."

"Pretty much. These pictures don't help identify him, but then, I'm not a cop."

"I need confirmation on his identity."

"That's up to the feds now."

"You have any DNA left behind?"

Debrow wiped his lips. "With a burned body? Nope." His finger shot in the air. "The ring."

"The ring?"

Debrow hurried to a drawer in the autopsy room. "When they brought him in, it was near lunch and I opened the bag to take a look at him."

"And he had a ring on?"

He smiled. "I extracted his ring from his finger and put it in a baggie, then decided to have lunch before starting."

"Steel stomach. You still have the ring?"

He turned around presenting a clear bag with a metal object in it. "When the feds came, I forgot to give it to them. I was about to send it over."

Lou took the bag. He recognized it from surveillance pictures Chad Cooper had taken. Knowing the mark's daily jewelry was important for identification purposes. "Can you get DNA from burned skin?"

"No, but it's all I have."

"Send it." Lou gripped his shoulder. "Call me immediately if they find something."

"What if it's not him? What if the feds come back asking questions?" Winston waited.

"You were acting on my instructions. I'll take care of it." Lou marched out of the room, needing to make one more stop.

## Chapter 34

"You're losing control of these young pups," Shelly said.

Lou glanced up at him. "What the hell are you talking about?"

Shelly sat on his stool. His jaw set. "You can see what's going on."

"We knew there would be ups and downs with the new crop. These kids have been coddled, growing up without the… *urgency* we had to face."

Shelly folded his arms. "Let me tell you something, Lou. If anything happens to that boy, you better take me out, too."

"Where was this concern when you were raising me?"

He chuckled. "You were a lost cause. And I don't hear you denying it."

Lou smiled, but in a less than humorous way.

The establishment was otherwise empty, the last two customers having just left. "I can tell you're anxious." Shelly changed the subject.

"End of a rough day. Like you said, things aren't going so smoothly, *Dad*."

"Anything I can do?"

"From inside your little prison? No, just keep being useless like usual."

"I'm the accountant of your little enterprise, so fuck you." Shelly pushed his boney bird finger in Lou's face with his tongue out.

As they laughed, a black kid no older than fifteen walked into the bar with wide eyes. Shelly instinctively moved toward him, but also positioned himself next to a pistol. The boy's skinny arm stretched out to offer something to Shelly. The old man cautiously took the note. As soon as the item changed hands, the boy shot out of the bar like a rocket.

"I'll be damned," Lou mumbled.

Shelly turned the folded note over and handed it to Lou. He leaned in. "Seems you were expecting this."

Lou's eyes lit up. Handwritten notes were the main form of communication with his insiders. He opened the paper to see only creases on a blank page. Nothing had been written – a very special message.

"Does this mean…?" Shelly didn't finish his thought.

Lou smiled, but not with relief. "I'm not sure. Could be a trap."

"I trust you'll find out." Shelly nodded toward the note with tired eyes. "I would vote on the trap." He reached out, placing his hand near Lou's but not touching it.

"Close up early. I'm going to stay a few more minutes." Lou studied the blank note.

"You're actually going to go meet him?"

"Have to. If the feds offered him a deal, then they have nothing, which is good. If he's wired, he's not going to get anything from me. I have a little time to think about it. Makes no sense to go home. Not that I have anyone waiting for me there."

"Companionship is overrated." Shelly nodded with a sad grin. "Lock up?"

Lou nodded. "Of course."

The old man collected a few things from behind the bar and shuffled to the kitchen to slowly climb the stairs.

Lou heard each creak of each board. To him, agoraphobia was mental weakness, not a debilitating fear. Some days Lou wanted to drag the old man outside and force him to walk around in the sunlight, but he didn't need the drama. Chain an addict to a pole, and he'll kick his habit – same with Shelly.

Lou was now the lone patron in the ghostly bar. One day soon it would all be his, and he cringed at the thought of retirement. He accrued enough money to live in luxury anywhere in the world. Yet, he couldn't be happy doing anything else. Lying on a beach? Visiting museums? Living in a nursing home like Big Hoover? Gambling, and early bird specials? Screw that.

The music had ceased, and the structure could be heard settling with cracks and pops in the silence. The hum of the refrigerator sedated him even more. Sitting straight, with both arms stretched out across the bar, Lou finally downed the remaining beer. The pot of coffee was old and cold, but he debated throwing it in the microwave.

He checked his watch. Either his contact was going to be there, or he wasn't.

Lou used his key to lock Shelly's door just after one in the morning. The weathered screen door slapped shut from the retraction of a strong spring. He drove his Mustang down Haynes, without another car within a mile of him. The radio played a tried and true song from the 1970's, but low enough so he could think. The beer made him tired, and he yawned despite the anticipation.

The cherry red Mustang had its pluses and minuses. Lou didn't like that people might remember his vehicle in any given circumstance, but the Mustang let law enforcement know not to interfere. He likened his vehicle to Starsky and Hutch's red and white Gran Torino.

Two minutes later, without a soul in sight, Lou felt safe enough to turn into the paved parking lot of a mom-and pop hardware store he knew not to have surveillance through continual checking. This had been their preplanned meeting spot for three years and it was only the second time using it.

A Volvo was the lone vehicle in the lot. Lou couldn't tell the occupant just yet. Careful not to roll over glass or debris, he drove straight forward as if wanting to hit the car head on before pulling his driver's side door inches from the Volvo's. The man behind the wheel rolled down his window. Gospel music flowed into the night air, mixing with Lou's Pink Floyd.

"Where have you been?" Lou questioned, turning up his own radio. The mash up of songs between cars sounded like gibberish, but was perfect to cover their conversation.

"I was on lockdown, man. They're looking for me." Gavin Jones had a shaved head and round spectacles.

"Start from the beginning." Lou held his gun just below the window.

"That morning, four agents show at my house telling me today was the day. Of course, I know today's the day thanks to you. Question is – how did *they* know?

"I have an idea."

"So, I can't contact you 'cause I got an agent on my ass all day. But, I still figure to handle things, dig? I get home from shopping and put my shit away, knowing your boy is in the house. But, I also knew the agents were also in place. I put away the groceries, keeping an eye out. Eventually, I sit down with my piece at the table. I figured when he showed his face, I'd shoot him, saying I had no other choice."

"That obviously didn't happen."

"Right. When he did show his face, I took my shot, but he was wearing a vest, which I didn't know."

"Ever since you told me who Cali Maddox really was a month ago, I've been trying to decide how to handle things."

"You think your boy finally told her what he really does for a living?"

Lou nodded. "How could he not? All this time he's been against me." He gripped the steering wheel with white knuckles. "Go on."

"So, with these guys still up my ass, I have no way to contact you. Should have aimed at his head."

"Keep going."

"An hour after your boy's arrest, I was on a plane to Virginia, cut off from the world. They took my phone, stripped my bling, and gave me new clothes. They questioned me and I faked some stir-crazy, bat-shit psycho-babble about being in the operation. I told them I was done. That might've backfired, because I they started looking at me like I was a nut-case."

"They weren't letting you go."

"Nope. I thought they would at first. Suddenly, the agents started acting goofy around me, telling me I had to wait in my room and couldn't have privileges. I got that sickening feeling. I trust that feeling. I got out of there before the armed guards came and they locked my door."

"Did they find out you were a mole?"

"Not sure. I'd rather just get out now, whether a free man or fugitive. I figure they're looking for me, so I left a little clue that I was heading to Canada, then I drove back here." Jones stared past Lou. "Probably this would be the last place they'd think I'd go."

"So, you risk leading them here, to me?" He looked around.

"We're good."

"You don't decide that."

"Be that as it may, as white people say... give me my money and I leave the country. And just a reminder in case you're looking to eradicate *me*..."

"Yeah, yeah. You have these imaginary recordings."

"That I should've turned over. Take a chance."

"Lou let his gun fall to his lap. "Do you know anything about the feds flipping Nick?"

"I don't. You said he didn't know who she was, right?"

"I suspected he didn't. Either way, they flipped him and faked your death. You say they took your bling. They put your ring on the corpse." Lou imagined holding Nick's head under water. "He betrayed me."

Winger hiked an eyebrow. "All you bitches betraying each other, seems to me. But, I can't talk, though, right?"

"You got anything else?"

"Yeah, I got something else I noticed. Your boy wasn't ready to do me. His gun had the safety on."

Lou's arm fell out the window. "Safety? So?"

"He came there to kill me, Rush. Why was his safety on just seconds away from pulling the trigger?"

Lou stayed silent in thought. "It was all for show?"

"It's like he changed his mind," Jones said. "The way he stood there just before I took my shot. Seemed strange."

"He's a strange kid." Lou was lost in thought.

"Like you said, that's for you to find out." Agent Winger stared at him. The man leaned his head slightly out of the window, into the streetlamp's illumination. "I want my money."

"You think I carry that amount with me, just waiting for you to appear. Give me time to transfer it."

"They found my fake passports." Jones kept a stone face. "I need that extra identification I gave you."

Lou set his jaw. A Kiss song began. "I got it, but I have to be careful." He pointed his finger hard at him. "Contact me when we can meet."

"Will do." Winger rolled up his window and cruised out of the parking lot.

Lou watched the taillights disappear down Haynes. The gun was placed back into the glove compartment. He released a breath and pulled at his itchy nose. His stomach rumbled. For the first time since catching his wife cheating, he found himself popping antacids again.

Chapter 35

The cell next to the bed jolted Nick awake. The bright screen read 2:13 a.m.

"It's Lou," Nick mumbled to Cali. They had agreed to sleep in the same bed to avoid all inconsistencies, but Nick wasn't sure about it. He felt stupid putting off the inevitable, but he couldn't just open his arms so soon.

"I'll get my cell." She turned on the lamp.

When Nick answered, there wasn't much to say on his end, except to agree and disagree. Nick finally said, "I can be there in an hour."

Lou disagreed with that estimate. "Leave now. Gary is outside your house. If you're not in your car in three minutes, The boys are coming in to get you. You don't want that. Follow him to the location." He hung up.

Nick faced Cali. "Lou wants to talk about Marcus, he needs me to follow Gary."

"You can't go alone."

Nick scooted out of bed to dress. "Have to. They'll come in to get me if I stall. No choice."

"I'll contact the team. Be careful." She dialed.

He put his hand over the cell in her hand. "This is in case something happens." He paused before he touched his lips to her.

Her lips parted as he backed away, but no words escaped. Her eyes instantly grew wet. "This isn't good to go alone, Nick."

"I gotta go."

Long had set up a team of three agents to be ready at a moment's notice, but they still had to assemble. Knowing the propensity of the Tribunal members scouting out a perimeter, having an agent watch the house was out of the question. The Bureau would send a helicopter in the next few minutes and find the car by process of elimination, as there were basically no one out that time of night. The ground team would have to arrive after the fact and hope they didn't get discovered.

Nick spotted Mr. Gary's idling Lexus up the block and jumped into his own car. Something had riled Lou up. He had a gun on his ankle and one in the glove compartment, but those gave him no comfort, as Lou knew his trade secrets. On the flip side, *not* having the weapons in his usual spots would raise suspicion.

He drove at a car's length behind Mr. Gary. He thought maybe they were going to Shelly's, but the Lexus never slowed as they cruised past the bar. They hooked a right where Haynes and Downman met, and he spotted the first squad car. Taking another quick right, the Stars And Stripes Boulevard led to the lakefront marina and private airport. In essence, he was heading back from where he came, but now on the other side of the levee. He spotted two unmarked cars with their lights off. With the lake on the left and the levee on the right, the road soon ended with a round-about where a casino boat had once docked. He could just make out a squad car parked near a dumpster. It was the only way in or out, and isolated to late night traffic. If the FBI vehicle even made it in, they would be spotted.

There was no obvious activity. Everything had shut down for the night. Cars were parked in various lots, but no other headlights were on the road. He followed the Lexus into the sporadically lit marina, slowing to a stop. Mr. Gary's extended arm pointed to a decommissioned lamp post to park under. Mr. Gary then drove farther into the lot, hidden behind a few cars close to the boats. The feds couldn't help him out here without showing themselves.

Two men appeared from the darkness, heading in Nick's direction. Their mere outlines told him that it was Lou and Mr. Gary. Marcus was nowhere to be seen, thankfully. Nick took out his firearm from the glove compartment and put it under his left thigh. The gun from his ankle holster was placed under the right one. Five seconds later, Mr. Gary climbed into the back seat while Lou took the front.

"You weren't shitting about your face," Lou commented. "The boys said they didn't touch you."

"Believe who you will. So, where's Marcus?"

"Don't say anything yet," Lou warned.

Mr. Gary pulled out a device that looked like a cell phone. He pushed some buttons on it as if making a call, then handed it to Lou who proceeded to wave it up and down Nick's body. The contraption didn't make a sound. After Lou swiped it around the car, he passed it back to Mr. Gary with a nod.

"Pro 10G cell and bug detector." Gary smiled while moving it around the back seat. "Love this thing."

"We should have just got in your car," Nick muttered, handing over his cell phone.

"I don't want any blood on my upholstery." Mr. Gary checked around the marina again.

Lou turned the detector off, then patted up and down his body. He got down to business, speaking under the volume of the music. "Marcus vanished without a trace. You're going to tell us what you know."

Gary Forche fiddled with his cell. "Hurry up, so I can get back to my snoring wife."

"You think I'm lying about not knowing." Nick watched the boats floating side-by-side quietly in the distance.

Lou sighed. "What I think is that you're protecting him, which is putting your own life in a precarious dilemma."

"You're right. I would protect him if I knew he ran. But, he didn't tell me shit. He knows the game. He gave me deniability." Nick tensed. Their silence could mean he was getting through to them. "If I had to guess, which I am, he couldn't handle Belinda, so he cut and run. He'll probably send for Kareena once he's settled."

Mr. Gary had no reaction to that theory. "You don't seem too broken up."

"Maybe it was you who had this done to me," Nick said, pointing back at his face.

"Not without my say." Lou shot Mr. Gary a look. "And stay quiet. I'm running this meeting."

In the mirror, Nick could see the old man silently mimicking Lou with an exaggerated expression. He looked out the window with a scowl.

Nick spoke confidently, "Ever since you murdered Cooper, he's been squirrelly."

Lou slapped Nick across the face like a lightning bolt. The cut on his lip opened again. "Why would you lie like that? No one in this car killed anyone."

Nick dabbed the blood with his shirt collar. "Jesus, you just cleared me with that thing Gary brought."

"*Mr. Gary*, you snot. Show me proper respect."

Lou explained, "You know the detector is only a precaution."

Nick nodded. "Marcus just skipped town. Mark that up as *undetermined* in your ledger."

"Ledger? Why on earth would you bring up a ledger?"

"I've known for years that Shelly keeps track of your... things. I actually expect to get it when I take over."

"At this point, Marcus stands a better chance of taking the reins," Mr. Gary spat.

Lou paused to shake away the thought. "Marcus wouldn't leave town without planning it. Without packing a single item. I'll tell you what I think..."

Nick felt something hard press against the back of his head, pushing it forward off the headrest. His peripheral caught Mr. Gary with his arm extended. A barrel pressed against the base of his skull. Nick asked, "Is this necessary?"

Lou opened the glove compartment. He slammed it shut, then held out his hand with a disappointed expression. Nick put his left hand in the air, then slowly lowered it to retrieve his gun from under his thigh. He handed it to Lou.

"Who doesn't trust who?" Lou let the magazine fall from the weapon. He ejected the round in the chamber.

"This can be a dangerous area this late at night," Nick said, dryly.

"Here's what I think..." Lou began again, but paused in thought.

"Marcus is gone, and we have issues with the Jones situation," Mr. Gary pushed the gun for emphasis. "This is just a little incentive to be honest with us."

"Yeah, 'cause no one gets questioned before getting killed." Nick glanced back.

Another slap grazed his face. Lou sighed. "I think Marcus contacted you and you met. Or you followed Belinda home. I think you and Marcus had a fight about it. Marcus was going to do his job, but you got in the way... again."

"*We* think that," Gary added, tapping the barrel on his head.

Nick tried to remain calm, this would put Marcus in the clear. "Listen to yourself. I've been on board with this

since I was a kid. If Belinda has to go, she has to go.
Cooper, too."

"You're a liar," Mr. Gary muttered.

"You want the truth?" Nick asked.

"No, I don't want the truth," Lou yelled in a whisper.
"The truth isn't why you have Gary pointing that at your
head. Why don't you lie?"

"The truth is..." Nick saw Lou's eyes widen. "I don't
know where Marcus is."

"Gary is just being Gary," Lou said, never taking his
eyes off Nick. "But, I actually know when you're lying.
And you're lying."

"I guess there's nothing more to say."

"It's time, Lou," Gary said.

Nick looked back and forth. "Time for what? You
can't do anything without knowing for sure. I swear, Lou.
What happened to Marcus, I don't know."

Gary yelled, "He wouldn't leave town without telling
you."

"Gary." Lou put his finger to his lips.

"He wanted out. He told me these fantasies he had
about moving to Alaska. He saw some movie and wanted
to live off the land in a cabin."

Gary advanced his gun farther into his hair. "A black
man from the East wanted to live in the woods? Marcus
was going to take care things, and you interfered. He
kicked your ass and now Marcus is missing."

A cell phone rang in Lou's pocket. He took it out and
eyed it with a scowl. He answered, pausing briefly between
orders. "Yeah. No. Don't pull them over. Let them in." He
hung up, looked at Mr. Gary. "We have company."

The threesome spotted a Black Jeep Cherokee with
tinted windows pulling into the marina. It parked about
forty yards away and sat a minute with glowing brake
lights. The engine finally shut off. Seconds later, two men

in casual attire with fishing gear and a cooler walked onto the pier and toward the slips of boats, out of sight.

Nick prayed that was the FBI playing it smart, but how many fishermen cast their lines at this hour? That wasn't to say they weren't going to sleep in their boat and head out later.

Lou held up his hand, his eyes glanced toward the Cherokee. "Gary, watch what you say."

"You brought me out here to get rid of me." Nick focused on the SUV as if something might be up.

"You're paranoid." Lou shook his head as if that was nonsense. "I don't blame you for saving your partner. I don't blame Marcus for not going through with it, if you were in the way. No one is getting penalized. This is nothing like before." Lou meant Cooper. He inhaled and calmly asked, "Just tell me where he is."

Nick moved his thigh, feeling the remaining gun on his skin. His fingers pushed his hair back. "I'll tell you if he contacts me."

Lou looked out the windshield. "Gary's right. You're a horrible liar."

"Not lying."

Gary twisted the barrel at the base of his skull. Nick reached back and swiped at the gun, causing it to fire, sending a bullet into the dashboard. "Shit!" Nick put his hand over the ear the bullet whizzed past. It felt like the bullet went *in* his ear.

Nick kept his eyes on the Cherokee, while a piercing ring stung his brain.

Gary lowered the gun and fell back against the seat. "It's his fault."

"Put it away." Lou said, strained. "We'll get the truth another time, and then we'll decide what to do with him."

Gary nodded. "Well, no matter when or where, you know how I'm voting."

Lou faced Gary. "We can't settle this until we find Marcus."

"I've never said this before Lou, but you're not seeing this clearly. Set up a trial." Gary leaned forward showing the gun again.

"We'll discuss that possibility tomorrow."

"We're going to find out what happened, and when we do..." Gary left the unfinished threat linger. He exited in a huff, staring at the Jeep.

"Lou and Nick sat in silence. After a long moment, Lou opened his door, stepped out, but leaned over to speak. "Son or not, you're going to be the next one we vote on."

Nick felt that Lou wanted to say more, but instead, his father shut the door.

Besides the bullet hole in his dash, the pair hadn't said anything incriminating and Lou admitted nothing. They weren't even hiding that they didn't trust him anymore. He drove off with a pit in his stomach and a humming in his ear. It didn't matter if that Jeep Cherokee was FBI or not, if they hadn't shown, he might be dead right now.

Chapter 36

Nick had barely slept after his near-death experience with Lou and Mr. Gary. He explained to Cali how they threatened him about snitching out Marcus, but watered down how close he had really came to dying. She confirmed that the SUV was not one of theirs.

But, despite the target on his back, the plan to barbeque wasn't canceled. They welcomed the normalcy, albeit with their anxiety in an endless holding pattern. Nick and Cali spent the afternoon in the back yard, avoiding certain topics of conversation. The barbeque came and went and the burgers had been nibbled on. When the conversation lulled, Nick watched Cali scoot from her chair to collect the paper plates. She brushed her hand across his shoulder and kissed his cheek, stopping to make sure they *saw* each other. A slight smile appeared. With a ruffling of his hair, she strolled inside with the plates.

From their first meeting at the church, it seemed there was no obstacle that could keep them apart – no deed could sour them against each other. He had to accept that Cali was in his blood. She flowed through his veins sustaining his life - a part of his biology – good or bad.

Various scenarios roamed through his mind. Did Jones try to kill him on Lou's orders? And could Jones have told Lou about Cali's true profession? If Lou suspected him of switching sides, he didn't get the opportunity to accuse him at the marina this morning. Lou arranged that impromptu meeting out of panic, trying to eliminate the guessing game of Nick's recent activities. He needed to use Lou's suspicion to his advantage.

Nick had felt safer staying indoors most of the day, so as not to give a sniper a good shot. However, if a bullet had his name on it, he couldn't dodge it forever. The sun hadn't descended yet, and the afternoon was finally cooling to the point of tolerable. With Cali inside making a dent in the clean-up, Nick let his eyelids drop in fatigue.

The hinges on the back door creaked open. He liked that there was ample warning in case of an intruder. Cali walked out. "Guess who's here?"

Nick looked up to see Belinda wearing a pair of dark sunglasses, standing behind his possible fiancé. She waved, sheepishly.

"Everything okay?" Nick asked.

Her face pinched, almost trying to smile. "I don't know." She looked between him and Cali, hesitating a moment.

Cali graciously took he hint. "Oh, I have a call to make inside. I'll be back, guys."

Belinda stood a few feet away from the table, sheepish like a child. "Can you take a ride with me. I need to show you something."

"Show me what?"

She took a broad step forward, whispering, "Marcus…"

"He sent you?"

She nodded with closed eyes.

Nick stuck his head in the back door and yelled to Cali that he'd be back shortly. Without further explanation, Belinda led him to her car. Nick settled into the passenger

seat. He noticed Belinda's eyes were swollen, and her
fingers had a slight tremor while starting the engine.

"Something wrong?" Nick asked.

"He needs to see you." She cleared her throat.

"You're going in the wrong direction," he pointed
out.

"He moved. Don't want to say out loud."

Nick understood the precaution. He sat silent as they
headed down the I-10 toward Slidell, knowing there could
be any number of places Marcus could have chosen.
Belinda checked her rearview before pulling onto an exit
ramp that had practically been destroyed. Her car slowly
dipped onto dirt before hitting broken concrete and gravel.
She barely fit around the barricades warning that the road
was closed.

"What the hell is back here anymore?"

"His idea."

"Belinda, there is absolutely jack shit back here. You
got this right?" Surrounding them was nothing but forestry,
neglected road signs and rubble from structures torn down
long ago. Concrete slabs were marked with graffiti and
several charred vehicles sat abandoned on the shoulder.
Nick got that queasy feeling in his stomach.

The car pulled to the side. "There." Belinda pointed
beyond a large foundation that no longer held a building.

Nick strained his eyes, then glanced back at Belinda
who faced him, holding a gun pointed in his direction.
Tears streamed down her eyes.

"What are you doing?"

She moaned and sniffled. "Lou told me he wouldn't
kill me if... if..."

Nicked brushed aside the shock. "You can't believe
him, Belinda. Once you kill me, you think he's going to let
you live? You'll be the next one out here."

She shook her head vigorously. "No, no, he promised that I would take your place. This would prove it to him. There's no other way."

The air conditioning was on full blast, but Nick's shirt was soaked. "I can tell you don't want to do this. You are so in over your head."

She beat the steering wheel with her free hand. "Don't you think I know that? This is my only way out."

"No, he *told you* this is your only way out." He remained calm, so she would remain calm. "Imagine this, Belinda – imagine you order me out the car. You pull the trigger and I die right here alongside the road. Imagine that moment."

"Nick, stop."

"Imagine if you can't take it back. Picture me lying there." He pointed out the window. "Imagine you holding the gun. I – am – dead. You just killed your partner – a friend. Do you want to take it back? Do you want to wish it never happened? That we would've found another way?"

Belinda's head nodded. The gun vibrated. "I've killed before. I'll be okay."

"You know this is different. Let's find another way."

"Get out the car." It was barely understandable.

"Don't…"

She screamed. "Get out the car!"

Nick opened the door, quickly going over every option. He could run into the bushes, but it was way too dense to put any distance between them. If he ran up the road, she could pick him off fairly easily. He knew her to be a good shot, but in her emotional condition…?

Once Nick closed the door, he waited for Belinda to get out as well. Instead, he heard the locks on the door engage. He bent over to see Belinda with her face in her hands, bobbing against the steering wheel.

He knocked on the window. "Belinda, let's figure this out together. We'll get through this."

She let the window down an inch so she could speak. She stopped crying and her voice became calm. "You're a good guy, Nick. You treated me better than many men in my life. I appreciated that."

Nick slid his fingers into the crack in the window, trying to pull it down. "No, Belinda. Don't…"

"Bring that bastard down, Nick." She placed the gun into her mouth.

"Belinda, no." Nick pounded on the window, but it held. He looked to the ground for a rock big enough to break the glass, then he heard it. The gun exploded in her hand, and he closed his eyes just as the bullet tore through her brain stem.

#

"You were never there," Cali said while seated at the table in their backyard, just an hour after Nick had left with Belinda.

The sun had descended. A cold beer sat untouched in front of Nick. The radio blared a little louder than it should. His heartbeat had finally steadied. He replayed Belinda's suicide over and over. He slumped in the chair, staring forward. "I can't believe we just left her in the car."

"We didn't just leave her. Thank God I followed you."

He interrupted, "Which worked in this case with her, but never do that again."

She agreed with a blink. "Long had an anonymous tip called in to the police. It has to be this way."

"Lou sent her to kill me." He reached for his beer, but only turned the bottle.

"Means he's scared. Long wanted to pull you when I called him at the scene. He doesn't think you have a shot at finding the ledger at this point."

"And what? Charge me? The ledger would be destroyed for sure."

She held up her hands. "I convinced him otherwise. You're his only shot. He knows it. But, now I'm worried. I'm considering that European idea more and more."

He looked at her, almost with a smile.

The unexpected clanking of the side gate caught Nick and Cali's attention. Nick quickly turned down the music, pushing the radio to the end of the table. He stood as Lou rounded the back corner of the house. Cali scoured at the sight of the hulking man in cargo shorts and an LSU shirt, but quickly switched into a pleasant mode. His watch was big enough to be a UFC belt.

"I didn't ring the bell figuring you'd be back here. You wouldn't have heard me over the music anyway."

"What brings you by?" Cali asked.

He frowned. "I have some bad news. Thought I'd come by personally."

Nick had no expression. His tone was dry. "We're going to keep playing this game?"

"Game?" His face screwed into a curious expression. "What are you talking about?"

"Anything new with Marcus?" Cali asked, not wanting to put it all out there yet.

"Still missing."

Cali appeared disappointed. "Want a beer? We can throw a burger on the grill for you."

"No, nothing for me. Don't mean to disturb your cookout." He took a chair opposite Nick, as if he didn't care about his intrusion. "But, like I said, I have some unfortunate news."

Nick waited.

"Belinda was found dead out by the decommissioned exit. Suicide from the reports I was given." Lou's hands gripped the armrest.

Nick looked at Cali. "I can't believe it." He was less than convincing.

Lou's lips curled up. "You're in shock."

"Coward," Cali finally muttered. She stood with her arms folded in a strong stance.

"Well, well." Lou did smile this time. "Do you expect us to have a real conversation here? You really expect me to say something to incriminate myself?" He chuckled.

Nick often noticed that in regard to fight or flight, Cali was like a Chihuahua boxed into a corner. She'd fight the biggest dog to the death. Shrinking wasn't in her nature.

"I, for one, can't believe she'd take her own life. In the heat of the moment," Lou began, "it's hard to tell what one might do."

"Come to finish the job?" Nick said. "Do it, or leave."

"I may have miscalculated the situation." He let his stare linger on Cali before giving his attention back to Nick. "We need to talk this out where I know we're safe. Why don't we go for a ride?"

Nick laughed out loud. He sat forward, then fell back into the chair. "That's just rich."

"Forget all that bullshit that's happened last night, and today. That was a mistake. We can settle this and get on with our lives like usual. You have my word nothing is going to happen."

"No." Nick stared at him. "I will never trust, or be alone with you again."

Lou hesitated, slapping the armrest. He wiped his jaw. "I drove by the coroner's the other day."

"Okay?"

Lou scraped at a dry spot on the table. "Gavin Jones?"

"Dead, we know," Cali said, playing along with the charade. Lou would talk with them, but only in a normal, cryptic manner.

"Someone shot Jones in the head, then set fire to his house."

"We heard about the fire. Tribunal?" Cali asked.

"Could be, babe." He focused on Lou. "Is there a suspect?"

"Turns out the feds came and got him." Lou reached over to examine the radio. "I guess they're going to pin this on the Tribunal again. The legend lives on."

"No for long," Cali stated.

Lou gave her a condescending look. "I have a feeling that all activities are going to cease and desist."

"Like the Tribunal is just going to stop?" Cali asked.

"How knows?" Lou's intensity seared through Nick. "The feds have nothing to this point, going off the grid would guarantee nothing in the future."

"This is pointless, Lou," Nick mumbled. "You'll get another shot at me. Just leave."

Lou gave an ominous smile to Nick. "We'll have that talk later." He strolled out the way he came, not bothering to close the gate on the way out. The Mustang growled with life in the distance, then tore down the street.

Chapter 37

The first thing Captain Lou Rush did that morning
was have Kareena prepare a missing persons report on
Marcus Hoover, arranging a statement to be made to the
public. They would have to deny that his disappearance
was related to Officer Chad Cooper, whose case was still
active as an open homicide. Kareena would also make a
prepared plea to find her boyfriend. Lou requested that a
trusted detective from Headquarters lead the charge. He put
out a BOLO on Marcus Hoover's car, and like kicking an
ant pile, every cop available, on duty and off, joined the
search.

Lunch hour approached. Lou's son betrayed their way
of life, and three attempts to rectify the situation failed, like
he was a friggin' cat with nine lives. Getting Jones to take
him out, while effectively ending that operation, seemed
like the perfect plan. Offering Belinda Nick's coveted spot
wasn't enough. Guess she really wasn't that ambitious. And
now, Nick wouldn't trust him if he had a lobotomy.

That reminded him, Jones was a loose end who was
probably bluffing about his evidence. He was an
experienced FBI agent for Christ's sake. When they first
met, Jones had summoned Lou while locked up in Orleans
Parish Prison two months prior and made an offer. When

he had exposed Cali Maddox for whom she really was, Lou agreed to the arrangement. However, he had a decision to make – which one would be eliminated? Cali Maddox was only doing her job, and her death could make things complicated. Nick, however – Nick was the worst kind of traitor.

He should have known Belinda would screw things up. If Nick were working with the feds, possibly watched, the eradication of his son would have to be a well-planned one… *or maybe not*. A thought struck him that if the Tribunal really was to go silent like he had threatened – if they stopped all activity – then, the Nick and Cali would be stuck in mud. The eradications were so few and far between, anyway. He contemplated a serious cease and desist.

A press conference was set for the early afternoon in regards to Marcus, in which Lou refused to participate. As a general rule, he steered clear face-time on television, and avoided the questions from random reporters about Gavin Jones and the charred body. He assumed someone from the FBI office leaked the hijacking of the corpse, just to keep suspicion off their new asset, Nick. However, those fools were unaware that Jones had become disgruntled and wanted out. Six years in a fishbowl was enough to drive him to Lou's side, where there was a finish line with a payday. The feds were counting on him to freak out when they release the news that the body found was of a dead agent.

Paperwork coated the surface of Lou's desk, all except for a space safely near the corner for his fresh, steaming coffee. Just as Lou reached for the cup, the burner phone in his top drawer rang. No one was approaching, so he felt safe answering. "Yeah."

The creaky voice of Gary Forche came out the speaker. "Metairie Cemetery. Took an Uber there, disguised in a hat, wig and glasses."

"Really? What's she doing?" He looked out the window into the squad room, just to see if anyone were paying attention to his office.

"She's still in the car. They drove down Avenue K in the cemetery. Stopped by Avenue S. I can't get too close, there's nobody out here, she'll see me."

"Is she getting out?"

"No." He waited a second. "They're just sitting there."

He sighed. "Alright. If she gets out, let me know what she does. Otherwise, when they leave, don't follow her. She Ubered for a reason. Don't validate her suspicions."

"You got it."

Lou pulled up from his desk and left the lieutenant in charge. Once in the Fifth District car, he put on a Cubs cap and sunglasses. The unmarked Taurus impatiently bucked forward as soon as the engine started, peeling out around the corner.

He made it to the Metairie Cemetery in only twenty minutes. His eyes widened as Cali left in the ride share car just as he pulled in. She wore a droopy hat and big sunglasses, unsuccessful in her attempt of not being noticed. Choosing to have her followed after their confrontation yesterday paid off.

The unmarked car continued farther inside and parked near the corner of Avenue's K and S. Lou walked with purpose ignoring the heat of the afternoon sun. The tombs were like beautiful, neglected little houses, weather-beaten, ornate, mysterious and final. As he passed each one, the family names etched in stone advertised the inhabitants. He stopped when he saw the name SANDERS.

Lou rubbed his jaw, looking around as if someone might be watching. Why would FBI Agent Cali Maddox be sitting in an Uber outside the tomb of Harold Sanders? Who was she to Slimeball Harry? He couldn't take yet another monkey wrench. At some point, the whole operation had gone off the rails, and Lou wasn't sure he could right the train.

The foundation of the Tribunal's success had been to never relax, to never let down their guard, but Lou was guilty of just that. Was someone watching him now? If he could do it to Maddox, then anyone could do it to him. He found the shade of an oak and looked at the calendar on his cell phone where he marked important dates and events.

"Son of a bitch," he mumbled. His body temperature rose when he saw why this date was important. While contemplating the day of Slimeball Harry's murder, the phone rang. It was the coroner's office. "Rush here."

"Captain, it's Dr. Debrow. How are you?"

"Depends. If you're calling about Gavin Jones, don't worry. We're good."

"Well, maybe you should come down."

Lou hesitated, not wanting to waste time. "Dr. Debrow, I have the information I need regarding that case. I don't need to come down."

"Still the same, maybe you should."

*Winger*. Lou exhaled in frustration. "Understood. I'll be there shortly."

"See you then, Captain."

Lou power-walked to his car, stopped at his bank to raid the safety deposit box for the fake ID package, and then sped off for the coroner's building. It was only a ten-minute drive, but seemed like an hour while trying to get around slow, sloppy drivers. He parked angled in two spots and entered the building with a manila envelope, noticing the same receptionist as before.

"Captain Rush, right?" She smiled wide.

"You got it, dawlin'. Dr. Debrow in?"

"You can go right back." She pointed at the door.

"Thanks."

Lou smelled the chemicals as he journeyed the vacuous hall to the room where Gavin Jones had supposedly been. He peeked in, but it was empty. He continued walking further and saw Dr. Debrow in a doorway of the autopsy room, as if his shoes were glued to the ground. Lou stepped to his side.

"Good to see you, Lou." The doctor twisted at the waist to push the door open.

"Where?" Lou folded his arms.

Debrow pointed, but didn't attempt to walk with him. "Go ahead in."

Lou took a step. "Thanks."

"Take your time." Debrow backed away, motioning for him to continue on while the hydraulics allowed the door to slowly close.

Lou felt trapped. He watched the entrance with caution like a soldier assessing an IED on side the road. Recent paranoia told him it was a set up. Would that be irony to be killed in a coroner's office?

Despite the location, he secured his weapon. He inched his way inside the cold room making sure no one was crouching behind him. Once the door finally closed, a figure appeared from an adjacent closet. Lou stiffened, holstering his gun. "This is the last time we're meeting."

Agent Winger inspected the doorway Lou had entered, opening it a crack to check the hallway. He wore a bandana, sunglasses, and he had let his stubble grow in. "I know. You're being watched so closely, I can't show up anywhere you go anymore. I remember you said Dr. Debrow was on board, so I came here."

"The place has cameras all over."

"Relax. Debrow said he'd disable them. I waited for him in the parking lot and told him this was important. He understood." He scratched his head looking around. "Can't believe I was just in here... dead."

Lou frowned, holding out the package. "Everything you need to leave the country."

Jones hopped up on an autopsy table as if standing was a chore. "I saw the money in my account. I knew when I approached you, I was making the right decision. Our business is done."

Lou folded his arms. "You open your mouth, I will find you and I will kill you."

Chapter 38

"The search for you is full on," Nick said into his burner as he drove alone down Decatur in the Quarter. Due to Belinda's suicide, he was given three days leave. The Mississippi River was on right, just beyond the old Jax Brewery.

Nick wasn't sure what architecture was French and what was Spanish, as a lot of the Quarter was rebuilt during the Spanish reign after the Great Fire of 1788. One might notice the street names are either in Spanish (Calle D Conti) or French (Rue Bourbon). He kept his eyes on the tourists meandering about outside his window.

Marcus gave him a definitive statement. "Lou is planning something, right?"

Nick upped the air-conditioning. "Things are bubbling over. It'll all be over soon."

"Things are going as planned on my end."

He gripped the wheel while coming to a stop in front a barricade guarded by two cops. A *second line* of dancers were crossing the street while a brass band intermingled. Several umbrellas popped up and down in rhythm to the trumpets and drums. "I'll do everything in my power to make sure you're safe."

"Oh, I'm safe. Bored, but safe."

They said nothing more as the second line came to an end. Nick's everyday cell rang. "I gotta go." He hung up with Marcus, then answered the second call. "Lou."

"Marcus' car is at Moisant," he said. "Don't know why I'm calling you, really."

"I assume he wasn't in the trunk."

"... in the trunk? No, he's still missing. J.P. are all over the place as witnesses if you want to show your face." J.P. referred to the Jefferson Parish police. "You coming or what?"

Nick hesitated. "On my way." The call ended before Nick could do it himself.

Formerly Moisant Field, the airport was named after the aviator John Moisant who died in a daredevil act on the same land in 1910. In 2001, Moisant was renamed The Louis Armstrong International Airport. Nick figured that was more for tourism than anything else.

Far from his district in the Quarter, Nick drove through Metairie, into Kenner and entered the long-term parking. They headed for the light show displayed by the Jefferson Parish squad cars and airport security. Nick spotted Lou in the distance. He was instructed to park just beyond the yellow caution tape wrapped around the rusting lamp poles, just a few feet from Lou's unmarked.

Despite being on leave, Nick bypassed the J.P. officers and was greeted by Lou's grim face. He had been talking with Sheriff Joseph Zucco. Behind Lou, a member of the CSU team was collecting evidence from Marcus' open trunk. It was empty.

"Any clue to where he is?" Nick asked immediately.

"Car seems clean." Lou put his hand on his hips, looking past him at an empty car. "CSU found trace, hairs and shit, but no blood. We're having video pulled, but they're on a forty-eight hour loop. It's possible we missed him. Judge won't sign a warrant to get the airplane manifests unless we can prove foul play. If he got on voluntarily, we can't do jack shit."

Questions and reactions would be critical in this game of who would blink first. To gain time and perspective, Nick brushed past his father to gaze into the trunk. His arms couldn't find a comfortable position. He palmed the back of his neck then turned around to walk past Lou, knowing he'd follow, taking them a good distance from everyone.

"Do you believe me, now?" Nick presented the car with a swipe of his hand.

"What I want is for you to tell me exactly who Cali is... or was." Lou stared at him as if disappointed.

Nick said, "Seriously? You want me dead."

"I've changed my mind on that. It was a rash mistake. I was pissed. But, I think we can find a way through this."

"Jesus." Nick spun as if to leave, but jumped to his side and whispered. "There's only one way this is going to end."

Lou dabbed his forehead with his sleeve. "I'm willing to let you make this right, son."

*Son.*

"I don't know what would be worse, death or being owned by you."

Lou's eyelids closed halfway as he stared at him, for the first time ever, not worried about bionic ears listening in. "I think Marcus is with the feds. I think he's spilling his guts."

Nick stood frozen. "You really want to work this out?"

Lou stepped up to Nick, taking him gently by the shoulders. His voice was barely a whisper. "You're my flesh and blood. I can forgive everything you've done to this point. They gave you no choice. We can use this to our advantage."

Nick almost succumbed, going pale. "How long have you known?"

Lou stood toe to toe with him. "Since Jones came to me." Lou put his palm behind Nick's neck. "I know they arrested you. I know they threatened you. But, it's not too late to prove yourself."

"You want me to take Cali out," Nick said.

"They have nothing or we'd all be rounded up by now." Lou softened. "If you come back to us, there's a chance you live to meet someone new. To have children. A chance for Marcus, too."

Nick forced his legs to relax, feeling the strain on his thigh muscles. "So, it's all out there. All the cards are on the table."

"Not quite. Who is Harold Sanders to Cali?" Lou's face was inches from his. "Who the fuck is Harold Sanders to your fiancé?"

Nick looked around, but no one was paying them any attention. "Nothing."

Lou's hand almost rose to Nick's throat, but he brought it back down. However, the intent was clear. "Tell me."

Nick took a moment. He needed the satisfaction of rubbing it his father's face. "Cali's real name is Tanya Sanders. Harold Sanders was Cali's father…"

## Chapter 39

"Now, the bastard knows everything, Cali. He knows you're really Tanya Sanders. He knows our history." Nick paced inside his house.

Her heart skipped. "How?"

"His spy saw you at your father's tomb. I'm not on the inside anymore. The ledger is the least of my concerns. Keeping us alive is."

Cali headed past the nurse's station to the exit. "How'd he take it?"

"He's pretty jacked up. Be careful on your way home. Wait, maybe you should stay at the hospital and I'll come there."

"Don't be ridiculous. I'll call Long and he can put a car on me. Plus, I'm armed and he's not going to try anything." Cali pinched the bridge of her nose through his silence. "This is so bad."

"We can't go one like this. He's waiting to see who's going blink first. He thinks he's holding all the cards."

"So, we use his arrogance against him. Shit, my battery's on fumes and I'm almost to my car. We'll talk when I get home. Love you."

Maybe it was fate, the universe balancing things out, or just a random series of events, but she often thought that her father died in order to bring Nick into her life. But, the other side of that coin meant Nick had indirectly delivered her father's murderer. Either way, both of their families had been destined for a head on collision since the first cells on earth started replicating.

Cali had no intention of calling Long. As far as he was concerned, the plan to get the ledger was moving along ever so slowly. Lou would pay for her father's murder, and it wouldn't be with a prison sentence. She briskly walked to her car facing the setting sun, wearing the sunglasses she purchased just for visiting her father. Agent Long wouldn't approve of her stepping out of character, but it was important to pay her respects. However, she had failed to remain invisible. Her mentor would berate her for being busted by Lou Rush's spy, just as Nick had wanted to.

The heat quickly penetrated her smock. She almost opened the car's burning hot handle when a white Taurus with Lou behind the wheel pulled to her side. She leaned back and waited with her hand near the purse's opening, just above her weapon. Her phone only had ten percent battery, but she let it record anyway. Her gun was at the ready.

Lou turned off the engine and got out wearing a bigger, more intimidating pair of sunglasses. "Glad I caught you."

"Why are you here?"

He waved a dismissing hand at her. "Don't pretend he didn't call you."

Cali looked at ground. "He called."

Lou smoothly walked around the car, stopping at her fender. "I'm impressed how you kept us in the dark for so long. You must have enjoyed making me look like a fool."

"You're a murderer."

"So, this is all about me, and what happened to your father. You're only using Nick to get your revenge."

"I love Nick."

"You can't have your cake and eat it, too. Winger is gone, and you're left with nothing. Soon, you'll be pulled. What then? What will you and Nick do?" He put his fingers up to his mouth in fake worry.

"Me and Nick being together wasn't about you. Nick had no idea who I was until the Winger arrest. Our secret relationship was him being worried you wouldn't approve, and he *needs* your approval."

"Don't ever become a psychiatrist. Nick doesn't want my approval. He gets satisfaction with disappointing me. I say left, he goes right."

"That's not true. He loves you, or at least at one point he did. But your being unavailable in his developmental years made him seek your approval. He thought he did something wrong to drive you away."

Lou laughed, shaking his head. "Bullshit. Don't pretend to know our relationship."

"Fair enough." She stared at him. "So, don't pretend to know ours."

"Your father killed the woman I loved."

"Bullshit!" Her voice carried. "*You* killed your wife. And you killed my father because they loved each other." She kept hold of the door handle, despite the pain.

"Joining the FBI to get revenge is pretty obsessive. Admit it." He ran his fingers along the fender of her car. "Today is the twentieth anniversary of your father's murder."

Cali set her legs. "You have a great memory of that. Interesting."

He stepped closer. "And it's just a coincidence that you and Nick end up together? The truth is, your father wasn't a very good man. He'd done things you wouldn't be too proud of. That's what got him killed."

Cali wiped the beginnings of tears, but said nothing. A man like Lou could snap at any moment. Rage tended to wash away all self-control and reason.

Lou's teeth flashed as he spoke. "Somehow, you got Nick wrapped around your finger in high school by opening your legs while he was a horny teenager. I know your M.O. Maybe you think he would reveal something to you in bed? Get your revenge by framing me for killing your father and then walking away, leaving him in shambles? Is that it?" His voice had grown loud.

She moved within inches of his chest. "Your opinion of my father means nothing to me."

Lou looked down with disdain. "Nick was a kid with a wet dick. He would have done anything for you." Lou stepped backwards, as if to leave.

"And he still will." Cali's kept her cool, speaking proudly. "We met at my father's funeral. You didn't know he rode his bike there that day, did you?"

Lou stopped with his back to her. "No. He lied to me."

"Amazing how if he doesn't show, none of this would be happening right now."

He turned back to her, fists clenched. "Amazing."

She squared with the large man, speaking clearly, "We made love all through my senior year before I moved to Alabama. You gonna call me a slut, now?"

"I thought my opinion means nothing to you." He paused to take a breath. "You did right by keeping it a secret. I would have done everything in my power to keep you out of my son's life."

"I pity you – never knowing what love really feels like. How it tranforms you. You are a sad, sad person."

His eyes bore into hers. "That may well be, but you have nothing on me. Nothing! There will be no more activity. None!" he yelled in her face. "As long as you're in the picture, we're going to be clean as a whistle. Good luck, Agent *Sanders*." Lou backed away, nodding as if a precursor to his head exploding. He slid into the car, not giving her a second glance. Lou's giant paws slammed onto the wheel and the car shook as his body rocked against the door. She thought he might have a tantrum.

Cali watched him drive out of the lot before allowing her knees to buckle. The two biggest secrets in her life had been revealed. She pulled out her cell phone and turned off the useless recording app. She called Nick with the last of the battery's power.

Chapter 40

*How dare that bitch.*

Lou sped away from Ochsner hospital without consideration of pedestrians or motorists that might've been in his way. The only thing that calmed him was the notion that he'd soon get his chance to kill both of them with his own bare hands.

His cell phone ringing barely registered. The screen indicated an unknown number, forcing him to calm. He cursed himself for letting her get under his skin. He pulled into a residential neighborhood and answered. "What?"

"You need to get to the Lexington Motel on Airline."

"What's going on there?"

"Not going to say over the phone. Just come to room twenty-three. Be discreet."

Lou pulled off the curb. "On my way."

The Lexington Motel was on Airline Highway, the old Metairie strip that used to be main route to get to Baton Rouge from New Orleans before Interstate-10 was built. The businesses were mostly auto repair shops, used cars, motels and vacant buildings. It wasn't a stretch where a nice, middle class family would want to stop for a bite.

Coming from Ochsner, it didn't take long before Lou pulled into the Lexington lot. A cautious tour around the building made him curious. There was no obvious activity. He scanned the doors until coming to number twenty-three. That was when he spotted Gary's car, as well as Chipotle's vehicle.

Lou was tired of walking into the unknown. Every situation had him on edge. If the other members knew exactly what had been going on with Winger and Maddox, they could rebel themselves. He palmed his sidearm against his waist as he approached the door. He stopped, checking left and right before knocking. "It's me."

The door opened with Gary on the other side. "Look what we found?"

Lou walked into the dark, stale room to see a sweaty Marcus Hoover duct-taped to a chair. When he saw Lou, Marcus closed his eyes hard.

Chipotle slapped Marcus' head. "I caught him trying to contact Johnny on his detail. They spoke for a while, and then I followed him here."

"What did Johnny say he wanted?" Lou asked.

"Money, according to my protégé. Said he was trying to get to France."

"France? No shit." Lou walked up to Marcus, almost touching his knees with his. "You believe Johnny?"

Chipotle shrugged. "Don't know. Never saw money exchange hands. We can question all the other youngsters to see if he approached them, too."

"And we will, but let's see what Marcus has to say for himself. Turn up the volume on the television, will you?" Lou yanked the tape off his mouth.

"Fuck you," Marcus said. "Do your worst."

"Well, well, well." Lou smiled. "My day just brightened."

#

The signal dropped while Cali was in mid-sentence. Her battery finally gave out. At least she had managed to inform Nick of Lou's confrontation.

Nick stared out from the curtains, waiting for Cali's Jeep to show, if not every Tribunal member. It was conceivable that if Lou had his way, she might never be found again. That would make Lou a dead man. That dark thought of killing his father to avenge her death made his vision blur. He would be avenging his mother's death, also, along with Harold Sanders and many others, too. It occurred to him their little club had only started to unravel with the new crop. The success of the Tribunal could only be attributed to the old guard that had the discipline and conviction - now it was contaminated by a conscientious, softer generation.

Every muscle in Nick's body hurt from prolonged tensing, like when cold and struggling not to shiver. It hurt to stretch, but he worked out the kinks while waiting. No sign of her, yet. Whenever the street was clear of cars, he paced. Ten seconds passed, and he searched the neighborhood again.

With a surge of relief, her Jeep Fit finally pulled into the driveway. The car didn't have bullet holes and she appeared calm. She waved discretely, spotting him in the window. He wasted no time in exiting the house and getting in the passenger seat. Cali turned up the music and they each leaned in to whisper, almost kissing.

"Thank God you're okay, Nick started. "We need to get you a car charger."

"Last of our worries."

He squeezed his eyes shut. "I know, but something that trivial has my head ready to explode."

"It's fine. I'm fine. I'm sorry." She stopped. "What do we do? Bring ourselves into the Bureau?"

"Let's think about it. My freedom hinges on that ledger."

"I have something for you."

"I don't know if I can take something else."

"I have one of your mother's letters." She reached into her purse. "The originals are still with the case files, but I made a copy of the one I thought was most important."

Nick took the folded-up letter. "I still can't believe my mom loved your dad," he repeated for his own benefit.

"Eventually, you'll get to see them all. I promise."

Nick swallowed hard as he began to read the loopy penmanship of the letter.

*Harry,*

*Here I sit again, all alone while Lou is working and Nick is in school. I can't call you or text or write an email. I can only write these letters and give them to you at our special place. All I want is for you to be with me. Can I break a pipe to get your over here? That wouldn't be a good idea. Lou has been suspicious lately. He's picking up on my good mood. You're the cause of that and he knows something changed. He's getting more upset with me and if he ever found out about us, I know he would kill me. I'm not joking. I know this, Harry. And you should be cautious, too. Just you continuing this relationship knowing the danger proves you love me.*

*I think about how you are the opposite of my husband. You're kind, loving, and thoughtful. I can't wait to see you again.*

*Love,*

*A*

Nick read the letter three times while Cali sat silent beside him. Her father chose not to reveal these letters during his trial – his affair, risking jail instead of embarrassing his family. Whether it had been his lawyer's

advice or his own sense of honor, it was a good risk in
hindsight. He tucked the letter in his back pocket and
thought back to how his mom's demeanor had changed
near the end of her life. She was *happy*. He had blocked out
the thoughts of Lou being responsible his mother's murder,
not wanting to believe it. Not anymore.

Still, Cali had kept this from him for all these years.
Did he trust her completely? Could she have another layer
he didn't know about? Or could Lou have some other
information on Cali that he hadn't even considered? That
notion was too far out to believe.

Nick's cell rang, jolting both of them. The Jeep
shimmied.

"Don't answer it," Cali said. "I'm with you. Let's
leave. Now."

Nick stared at the phone. "It's Marcus. I have to
answer."

Cali's eyes watered. "Okay."

"Marcus," Nick answered, watching Cali's concerned
face.

"You thought about my proposition?" Lou asked.

*Shit.* "Lou. Where's Marcus? Is he okay?"

"You're going to find out. You're getting picked up.
Be ready," the gruff voice stated.

"Put Marcus on."

There was shuffling. Marcus' voice came over. "They
don't know shit. Don't..." An abrupt noise halted his
words.

Lou came back. "See. He's fine."

"How can I trust you?" Nick glanced out the window,
expecting to see a Tribunal car. "I'm not going anywhere
with you. As a matter of fact, we're turning ourselves in.
This is over."

"You're not going in. We're going to settle all this
shit today. Look out your window."

Nick turned to see three vehicles blocking his driveway. Four Tribunal members had their weapons drawn. Mr. Gary was smiling wide.

He covered the phone to speak to Cali. "Where's the car that's watching you?"

Cali turned away. "I – I didn't call Long."

Nick returned to the call. "I thought you wanted to work this out, Lou." Nick stepped out of the car.

"That's what we're doing."

"This is considered kidnapping. A federal crime. The feds will be all over you if you do this."

There was a moment of silence. He heard a scuffling. "Get in the car with Gary. You try to fight back or escape, he dies. You think I'm playing? Try me." The call ended.

Nick turned to Cali as they slowly walked toward the guns with their hands in the air. "If we don't go, he'll kill Marcus."

Her head shook. "If we go with them, we're dead, Nick."

"If we run, we won't make it five feet."

She lost color, speaking into his ear. "We have to hope Long finds us."

Mr. Gary grabbed Nick by the arm and threw him into the back seat. Cali followed. All three cars eased onto the street at the same time.

Chipotle held a gun on them from the front seat. Classic rock played on the radio. Nick spoke low and close, "Listen to me… shortly after you moved away to 'Bama, I was in such a funk, that I started getting into trouble. One day I got caught shoplifting a Manning jersey from a sporting goods store."

"What are you talking about?"

"Shut up," Chipotle commanded.

Nick ignored him. "Lou made it go away, but he sat me down and gave me an ultimatum. He said my slate would be wiped clean as far as he was concerned... no punishment or lectures... if I gave up the Camaro."

"Is that why it's still in Shelly's garage? To this day?"

"I gave up the Camaro, otherwise, Lou's punishment would have been harsh. And when he lifted the ban, I refused to drive it out of spite." Nick exhaled.

"Why are you telling me this story?" She paused, leaning into his ear. "Is there something I need to know about the Camaro?"

Nick's lips touched her ear. "He'll forgive my betrayal if I murder a federal agent who's the love of my life."

Cali closed her eyes as a tear fell. "And if you refuse?"

Chapter 41


The three vehicles pulled into Shelly's lot, parking around the side near the back. Nick and Cali were manhandled as they were shoved into the back door. It took a while for Nick's eyes to adjust to the light, but when he got his bearings, the first person he saw was Lou. Both he and Cali were physically placed in a chair.

"They're both clean," Gary offered. "No one followed us, and the boys have our perimeter."

"It kills me that it's come to this," Lou said as he traced Nick's outline with his T-9 detector. Cali received the same treatment.

Nick looked past the two Tribunal members sitting at the bar and tables, to the lone figure near the front video poker machine. Marcus was tied to chair, unconscious. He couldn't see his best friend's face, but the dark stain in his lap indicated a fair amount of blood had dripped from his wounds. He could see his chest inflating.

Cali was visibly upset, but holding it together well, considering.

The place appeared normal, otherwise, with the closed sign lit up in the front window. Lou took his usual stool. Shelly came from the kitchen, standing behind the bar. His gaze lingered on Nick long enough to know it meant something. Lou hovered over his longneck as if asleep.

"You got us. Let Marcus go," Nick demanded.

"At last, we can finally talk freely. Nothing to hold us back." He waved his arms around the bar. "Twenty years," escaped from Lou's lips. "Twenty years without a mistake."

"There's still no mistakes. The feds have nothing."

Lou laughed louder than Nick had ever heard. "A federal agent is sitting right next to you!"

Cali finally spoke, and with strength in her voice. "I'm not kidnapped, Lou. I'm here of my own free will. It's not too late."

"Don't try to help yourself." Lou pulled something from his pants pocket. He held three tiny objects in the palm of his hand, raising them to Nick's face. They were listening devices. He placed them on the bar and smashed each one with an empty beer bottle. "Just found them in here. You're so stupid sometimes. You're engaged to marry the daughter..." Lou stopped, palming his eyes.

Nick slowly rose, holding his hands out in full view. He sat on the stool next to Lou. "Look at me."

Lou's head angled.

"I've loved her since I first saw her. Since I was eleven. How could I tell you when I knew you'd forbid it?"

He straightened. "Forget who she is. That's bad enough. You're engaged to an FBI agent. My only question is... did you know?"

"Or course, I didn't know. Not until I was arrested. She knows nothing. But, she's right. It's not too late. Don't make a rash decision out of pride or hatred of me."

Lou knocked him off the barstool with a punch to his chest. Nick stumbled backwards, however he didn't fall. The two men tensed, and waited.

Lou commanded. "She never loved you. She was using you to get to me." He was restrained and grim. "Wouldn't you agree?"

"Whatever her motives... you sent me to Jones to die before I knew she was an agent. My fate was sealed all along. My question is why? Why did you put a hit on me, Lou?"

"When Jones told me who Cali really was, I figured there was no way you didn't know. My imagination ran wild where I pictured you and her talking about the Tribunal, laughing about how you'd take us down. I believe you now."

"And your first reaction was to kill me?"

"You're working for them, aren't you?"

"They didn't flip me. I pretended to go along with her plans. To know when shit was going to go down." His drying sweat felt cool, like an air conditioner was on him.

"Is that right?"

"Yeah, but I found myself in over my head. Cali told me they knew Jones was your mole."

"The hell you say?" He mocked.

"It happened just like that," Cali confirmed.

"Is it that far-fetched?" Nick regained position on the stool. "I decided to give them myself to relieve the suspicion. They didn't have anything, and I wouldn't give anything. The Tribunal would be in the clear. That would be that."

"*That would be that*," he spoke slowly into his beer.

"I never had any intention of giving you up or the Tribunal."

"No, getting arrested by the FBI was your ticket to witness protection." Lou exhaled. "Sometimes, I wonder how you can even be mine. Maybe you're Harry Sanders' son. Hell, if I didn't do the DNA test on you as a baby, you could be fucking your sister right now. But, no. You're mine."

"So, you knew about the affair mom had with Sanders?"

"Of course, I knew. We talked about it and I forgave her. When she told Slimeball it was over, he couldn't handle it. He killed her. I thought it best to keep her affair out of the news."

"I thought we were talking honestly."

"You were always easily manipulated." Lou raised his eyebrow. "You disappoint me on every level. You always have. But, you can make up for it."

Nick spotted Shelly watching them at the far end of the bar. He had a defeated look on his face. His pawpaw had aged exponentially. Nick said, "Shelly, did you know he wanted me dead? Is that why..." He stopped before implicating his pawpaw.

"I had no idea," he responded. "Just a feeling."

Nick continued to protest. "I thought I'd be on the inside. It was the best way."

Lou's quick right fist knocked Nick off the barstool and onto his back with a thud. "You had to have been planning this for years. It ends now."

"It's the Camaro all over again." Nick touched his lip and saw blood on his fingers.

"You have options here, Nick."

"Does Marcus have options?" Nick felt nothing but his heart racing. "Take me somewhere and kill me, but you'd be stupid to make a move on Cali or Marcus. What happened to caution? To planning? This is stupid."

"Why was Marcus talking to the junior members? What are you planning?" Lou asked, as if considering.

"After bailing on Belinda, we wanted to get him out of the country," Nick boomed. "He knows nothing. Have I pressed you for any info? Have I tried to lure you anywhere you're not familiar with? Cali and her buddies are ready to toss me in federal prison because I'm not giving them anything."

Lou stared at him in silence. Nick saw a glimmer of doubt.

"You're not buying this shit, Lou?" Gary yelled from the table. "He's a traitor. I knew you'd be soft on him. He's breaking every rule."

Marcus didn't register as he was still unconscious, or at least pretending to be.

Lou spun to face his old friend. "If you're not going to help, then shut up."

Gary fumed. "Nick is right about one thing – you're getting careless. This is bullshit."

Lou pointed. "If Nick is committed to the Tribunal like he says, then he'll perform a little job for us."

"Job?" Nick asked.

"It was *your* idea." Lou smiled.

"You want me to eliminate Cali."

"You know she's only with you to bring me down. She doesn't love you." Lou invaded Nick's personal space. "That is how Marcus will keep his life. That is how you will earn your trust back. I'm going to give you a gun. Check that it's loaded if you don't trust me. If that gun points anywhere other than at Cali, you will be shot dead where you stand. And then we'll kill her, and we'll kill Marcus. Your bodies will never be found. You kill her, then Marcus goes free, and so do you. Weigh your options, son. Three deaths? Or one lying agent who would dump you once I was in jail."

*He wants me to think I'm going to live*, Nick thought. "Okay, I'll do it."

"You'll do it," he repeated as if not believing it.

"But, I have to warn you about something first. They know about the ledger. I found it and made a copy. I sent it to Agent Long."

"The ledger?" Lou shook his head. "You didn't find it. Never will that book be found."

"Okay, keep thinking that. They have a case Lou. They're going to issue warrants any day now."

Lou laughed again, but without confidence. "They got nothing."

Cali spoke again, choosing the right moments. "We have audio and witnesses. You think me and Jones were the only undercover? They're ready to take you in. I mean, like now. You need to disappear. I'll bet my ass the feds are going through Nick's house as we speak."

Nick wondered if they were mixing lies, overlapping excuses, but it was too hard to keep straight when fighting for your life.

Lou focused hateful eyes on Nick, but then spoke toward his own father. "Shelly, you better go upstairs. It's about to get unpleasant. Maybe having to live with the ghost of a dead FBI agent will cure your agoraphobia."

Tonight would be the end, whether on Shelly's floor, or if they took him to an unmarked grave. Nick charged in a growling attack, taking Lou down amongst several barstools. The old cop fell hard.

Nick connected on three punches before his body flew into the air as if sucked up by a turbine engine. He had forgotten about Mr. Gary and Chipotle that were brought as security. Nick hadn't a chance to defend himself. A glimpse of a bottle flying toward him made contact with his head, but he didn't hear if it shattered.

Two of the men caught Nick before he fell to floor. His double vision prevented him from gaining balance, and his mouth couldn't form proper words. They dragged him across the floor with Lou spouting nonsensical orders. Shotgun blasts went off from his left side. Then, lesser audible gunshots rang out. A window shattered. The smell of gunpowder filled the air. Another shotgun blast, and the mechanical cocking action came from behind the bar. A cacophony of noises and movement blended into a surreal drug-like state. Nick was suddenly aware that he was tangled in a chair next to an overturned table.

The motion stopped, and Nick spun on the floor covered with broken glass. He could just make out Shelly holding a shotgun in the doorway. It was the closest he ever saw his pawpaw to going outside without the car. Nick could have sworn the old man said, "They took Cali."

Nick twisted onto his back, and just that fast, his world slipped into blackness.

Chapter 42

It felt like a pillow of tacks. Nick opened his eyes to find himself face down on shards of glass. He lifted his head, seeing where blood from his face had pooled. The lights were off inside Shelly's and no cars were around, but his grandfather watched from the crack in the door. Was he waiting for Lou to come back?

"You okay?" Shelly yelled. The old man closed the door, locking it up. Shelly had just betrayed his only son, taking sides with his grandson. There was no going back.

Nick rolled his hips and felt his back pocket for his phone, but only found his wallet. He finally spotted the shattered screen a few feet away as if it had been stepped on. Nick's trembling fingers pushed the side button and waited for it to power up. It said 9:37 p.m. under the cracks.

He should have been grateful to be breathing, but Cali was his only concern. He stood, falling forward onto his knees. The blow to his head threw off his equilibrium, but he managed not to stumble on his second attempt. He made it upright to see three bodies on the floor. Marcus was one of them.

"Marcus is alive. He's just out." Shelly sat at the corner table. "Gary and Chipotle wasn't so lucky. I killed them dead. Lou managed to take Cali."

"Where would he take her?"
"That's what we need to figure out."

#

Nick continually checked on Marcus, who was breathing steadily with a strong pulse. A large lump on the back of his skull told him that he had been hit pretty hard. Nick sat opposite Shelly who had set up a bottle of whiskey between them. Crimson splatters appeared by his shoes like raindrops. He wiped his face to find his palm smeared with blood. His pawpaw tossed him a clean white towel.

Feeling nauseous and seeing pinpoints of light, Nick staggered to the bathroom and splashed water on his cuts and swollen face to avoid passing out. *Wasps*. Diluted pink mixtures of blood and water coated the white sink. His face looked as if he hacked at it with a dull razor. He pressed a towel against his skin to absorb and clot the cuts.

Would Lou really kill an FBI agent? Under these conditions, while the walls were falling all around him, of course, he would. The Tribunal had ultimate power because they never feared consequences.

Nick stopped for a breath. He had to suppress the raging anger, and the irrational behavior that would accompany it. The trickling blood subsided. He threw the ruined towel into a corner. It was time to find out what Shelly knew.

He returned to the room to see Shelly had placed a few clean bar rags under Marcus' head. All the lights were off. Nick zeroed in on the old man sitting at one of the tables with the glow of a cigarette floating weightless. As Nick drew closer, he could see a bottle of whiskey next to the ashtray. "Do you know where he took Cali?"

"No, but once he's settled, he going to call." Shelly pointed at his cell phone. "He's gone too far this time. He can't come back from this. Anything he threatens, it's real."

Nick stared, ready for action. "How do you know he'll call, and not just kill her?"

He took a drag from his cigarette. "You say you know your father… but, I know him better. He's not going to kill Cali unless you're there. He's beyond rational at this point." Shelly kicked out a chair for him to sit.

"We should get Marcus some help."

"That would invite all kinds of law enforcement to our doorstep, and then you're screwed. Cali's screwed. He'll be fine."

"So, we wait?"

Shelly blew a cloud of smoke. "You took down the Tribunal. He has nothing left."

Nick accepted the chair. "Never thought it would end like this, Shelly."

"Call me pawpaw… just once."

"Too late to be that kind of family."

"I love my son, but I hate him, too. Funny thing, if the first eradication would have been anyone else other than Cali's father, we probably wouldn't have any resistance."

Shelly pushed the bottle to Nick. Despite the distaste for hard liquor, Nick took a pull that stung his split lip. He fought with a sour expression and gasp. "That has a bite."

"There's something wrong with the males in this family."

Nick nodded. "Did your father have issues, too?"

"My father died before I was born. My stepfather disciplined me to within an inch of my life and then comforted me in a way a grown man shouldn't."

"Jesus."

"I killed him. I made sure people saw me buying a movie ticket with my best friend and entering the theater." He glanced at the phone. "Gentlemen Prefer Blondes. Saw it twice already so I'd know details. I snuck out the side door and rode my bike back to the house. My mother was with her church group. He was passed out in his recliner. His disgusting mouth gaping. I took a gun from his nightstand. He threatened me with it often. I placed the barrel in his mouth and blew him away. I put it in his hand. I walked out of the house and rode my bike back to the theater. My best friend let me back inside."

Nick checked the phone, too. "You got away with it."

"I told your father that story one night when he was fifteen, when I was drunk as a skunk. You can say I planted the seed in his head for this whole thing. He seemed to understand why I wanted to pummel him, your father, instead of hugging him. I never showed him affection. I couldn't bring myself to. My stepfather killed that part of me. Best thing I could do was distance myself."

"And mawmaw?"

"She left me when Lou was a baby and moved north. New York last I heard. She was a… complicated woman. There was something manly about her, if you get my drift. She pretty much rejected your father, like a bad organ.

"Sorry about that, pawpaw."

The old man smiled. His eyes were wet. "I wasn't a good father. Didn't know how to be."

"You're saying it's not his fault he's a shitty father, too?"

"I'm saying things would have turned out different if I treated him better. I was an ignorant, selfish parent. I'm the worst kind." He took a drink.

"How can you love anyone else, if you don't love yourself?" They sat on that sentiment. "Where is he, Shelly?"

"I have a hunch, but let him call." His grandfather's eyes settled on him, twinkling in the dark. He huffed with a smile. "You have a good head on your shoulders. Most normal one of all of us. He even fucked up in fucking you up."

Nick touch at his tingling lacerations. "I love her. You and Lou might not know what that feels like, but it's worth dying for."

"All Lou knows is power."

"Power tends to corrupt. Absolute power corrupts absolutely."

"Churchhill?"

"John Dalberg-Acton."

"Never heard of him. But, good things have come from this."

"Cali's father was an innocent man. Are you saying his sacrifice was justified?"

Shelly grimly nodded. "Ask that question to any of the hundreds or thousands of people still alive because of that sacrifice."

"He's going to kill you the first chance he gets. And you're a sitting target."

"I've lived longer than a man with my sins should have." He reached over, touching a shotgun leaning against the wall. "I killed two tonight. Let the rest of them come at me."

The cell phone lit up, buzzing to life. Nick's eyes lit up as Shelly took the call. His pawpaw kept his gaze on Nick as he nodded, saying yes now and then. He put the phone down, and it went black.

Chapter 43

"So, where is he?" Nick was ready to bolt out the door.

"He's waiting for you." Shelly stood with the shotgun in hand, motioning for Nick to follow him. They took their time walking to the rear of the bar and into the connecting garage. The Camaro was already uncovered, with the tarp bundled near the trunk.

"It's time you drive your car." Shelly presented it with his hand like on the Price Is Right.

"So, where is he?"

Shelly appraised the classic, also. "How many years we worked on this behind your father's back?"

Nick exhaled. He wanted to take Shelly and shake him, but he could only play along. "On and off for years. The first lie I actually felt guilty about. Amazing he never busted us on it."

"He knew. That was one battle I fought for. He rarely let me win any, but he let that one go."

Nick's eyes widened. "He was so hurt when I refused to work on it with him anymore."

"True, but he was also blessed with the *don't give a fuck* gene. He didn't mind your keeping secrets as long as he knew about them and they were harmless. He let us have this."

"I loved the time we spent on it."

"With most grandparents and their grandchildren, there's a softer touch there. I developed an affection for you that I avoided with Lou."

"Too bad you didn't feel that way in your younger days."

"In my younger days, I was a racist, abusive, a chauvinist, and a bigot. My agoraphobia is my penance. My punishment."

Nick got into the driver's seat and Shelly followed by carefully slipping into the passenger side. The smell of Armor All wafted at him. He touched the key already in the ignition. "Where is he, pawpaw? Please."

He continued in a whisper, "Your grandmother inherited a house that she abandoned along with me and your father. After she left, I moved in here, but I maintained the old place. I paid the property taxes in her name."

"One time, Lou showed me a house over by Little Woods Elementary when I was a kid. Said we almost lived there."

"That's the one. I pay a service to cut the grass and I keep insurance on it, but no one lives there. It was used for quite a few eradications. It's looking rough on the outside, I can only imagine the inside. Lou sends a member there every six months or so to check for listening devices and such."

"And it's empty."

"Not at the moment." Shelly stepped to the wall to open the garage door.

"Do you have a gun?" Nick asked out the window.

"One in the glove box. One under your seat. One under the passenger seat."

Nick nodded. "Nothing like being prepared." He looked inside the glove box finding a small Ruger LCP, with a six-round magazine. "Nice. How long has this been here?"

"Just put it there before you showed." Shelly got out of the car as Nick started the engine. He leaned in, touching Nick's forearm. "I used to get beat up as a kid. I'd avoid the beating if I could make it home in time, outrunning the boys on their bikes. I'd watch them circling in the street from the window."

"Your agoraphobia."

"I think those were the seeds. When I was in my forties, already a home-body, I was robbed at gunpoint outside the very house you're going to. Thought I'd die. Never told Lou. I think that's when the agoraphobia took hold."

Nick suddenly realized why he had been procrastinating. Shelly had said he'd give the story about his agoraphobia before he died. He got an ominous feeling he'd never see Shelly again. He touched his hand. "Thanks pawpaw. One more favor, use the smelling salt to wake Marcus. Tell him where I'm going. He'll know what I want him to do."

## Chapter 44

Nick had to assume the FBI might be on Cali's tail at this point. There could be a helicopter hovering far above Shelly's. Leaving out the back, while under the cover of several large and leafy Magnolia trees, Nick drove the purring black, immaculate Camaro with its lights off in the opposite direction, toward Little Woods Elementary, taking side streets all the way. Marcus was safe; now to get Cali.

Just for good measure, Nick zig-zagged. The feds would be easy to spot as no cars were on the road. Agents could be watching all the major intersections, or worse yet, the helicopter had infrared and hadn't fell for his ploy. It could be directly above, but maybe he was giving them too much credit.

A half-mile away from his destination, Nick spotted a squad car on side of the road. Not unusual for a cop to take his car home, but this one was occupied by two people – an elder and his protégé, Nick figured. The ominous shadows watched him. Just a few more blocks revealed another uniform on his Harley, parked in a random driveway. He spotted a third car on the shoulder of the road with two members. It was an all too familiar scenario. His stomach sank.

Nick wouldn't be shocked if every remaining Tribunal member surrounded his grandmother's old house. They were preparing to assemble for a trial. It would be Lou's show. For Cali's sake, there was nothing for Nick to do but continue on. Within the minute, he had pulled up to the curb. The memory of seeing it as a kid came back. It would all end here.

The gray-bricked ranch house was falling apart, a long way from the no frills, simple home he remembered. Nick pulled onto the cracked, empty driveway, feeling the convergence of the elders he had just seen. On closer inspection, a length of gutter hung on by a thread. The windows were barred like a prison. The home had deteriorated, and the overgrowth seemed to be holding the walls together, taking over like an ancient city in the Amazon Jungle. However, the lawn was mowed as Shelly had said.

The details from Harold Sanders' murder made an unwanted visit. He expected this ghost from his past. The vision of the Spiderman sweatpants led to memories of his mom. He turned off the engine and waited for movement. No lights illuminated the inside. His body shook as if freezing. Lou's Mustang wasn't in sight, but he wouldn't be so stupid as to leave visual evidence.

Nick finally got out of the car.

He looked around the neighborhood, not seeing anyone stirring at this early morning hour. If he was going to die, so be it. He entered the front door, which needed a little extra push as it rubbed against the peeling floor. A stale, moldy decay infiltrated his nostrils. The moonlight revealed that the inside was just a shell, without any furniture. He inched inside, sloth-like, keeping his guns hidden.

"I warned you about her," a voice said from the back room. His arm hair stood on end. Lou's large figure appeared in the hallway with a gun pointed. "Toss your sidearm."

"Do you have Cali here, Lou? Tell me you didn't kill her."

His face contorted with deep shadows. "She might be back there. She might not be."

"Cali!" He yelled, "The feds know you took her, Lou. It's all over."

"I said toss your gun."

Nick threw it to the side. "This is your last night of freedom. You have to know this."

"So, I guess that makes me a very dangerous fellow." He took a step. His face hit a sliver of moonlight from the window. "Once the boys are sure you weren't followed, they'll come here to begin your trial. It'll be a brand new start for us. The Tribunal will continue."

"You're going to vote to kill me. You'll have your wish."

"You don't know the pleasure I'll get from Cali seeing you eat one of my bullets."

"So, she's here. Where? In the back room?"

"Give me the guns Shelly let you have." Lou's finger circled at his body as if encompassing all his hiding spots.

Nick hesitated, but knelt down and pulled off his holster, sliding it toward him. "This is it."

"In your waistband. Give it."

Nick put his hand behind his back and pulled out another weapon, also sending it to Lou's feet as if bowling.

Lou stepped over one of the guns. "After you and the bitch, I'll go deal with Shelly. My father is a bigger traitor than you. Killed Gary and Chipotle." Lou moved sideways to the window and bent to gaze out. "They should have been here by now."

"Why not just kill me now?"

"You're not above our rules." He pointed the gun.

"It's not about rules. It's about power. You want to show the remaining members that you're in charge. That you run things." Nick laughed to himself.

"You got too much of your mother in you."

"Thank God." Nick held his hand in plain sight, then slowly reached for his back pocket. "I want to show you something." His hand returned holding the folded letter.

"What is that?"

"Come see." Nick stood his ground.

Lou moved close, but stopped when he got within arm's reach. Nick handed over the paper. Lou leaned into the moonlight. His eyes popped up to Nick, then back down. "Where did you get this?"

"Cali." Nick's hand stealthily pulled an extra gun from his waistband while Lou was distracted.

Lou noticed the firearm and tensed. They stood ten feet away from each other with their guns aimed to kill. Lou smiled. "Well, well. How will this standoff end?"

"That letter is proof mom was scared of you. She predicted you would kill her."

"No court would ever see it that way. Sanders killed her in a fit of jealousy."

Nick glared at him. "I read the ME's report on her autopsy. She was strangled by a large set of hands. Sanders had lean hands, not large like yours."

"You want to believe that because it's convenient."

"You found out mom was cheating on you. You killed her and framed Sanders. When he didn't get convicted, you satisfied your fake vengeance by killing him in front of me."

"She was a whore."

Nick took a breath. Everything slowed. "I found your ledger and I passed it on to the FBI. It doesn't look like your pals are coming. You're done. Put the gun down."

"If they had the ledger, you wouldn't be here alone."
Lou took three broad steps backward. "Why are you trying
to get me to admit things I didn't do? Are you wired?"

"I'm a witness to Harry's murder. A reliable one."
Nick's arm stiffened with the gun. "It's over, Lou." Tears
blurred his vision. "You killed my mother. Now, I'm going
to kill you."

His hands dropped ever so slightly. "Oh, Nick. Poor,
pathetic Nick. You and Cali are the only ones not leaving
this house alive."

"Are you too psychotic to see that it's over?"

"Then, shoot me. At this distance, in the dark. As
tense as you are; you think you can get an accurate shot and
I won't? I've killed so many more men than you."

"Pull your trigger." Nick countered.

Lou's face relaxed. "What if Cali isn't here? Will she
ever be found? You won't shoot me."

Nick noticed a figure appear behind Lou in the
doorway, but tried not to let on. The silhouette was that of
Cali. She picked up one of the guns Lou had kicked to the
side. "Nice bluff, asshole. You don't have me anymore,"
Cali said, walking in the room. "Now, I got you."

"Fuck!" Lou spun around. "How...?"

"You left me on the floor in a room with broken
glass, genius. Cut right through the tape." She held the gun
on Lou with bleeding hands while making her way to a
clear spot in the corner of the room.

Chapter 45

Nick's relief upon seeing Cali almost buckled his knees. His chest vibrated with every beat. "Cali, thank God. I thought I lost you."

She was breathing heavy, rocking back and forth as if she had ran a mile. "Takes more than an egotistical douchebag to kill me."

"Oh, that's just wonderful." Lou backed away to the far wall. Nick regrouped and held his gun high. "You going to kill me now?" Lou clenched his teeth. "You can't prove a damn thing. Nothing happened here."

Nick let himself smile. "The elders have been decommissioned by the rookies. Marcus turned them all against you. They abandoned you, Lou. Cooper and Belinda were the last straw."

"That's what Marcus was doing with the rookies," Lou spat.

"I'm undecided on what to do with you, Lou," Cali said. "There's no statute of limitations on murder. Nick is an eyewitness to your killing my father. I have the letters. It's premeditated."

"You could have just arrested me if that were the case."

"We wanted more."

"And you still got shit."

"Got your ledger," Nick repeated, needing his defeat to sink in.

Cali's head flinched toward Nick at that news, but she still focused on Lou. "You are done, mother fucker."

"You're two bumbling fuck-ups." Lou straightened his arm with the gun, while his lumbering frame dropped into a roll. He fired.

Without hesitation Nick fired back, but he couldn't tell if he hit anything. Cali's gun went off, also. Several more shots exploded from Lou's area in the darkness. Nick felt a graze on his leg. He continued to fire while collapsing. Sharp bursts continued from where Cali had been, creating a triangle of chaos. After the barrage ended, dusty smoke floated in the moonlight.

"Cali, you okay?" Nick shouted into the haze.

No answer.

Suddenly, a huge body pounced on Nick, pinning his shoulders to the floor. The searing hot barrel of a gun burned into his forehead. Lou's hands shook as sweat dripped onto Nick's bleeding face.

"I should have killed you the same night I killed your mother."

"I will see you in hell," Nick barely whispered.

"She was a whore, Nick. She cheated on me... on us." Lou sucked in breath like a madman. "The Tribunal will continue. You did all this for nothing."

"I hate you."

A foreign voice echoed in the house. "I hate you, too. If that matters to anyone." It came from the threshold, behind Nick's head.

Lou looked up, showing the whites of his eyes. His recognition was deep and guttural. "Marcus."

Nick tilted his head back to see an upside-down, battered and bruised Marcus holding a gun on Lou. "About time you woke up and got here."

"My head is pounding." Marcus stayed focused. "Shelly used smelling salt on me right after you left. All the boys shut down their mentors without a problem. The old dinosaurs are zip-tied in their back seats."

"What are you talking about?" Lou continued to point his gun while on top of Nick.

Marcus explained, "The seven other members of the new Tribunal didn't take too kindly to killing Cooper and trying to kill Belinda."

Lou backed off of Nick and stood in the center of the room, moving his gun back and forth between them. The doorway filled with a line of young cops stepping into the house until they had Lou surrounded.

"Cali," Nick yelled into the darkness. "Where are you? Are you okay?"

"I'm here." Cali stepped into the circle of cops with a limp. "I didn't know you were inviting company."

"You shot?" Nick asked.

"Twisted ankle. I'm fine."

Nick faced Lou. "You're not my father," he growled. "You're a stranger. A monster. Marcus is my real family. Cali is my family."

"Isn't that sweet. You're all fucked," Lou huffed, "I own this city. You let me go, and you have a chance to leave town alive."

"Hard for us to negotiate for our lives with your holding that gun," Marcus said. There were multiple weapons pointed at Lou.

Lou took a second before he threw his gun down and held up his hands. "I'm serious. It's not too late for everyone here to leave with our lives and our freedom. The feds don't know we're here or *she* wouldn't be alone. The NOPD will want to sweep all this under the rug. They don't want the embarrassment."

Nick stepped next to Lou, slowly raising the gun to his head. Lou stared at him, not looking away. Lou hissed, "Do it."

Marcus pleaded, "Nick, don't..."

"I want to enjoy this." Nick pulled the trigger with a cold, crisp click. Lou's shuddered, dipping on weak knees. "How's that feel, bastard?"

"Nick, stop." Cali crossed the circle of cops with her gun trained.

Marcus intervened and put his hands on her shoulders. "I won't let you do this."

Nick put bullets back into his revolver with shaking fingers. "He's right, Cali. I need to do this. For real."

Marcus shifted to Nick's side. "No. You're not going to do this, either."

"He's *my* responsibility. My... problem."

"That's why you're not going to." Marcus stood between him and Lou. "Am I your brother?"

"Of course, you are."

"*Am I your brother?*" He asked harder.

"Yes. You are my brother."

Marcus held the back of Nick's neck, putting their foreheads together. "You cannot do this. Cali cannot do this. You will never be able to live with yourselves, much less each other. This will always be hanging over your heads, eating away. This will *change* you." He turned Nick's shoulders around to face the door. "Take Cali outside."

The hardened group cops watched as Cali helped pull Nick reluctantly toward the front door. Nick resisted a moment, but eventually caved and staggered with his arm around Cali to the freshly cut lawn. Cali leaned against him, both facing the door, which was open a couple of inches.

"Is Marcus right?" Cali asked. "I feel like I'm being cheated."

"Like you won't have closure…"

"…if I don't do it myself."

"He's the one person outside of you, that I trust. We had tunnel vision. Marcus has a clear head. I think he's right. I think it's fitting that his creation ends up being what destroys him."

Nick directed Cali to the window, prying the dry-rotted plywood off with his bare hands. Cali joined him at his side. They saw Marcus take the first shot, and Lou fell to the ground. One of the other members fired, and Lou's body jerked. He tried to roll and slither across the floor. Another shot, and then many more, causing Lou's meaty frame to tremble before becoming motionless. They stared at the smoke gathering strength like a rolling fog. The pops grew closer together until they were indistinguishable. It sounded like the Chinese New Year. It ended just as suddenly. There was no way to count, but one hundred bullets would be a good guess.

Nick held Cali in a tight embrace, swaying back and forth.

Moments later, each officer exited, coughing and taking in the fresh night air. They walked by in a line, wiping their eyes and nodding at the pair huddled against the brick wall. A few patted them on the shoulder.

By the time the authorities will have found the body, without any traceable bullets, shells, or witnesses, Nick had no doubt that any of them would ever get prosecuted for the murder of Captain Louis Rush, NOPD.

Chapter 46

No one said a word as Cali drove the Camaro toward the bar to check on Shelly. Marcus kept his eyes closed in the cramped back seat. Nick had voiced his concerns about a possible suicide after the agoraphobia story. Cali kept her hand in Nick's, squeezing every so often. Amy Winehouse played softly on the radio.

Nick finally spoke. "You know when I mentioned the ledger, Lou didn't act like it was an impossibility that I had it."

"So?" Marcus moaned from the back seat. "Doesn't matter now."

"Big Hoover said something during our last visit that stuck in the back of my head." Nick spoke over his shoulder. "He said Lou had a hiding spot that no one would ever find."

Marcus nodded. "I remember. You're not thinking he still uses that same spot my dad knows about?"

Cali and Nick looked at each other with renewed vigor. Marcus instinctively grabbed the *oh shit* bar as Cali performed a fish-tailing u-turn to head toward the interstate. With barely any cars to impede them, they made it there in minutes. No headlights followed as they pulled

into the receiving area of The Brightstar nursing home.
Nick put on his hazards before the threesome exited the car.

"We all look like shit," Cali said.

Nick checked his reflection in the window. "Yep."

"Who cares." Marcus slicked his fade back.

Nick walked with the aches and pains of an old man,
but he'd never complain in front of Mr. Mike. He knocked
on the sliding glass entry doors that weren't operational at
that hour. From the darkness within, a figure materialized,
growing closer until they saw a uniform. The Brightstar
employee slapped at the wall and the lobby lights came on.

"Can I help you?" the Hispanic man asked from
inside the glass, his face grew curious at the condition of
his visitors.

Marcus and Nick held up badges. "Nick Rush,
NOPD. I need to see a resident. Mike Hoover in 3H."

"Can I ask what this is regarding? There *are* other
resident's safety I have to think about."

"No one else will be disturbed…" Nick looked at his
nametag. "… Officer Santos."

"I'm not a cop. Just a security guard."

"You mind letting me in to see Mr. Hoover?"

"We have visiting hours, officers, sorry. It'll have to
wait."

"That's my father." Marcus banged on the glass, then
brought his hand up to his temporal lobe in pain.

Speaking loudly, Nick said, "It can't wait. As a
resident, by law, apartment 3H is considered Mr. Hoover's
home, and as such, Mr. Hoover is allowed visitors at any
hour of the day or night unless otherwise specified by his
physicians. Now, if you don't want to explain to your
employer why a law firm is bringing suit against Brightstar
and all the media coverage that would bring, then I suggest
you open up this fucking door and let us see Mr. Hoover."

He looked to have finally woke up. "Alright, alright. I got you. I'm going to call him first, though. How's that?" Santos backed away while still facing him.

"Hurry, then."

Nick could just see him dialing into a phone on a desk. The guard waited for a minute, then his mouth started moving quickly. He nodded with a quick smile before hanging up the phone. Santos hesitated, then side-stepped out of view to disarm the security system. He pulled out his keys and partially opened the doors. "He says you people are trouble, but to let you in."

"Thank you. we won't be long, and we'll be quiet. I promise." Cali smiled.

Nick brushed past the man to the elevator in the darkened hallway. The metal doors opened immediately. Marcus pushed the number three on the panel. The air smelled of ointment and lotion.

After the carriage expended extreme effort to rise three floors, the threesome exited the bland elevator, walking briskly down the hall. Mr. Mike opened the door wearing a bathrobe just as Nick approached. His glasses weren't on. For a moment, he forgot Mr. Mike was blind.

He held onto his walker while leaning forward. "I know that smell. Someone fired their weapon... a lot. Marcus, what happened, boy?"

"I'm fine, Dad. I'll tell you about it later. I'm going to get some aspirin from your bathroom." Marcus disappeared.

Nick stepped inside the dark room illuminated by one small lamp, which was turned on for his benefit. "Sorry to wake you."

"Not a problem. Not that I sleep through the night anyway. I was actually taking a piss when the guard called. I'm pretty good at aiming, believe it or not, but that phone ringing at this hour distracted the stream just a bit." He laughed.

Nick jumped right in. "When we were here before, you said that Lou hid his porn and other stuff where no one would ever find it. Where were you talking about? You only knew him at the junk yard, right?"

Mr. Mike stared past him. But, then he spoke, "The car. He welded a thin sleeve on the custom oil pan on the underside of the car, you understand. Just clear of the oil plug." He used his hands to demonstrate. "He could only keep small things like weed, maybe a couple of girlie books, but if you knew nothing about cars, you'd never see it. Blended right in."

Nick grabbed Mr. Mike's hand. "Thank you. Thank you. We have to run. Me and Marcus will be by again soon and I'll explain everything."

Marcus stood in place. "Actually, I'm going to stay here. Explain things. Rest."

Nick drew Marcus into a hug. "Take care, brother. Love you."

"Love you, too."

Cali followed with her own embrace. Without another word, they filed out of the door.

"Good luck!" Mr. Mike said into the hall from the threshold.

"Why don't you do the honors of checking in," Cali said while entering the elevator. "I don't want him to know I'm with you."

Nick called Agent Long as the elevator struggled to descend. He answered quickly, as if he slept with his finger was on the button. "This is Long."

"It's Nick. Find Lou's Mustang and you'll find the ledger. It's welded to the underbelly of the car."

"I'll get my team on it. Any ideas?"

While speaking into the cell, he glanced at Cali. "I haven't talked to Lou in a while. I have no idea where the Mustang is. I know it's not at Shelly's."

Long hesitated. "I'm at Shelly's, now. The NOPD just removed three bodies, two shot to death – one suicide. You wouldn't know anything about that?"

"No. Who's the suicide?" He tried to sound surprised. "Not Shelly?"

"It looks like your grandfather killed the two cops, then killed himself. Sorry."

Nick hung up, immediately receiving an embrace from Cali.

Chapter 47

Two days later.

Nick pulled the Camaro to the curb of Conti Street in the French Quarter, just a block off of Bourbon Street and three blocks from his stationhouse. He hated traversing the Quarter due to oblivious drunk tourists and the narrow one-way streets, but today was a necessity. Four squad cars were already parked nearby. Police tape had been wrapped around a lamppost extending to the side-view mirror of two of the blue and whites. Gawkers were kept a safe distance away, but they all had their cell phones out. Nick ducked under the tape and showed his badge to the uniform standing watch.

The door to the covered parking garage was open, but not the larger vehicle entry door. Nick stepped inside to see Lou's Mustang spread out in pieces along the concrete floor, tagged with numbered cards. He immediately spotted Agent Long near the oil pan, and a white-wall tire.

"Heard they found your father this morning," Agent Long started.

Nick nodded. "They're still processing the scene. I imagine we owe you a thanks."

His squint opened enough to see his eyes. "Oh?"

"You know why. My questioning lasted hours instead of days. And the questions were softballs."

He shrugged. "The Bureau got what it needed."

Nick smiled. "But, I'm sure more questioning will come at some point."

"It's easier not to ask the questions than to bury the answers." Long smirked, letting it go. "Seems denial is going around," he said, referring to the junior members of the Tribunal.

"So, where is it?" Nick asked while cautiously stepped through the maze.

"Nothing." Long knelt while pointing. "We found the sleeve on the oil pan like you said, but nothing was in it. It's not here."

"Damn. But, why take it apart in here in the garage? You could have towed it back to your forensics garage." Nick looked around at the inventory of what used to be Lou's baby.

"If it was somewhere else in the car in a hidden compartment, we didn't want to take a chance that there was some kind of self-destruct mechanism when we started the engine or set up a tow."

"What, like a vile of acid that would break on it, Davinci Code style?"

"Something like that. But, it's not here." He noticed Nick's far off expression. "You thought of something. What? What is it?" Long asked.

Nick almost fell over when the thought hit him. "Follow me."

They walked out of the garage, slow with Nick's recovering injuries, into the shaded side of the street. They approached the Camaro, stopping before the bumper. Long looked at Nick. "You don't think? No shit?"

"This is a custom oil pan, too. Lou worked on it before Shelly and I took over. It has to be here." Nick fell to his knee, keeping his other leg straight while turning over onto his butt before lying flat on his back. He shimmied halfway under the Camaro, stretching his arm to reach the oil pan. After fumbling with a narrow, spring-loaded lid, his fingers nimbly pulled out a rugged, half-inch, black and white accountants ledger notebook. "This what you're looking for?"

"Well, I'll be damned."

Epilogue


Two years later.

Cali had resigned from the Bureau immediately after the inquisition began, as did Nick from the NOPD. The FBI, in conjunction with the NOPD, went decidedly soft on them, given the circumstances they didn't want to come to light.

They had become New Orleans celebrities, interviewed on many national shows. The details of the investigation remained sealed, but their redacted accounts had stayed within the parameters set by the Bureau. Nick and Cali had also written a book; one that cleared the FBI's scrutiny. With every month, their bank account grew, securing their future. The Tribunal's offshore accounts, totaling just over five million dollars would eventually be dispersed to the victim's families.

For the past two years, the ledger had been dissected and deciphered, used to build a solid case against the remaining elder members of the Tribunal. Three had committed suicide, or at least that was the finding. Suspended sentences were given to the new recruits in exchange for their testimony. The D.A. was successful in arguing that the junior members feared for their lives if they didn't cooperate and were basically brainwashed.

However, none of them would ever put on the uniform again.

Gavin Jones was found in Mexico a week after Lou's death, just over the border. He accepted a plea deal in exchange for life in a minimum-security federal prison. The kind where politicians and lawyers have ping-pong tournaments. Each of the four remaining original Tribunal members would be tried together, as all of them pled *not guilty*. There was no deal offered. The date of their must-see trial had been set for five months from Nick and Cali's wedding.

Nick and Cali had bought a house in the Garden District, just a few blocks from Saints quarterback Drew Brees, and a few other Hollywood celebrities that had fell in love with the city. They took their time in planning their nuptials, deciding to keep it small and intimate. Shelly handed the bar down to Nick in his will, but he didn't want it as vandals got to it often. The land quickly went up for sale and was snatched up by a popular car dealer who wanted to refurbish the bar for tours.

Marcus had started a security firm and bought into a brick and mortar comic book shop. It was a secret dream come true. He relaxed after it was determined that Lou's death wasn't going to be solved. All of the one-hundred and three bullets pulled from his body couldn't be traced to any known weapons in the database. The younger Tribunal members used throw-away weapons to kill Lou, and those were now most likely at the bottom of a bayou, lake, or river.

Marcus and his girlfriend finally bought their house, directly behind Nick's, where their backyards met with a privacy fence. A gate had been added so they didn't have to circle the block or climb over. Mr. Mike remained a constant in Nick's life, visiting at least once a week. The last time he had seen Mr. Mike was at the tuxedo fitting.

While in the church rectory, Nick watched Marcus approach in the mirror's reflection. He turned, and they fell into a hug. Not that macho man-hug with a closed fist, but an all-encompassing embrace, complete with rocking. When they broke free, they each had to laugh away the tears.

"Wedding day." Marcus gripped Nick's shoulders.

"Unbelievable. Could you have imagined this day two years ago?"

Marcus sat on a love seat. "Honestly, I thought the only way I'd get out of this was in a body bag. If you think about it, we were initiated into it without our consent. They groomed us."

"They did groom us. I tried to convince myself I made the decision to become a cop." Nick straightened his bowtie. "They made it seem glamorous for lack of a better word. As smart as they were, they had to have known new blood would be the end of them."

"They didn't think that. They thought they were gods."

Nick smoothed the back of Marcus' jacket. "I love you, man."

"So gay." They laughed, this time pushing each other away instead of hugging.

"Cali's pregnant." Nick blurted. "Two months."

Marcus' mouth sagged. He caught his breath. "Congratulations. Wow." He put his hand over his forehead. "What a coincidence. I was going to wait until you got back from your honeymoon, but, Kareena..."

"No..."

"I'm not supposed to tell anyone yet, but... one month." He nodded.

"Such a follower."

"C'mon." Marcus stood. "It's time."

Mr. Mike slowly walked Cali down the aisle of their small church wedding. His bad knees suffered through the

short march, but the smile never left his face. He promised
Cali he would dance with her at the reception, but then he
had to get back to the home. Nick dabbed at his wet eyes. It
was a sight Nick never thought he'd live to see.

Before he could blink away the tears, he found Cali
standing next to him, the veil lifted, falling behind her
perfectly swept *brunette* hair, having returned to her
original color. The priest welcomed them, as well as
everyone in attendance. Her green eyes sparkled; her face
glowed with the beauty and youth of when they first fell in
love.

*What he wouldn't do for her, if she would only ask.*

Today, she asked if he would be her lawfully wedded
husband…

"Yes, will all of my heart," he answered.

## Acknowledgments

I'd like to thank Detective Bruce Brueggerman with the NOPD for answering my annoying questions. Betsy Glick and Craig Betbeze with the FBI for sharing their knowledge of the Bureau and the New Orleans Field Office.

Also available by E.J. Findorff

Unhinged

Kings Of Delusion

A French Quarter Violet

Where The Devil Won't Go

The Unraveling